The Hotel at Honeymoon Station

BOOKS BY TILLY TENNANT

The Summer of Secrets

The Summer Getaway

The Christmas Wish

The Mill on Magnolia Lane

Hattie's Home for Broken Hearts

The Garden on Sparrow Street

The Break Up

The Waffle House on the Pier

Worth Waiting For

Cathy's Christmas Kitchen

Once Upon a Winter

The Spring of Second Chances

The Time of My Life

The Little Orchard on the Lane

An Unforgettable Christmas series

A Very Vintage Christmas

A Cosy Candlelit Christmas

From Italy with Love series

Rome Is Where the Heart Is

A Wedding in Italy

Honeybourne series

The Little Village Bakery

Christmas at the Little Village Bakery

TILLY TENNANT

The Hotel at Honeymoon Station

bookouture

Published by Bookouture in 2021

An imprint of Storyfire Ltd.
Carmelite House
50 Victoria Embankment
London EC4Y 0DZ

www.bookouture.com

ISBN: 978-1-80019-678-0
eBook ISBN: 978-1-80019-677-3

In memory of Storm Constantine

Chapter One

Elise was going to love this.

Emma fixed the bunting to a hook she'd just knocked into a fence post, and the thought made her simultaneously happier and yet sadder than she could remember being in a long time. The sad bit she'd do her best to hide. Her younger sister had worked hard and she deserved this glorious, golden, once-in-a-lifetime opportunity. She'd been more diligent than the other students, had gone out of her way to display knowledge way beyond her course, had proved her passion, her hard work and her indispensability, and, as a reward, she'd been chosen out of her cohort of fellow post-graduates to take the final space on a research team as a paid intern. She'd be gone for a year at least, maybe longer, and while Emma would miss her she wasn't going to let Elise get caught up in that grief.

There was another part to her sadness too, a part that felt far more selfish and unreasonable. As she toiled in the spring sunshine, hanging bunting, positioning garden chairs, tables and parasols, dusting plastic picnic-ware and making various other party preparations, she was forced to reflect on how, at the moment she was about to say goodbye to her little sister, she would also be forced to recognise her own shortcomings. She wasn't going to let Elise see that either. If she dared let any of those bitter thoughts slip, Elise would try to reassure her that life had cut them a different stack of cards, and that Emma shouldn't see the static nature of her existence as failure. But, in the end, Emma couldn't view her distinct lack of achievement, or even ambition, as anything else. Elise – eight years her junior at twenty-two – was destined for great things. Emma… not so much.

She was shaken from her reverie by the sound of Aunt Patricia's voice, and perhaps that was a good thing. Today was not the day for maudlin thoughts.

'Done over there yet?' she called from the far side of the garden where she was busy setting a table that they'd moved to the shade of a cluster of maple trees. It was early in the season and not yet the furnace-like temperatures of a midsummer day, but it was still warm and bright enough to be uncomfortable sitting for long in the glare of the sun.

'Nearly,' Emma said, shaking off her melancholy.

Patricia raised her eyebrows, giving Emma a look that never failed to remind her of her mother. Patricia's hair was a soft grey, almost white, but it suited her. Her skin was fair and her eyes green-grey, and her movements were always delicate, like a ballet dancer's, even when carrying out the heaviest chore.

Emma had supposed, over the years, that had her mum still been alive, her ginger hair would have been turning white now too, and her movements would have been elegant and considered like her twin's, her grey-green eyes shining with the same kindness. Her mum and aunt weren't identical, but they were so alike people said they might as well have been. No matter how many years she'd been gone, Emma would always look at her aunt and see the echoes of a mother she'd lost at the age of eight – a mother Elise had never even known.

At eight months pregnant a collision with a car had put her into a coma she'd never come out of, and Elise had been born by caesarean, into a world where everyone had overcompensated to make up for her tragic beginnings. In her darker, less charitable moments, Emma would blame that for the fact she had failed while Elise flew, but in reality she knew that wasn't fair. Elise had suffered in different ways. She had never known her mum, but she had still suffered a loss as tragic as Emma's.

'Looks pretty good,' Patricia said, coming over. 'You've got an eye for this kind of thing – I always said so.'

Emma smiled. 'Oh I don't know about that…'

'You don't give yourself enough credit. Didn't you have balloons to sort too?'

'Over in that box.' Emma indicated a trestle table still groaning with things in boxes and bags they needed to put out before her dad brought Elise over under the pretence of having a quiet family farewell dinner. Elise had said no surprise parties, which meant that this party might not be much of a surprise considering she'd spotted the possibility of it happening. But it wasn't every day your brilliant baby sister got the chance of a lifetime to study a largely unknown volcano in Iceland with a renowned professor and a team of eminent scientists, and if Emma couldn't throw a surprise party to celebrate that, she didn't know what she could throw one for. Of course, studying a volcano in Iceland wasn't everyone's idea of a dream opportunity, but for Elise it represented all she'd been working towards since first setting foot on the university campus.

Emma's mind went back to the day Elise had come over to her house with the news. She'd never seen her sister so excited – in fact, she didn't think she'd seen anyone look that excited about anything before. She cared not a jot that she'd have to spend a year in a village (more of a hamlet, really) whose name she couldn't pronounce and whose only source of electricity and heating was geothermal energy produced by magma under the ground they'd built their houses on. In fact, she absolutely loved that the village had a name she couldn't pronounce and that it was heated by molten magma, but then, Elise would. Emma had pondered what might happen if that magma ever came to the surface, and at the thought of that her sister had gone into near-raptures.

Elise had always been the curious one, the adventurous one, the child filled with wonder at the world. Emma had happily taken on the mantle of responsibility and stoic practicality to indulge that wonder, often giving up her own school trips and outings so their dad could afford to pay for Elise's. She'd pretended she hadn't wanted to go so that nobody would feel guilty, and she'd do it all over again if she had to. If anything, their celebration today and the reasons for it were reward for that sacrifice. Elise was off to start the realisation of her dreams and Emma couldn't be happier for her – her little sister had been robbed of any memories of a mother and it was the least she was owed.

'I suppose I'd better get some blown up,' Emma said. 'We're running out of time.'

Patricia cast a glance at the box. 'It'll take you ages – I thought Dougie was coming to help us.'

Emma's whole body tensed at the mention of her boyfriend. 'So did I. I've called him three times but he's not answering his phone. If he's too busy to help set up that's fine, but I don't want him to rock up late and spoil Elise's surprise.'

'Do you want to take a quick trip to the lake to see if he's there?'

'No – there isn't time,' Emma replied, though that wasn't the real reason she didn't want to go. She already knew he'd be there and she knew that catching him there would provoke the kind of almighty row that would completely ruin the day. For herself, she didn't really care, but for Elise's sake that could not be allowed to happen. 'I swear he's at that fishing lake more than he's home these days. I ought to suggest he gets engaged to a passing carp – they see more of him than I do.'

'I rather think a carp might struggle to take the vacuum cleaner round your house.'

'Hmm,' Emma said. 'Me too, and if you're saying what I think you're saying then you might be right.'

'What do you think I'm saying?'

Emma gave a small smile. She could speak frankly to her aunt, who'd always treated her with respect and as an equal, even when she'd been very young. Growing up, Emma had appreciated that and she still did – now more than ever, if only because Patricia had become one of her most important confidantes and counsellors. But even so, there were some things even her aunt couldn't help her sort out.

'That he's only marrying me because I look after him and more or less let him do whatever he likes?'

Patricia frowned. 'If you know this, I don't understand why you don't do something about it. Knowing that can't make you happy.'

'Do what?'

'Tell him.'

'I have,' Emma said wearily. 'More times than I can count.'

'Then you haven't told him in a way that makes him take you seriously.'

'He doesn't take anything seriously – that's the problem.'

'And you love this man? Sometimes I wonder, Emma…'

'Well they do say love is blind,' Emma said wryly. 'They must have forgotten to mention the part where it's stupid as well.'

'If I were you I'd tell him to buck his ideas up or it's the end of the line. An ultimatum is the only way.'

'It's not that easy.'

'It's not that hard.'

Emma ran a packing knife along the Sellotape sealing the lid of the box and pulled it open. 'He knows I'd never chuck him out – that's why he doesn't take me seriously.'

'He thinks he knows. Say it like you mean it – call his bluff; pack a suitcase or something.'

'I don't know…' Emma let out a sigh. 'Sometimes I wonder if it's me. Perhaps I'm too uptight about it all. I knew what I was getting when we moved in together – he's never been the world's most driven man, and in that way we're not so different – we just manifest our lack of ambition differently.'

'There's a difference between a lack of ambition and downright laziness,' Patricia said.

'He does what he needs to do… eventually.'

'Like today? How long have you been planning this party?'

'Couple of months.' Emma looked at her feet, starting to feel like a chastised toddler.

'And how long has he known that he'd have to be here to help?'

'He didn't *have* to—'

'You asked him to and he said yes. In my book he's committed to it and he has an obligation to see that commitment through. He lets you down again and again and you make excuses for him.'

Emma looked up to see her aunt was regarding her with a keen questioning stare, but she had no convincing response.

'Your uncle will be back shortly,' Patricia said. 'Once he's set the drinks up I'll ask him to help with the balloons.'

'Dougie will probably be here soon too,' Emma said quickly, although she didn't feel that optimistic.

Patricia raised her eyebrows again, and Emma had to admit that she had a point.

Patricia's lawn was dotted with daisies and buttercups, the odd dandelion or coltsfoot poking a shaggy head above the carpet of more delicate flowers. Patricia had always let the first weeds of the season take hold and left mowing the lawn for as long as she could stand – it was important spring food for the bees, she said, and she wouldn't deprive them of that for the sake of a pristine garden.

Emma had always liked the way it reminded her of a country meadow – there weren't so many of them in the little ex-industrial northern town of Wrenwick where she lived. There were some stunning moors on the outskirts of the city, but they were wild and bleak and often obscured with rain or cloud, and there were pockets of man-made greenery here and there, but they were the types of green spaces where you still knew you were in suburbia – houses and blocks of flats showing above the treeline, with concrete paths and council bins every few yards overflowing with uncollected rubbish. It was nice enough to walk there, but you'd never be fooled for a moment that you were in the countryside. A crowd of grateful little bees were exploring Patricia's flowery larder now, bumbling from plant to plant, settling for a while in the sun before moving on to the next.

Her aunt Patricia and uncle Dominic had a bigger house than either Emma or her dad, who both lived in turn-of-the-century terraces which had once belonged to a mill owner and which he'd used to house his workers. Patricia and Dominic had a detached house on the outskirts of town, and they often hosted family get-togethers, so it made perfect sense to have their party here. Emma's dad and Patricia had continued to have a close bond even after the death of Emma's mum – partly, Emma had always supposed, for the sake of her and Elise, but also because there was genuine affection between Patricia and her brother-in-law. She'd looked out for him after Felicia was gone and had comforted him, never asking for anything in return, despite the fact that she'd also lost her twin sister. She'd taken an incredibly active role in the raising of Emma and Elise and, having no children of her own, had almost become their surrogate mother.

Emma and her aunt were putting the finishing touches to the table decorations now. Emma had put Dougie firmly out of her mind and her tummy flutters were now at full pelt as the excitement grew about the arrival of her sister. Today had to be perfect, and if it had anything to do with her it would be. While they'd been working, her uncle Dominic had arrived and was bringing crates of beer and wine from his car.

'Don't worry – I've only brought a few bottles of the home brew,' he said in answer to Patricia's frown. 'The rest is all shop-bought.'

'Thank goodness,' Patricia said under her breath. 'First sensible thing he's ever done without having to be told.'

'It isn't that bad,' Emma said with a laugh.

'I don't think it's that bad either, in all honesty,' Patricia agreed, 'but it's not for everyone, and you can't just offer naff old home brew at a party – you've got to give people proper stuff to drink. If Dom had had his way he'd have been scaling up his shed production to something rivalling Guinness and he'd be trying to force it on everyone.'

Emma's reply was cut short as Dominic came back and gave an approving look at the garden. 'You've done a cracking job here, ladies. Need me to do anything?'

'Are the drinks all in?' Patricia asked.

'Yep. I think that's all my jobs ticked off.'

'I think we're nearly done too, aren't we?' Emma glanced at her aunt, who nodded agreement. 'Just the balloons if you don't mind helping out with those.'

Dominic scratched his head and swept his gaze over the garden again. 'Dougie here?'

'No,' Patricia said in a stony voice before Emma had any opportunity to reply herself.

And while getting angry might feel good for a while, it wouldn't change anything and so she'd vowed not to. She was annoyed, of course, but that was a different thing entirely. She was frustrated that Dougie had failed to see what today meant to her, and she was also sad that what meant a lot to her meant – if the evidence was anything to go by – absolutely nothing to him, because it meant she herself meant nothing to him.

She'd left phone messages and texts. She'd allowed herself, on the odd occasion, to imagine that he'd been genuinely held up, and she'd even aired the worry to her aunt that he might actually be in trouble (though Patricia had given that theory short shrift, reasoning that if Dougie ever had trouble Emma would be the first person he'd come to, expecting her to sort it out). In the end, even if he wasn't able to get here for the setting-up, Emma could only hope he'd arrive with the rest of the guests in plenty of time for Elise's surprise. She liked to think that, knowing this was important, he'd at least make the effort to do that much. But these days, Dougie doing anything that selfless was an increasingly vain hope.

'I'm going to get changed if we're done here,' Emma said. 'Mind if I borrow the spare room?'

'Help yourself,' Patricia said. 'I'm going to freshen up too before the guests start arriving.' She turned to her husband. 'Can you keep an eye on things here while we get ready?'

'If you can trust me not to start eating the food while you're missing,' he said. 'I don't mind telling you my stomach thinks my mouth's gone on strike.'

Patricia gave the sternest, most comical mock frown. 'Don't you dare! I'll know if so much as a slice of cucumber has gone missing!'

'She will as well,' Emma said with a laugh. 'She nearly broke my fingers earlier when I went in for a carrot baton.'

'In that case I'd better try and manage a bit longer,' Dominic said. 'But don't blame me if you find me fainted clean away when you come back down.'

'Honestly…' Patricia said as she and Emma began to walk back to the house, 'he should have been on the stage; he's such a drama queen.'

Emma grinned, and then turned to shoot her uncle a face of sympathetic solidarity. He returned it with a silent shaking fist to his wife's back and Emma burst out laughing.

'I don't need to ask to know what you're doing!' Patricia called blithely, not even bothering to look back.

Patricia and Dominic were amongst the handful of people Emma loved most in the world and she loved them at this moment just about more than anyone. It was moments like this that had made them so important to her, because after her mother's death Emma had needed not only emotional support, but, as a child of only eight years old, she'd desperately needed to find some joy in her life again. Dominic and Patricia had given her that in spades. They'd supported her during her darkest days and they'd shown her light again when her shell-shocked father had been unable to. Emma's dad had struggled to process even the smallest things his new life as a single father had demanded of him and for a while he'd become selfish, resentful, unwilling to acknowledge that anyone else's grief might be as vast as his.

He hadn't meant to be – Emma knew that now – but as a girl it had been hard to understand that he was expressing himself in the only way he was capable of – shouting into the void, demanding answers from a universe that refused to give them. His wife had been taken and he'd wanted to know why. Emma and Elise's mother had been taken too, but Emma had often been so wrapped up in her dad's needs that she'd been robbed of the time she'd needed to process that. She'd known that it hurt, but it had taken a long time to really understand why.

In the end, Patricia and Dominic had provided the space and time for her to do that. She and Elise had spent many weekends at their house, just being silly and spoiled and carefree and all the things kids were supposed to be. Her dad had got better as the years went on, but he'd never really been the same since Felicia's death. And as adults, if ever Emma or Elise had needed support, it was Dominic and Patricia who had almost always provided it.

Up in the spare room Emma slipped on a long floral dress. It was baby pink and white and about as girly as she got, but it had been hanging in the wardrobe since she'd bought it on offer at the tail end of the previous summer and this was the first time since that the weather had been good enough to wear it. She didn't need any more reason than that and had happily pulled it from her wardrobe this morning to iron it for its maiden outing.

The colour was delicate but it suited her winter complexion – though she'd have loved to wear them, stronger colours overpowered it. Her mousey hair had been given a helping hand to something more impactful with the aid of a bottle of blonde hair dye, but the sage green of her eyes was the same as her mother's and aunt's. She had a figure so straight up and down that an unkind classmate had once teased her she could iron clothes on it, to which another had added that she'd look like a boy with short hair – and in a world of Kim Kardashian-style booties it was deeply unfashionable. Still, she'd got used to the way her body looked and she'd even learned to love it; if only she'd been born in the roaring twenties she'd have made one hell of a flapper girl, cutting a dash at all the best parties. Perhaps a little unconsciously, to redress the balance somewhat, she tended towards ultra-feminine looks, wearing all manner of soft pastel fabrics and leaving her hair in loose curls.

She gave herself one last glance in the mirror now, fluffed her waves, touched up her lipstick and hurried back downstairs so she'd be ready and waiting to direct the first guests to their hiding places.

Patricia was already in the garden, looking gorgeous in wide-legged linen trousers and a vest top that showed off a figure earned by daily yoga. Her features mirrored those of her nieces in the uncanniest way; the same features that Emma recognised from old photos of her mum. These days, photos often felt like the only way she could recall what her mum had looked like – as the years had gone by Emma had struggled more and more to picture her, no matter how hard she'd tried to hold on to the memories.

Her aunt looked up from an extension lead she was plugging in. 'You look lovely.'

Emma smiled. 'I was just going to say the same thing to you.'

Dominic came out from the kitchen and handed her a drink. 'Thought you might like a nice G&T to get you started. You've certainly earned it today.'

'I feel as if I have.' Emma took the glass and sipped, savouring the ice-cold crispness of a perfectly mixed drink. 'It's not even my party but I'm as nervous as hell. I suppose I just want it to go well.'

'Everyone knows how much you care about Elise,' Patricia said. 'It's understandable you'd want her send-off to be perfect.'

There was a sound from the garden gate and they turned to see three girls trying to undo the latch. The guests had been instructed to come straight round the side of the house to the garden, so Emma and her aunt and uncle weren't surprised to see Elise's university friends letting themselves in.

'Hi!' Emma dashed forward to give them a hand undoing the gate before ushering them in. 'I'm so glad you could come! You found us OK?'

'The taxi driver did,' one of them said with a light laugh. 'We wouldn't have had a clue.'

'Well, however you found us, we're glad,' Patricia said. 'Elise will be thrilled to see you.'

'Yes,' Emma agreed, 'it'll mean a lot to her that you're here.'

'Oh, we wouldn't have missed this,' another girl said. Emma vaguely knew them as Abigail, Sana and Olivia; she only wished she could remember who was who. 'Even if Little-Miss-First-Class-Degree did show the rest of us up.'

The third girl laughed. 'I think that might be something to do with her actually working and us having too many mornings in bed.'

'Oh yeah,' the second said with a grin. 'That'll be it.'

Emma's proud smile grew. Elise had worked hard but she was clever too – and nobody minded admitting she was the brains of the family.

As Patricia started to fill the girls in on the plan for the afternoon, two more guests arrived – tutors from Elise's sixth-form college days. They were quickly followed by more family members (cousins from their dad's side) and colleagues from the restaurant Elise had worked at to finance the last year of her studies. Then came Elise's geography teacher from school and his wife – Elise had always said had it not been for Mr Baker firing her interest in the physical landscapes of mountains and lakes and the way the earth had been formed, she would never have gone on to her degree course in earth sciences, and she wouldn't currently be about to embark on her dream job as a volcanologist.

Some old school friends came next, followed by more family members, and soon the garden was buzzing. As people who knew each other chatted and those who didn't got acquainted, Patricia checked her watch and then hurried over to Emma.

'They'll be here in five minutes!' she said. Emma didn't need to ask who she meant and couldn't help but note that her aunt, who'd been calm all morning, was now showing almost as much excitement and nervousness as Emma. 'Shall we get everyone in position?'

Emma glanced around the garden. 'It might take that long to get everyone organised so perhaps we ought to, just to be on the safe side.'

'And knowing Elise she'll decide to turn up early.'

'There's that,' Emma agreed.

After calling three times for everyone's attention, Emma and her aunt finally got started. They directed one giggling group to the summer house (and if Elise didn't hear them giggling when she walked in then she probably needed a hearing aid because they didn't seem to understand the concept of quiet or surprise). When the summer house was full they sent another group to stand in a gap between it and the fence behind it. The third group were directed to the far end of the garden to hide behind a wall of fruit trees, and the last ones stood around the corner of the main house. People continued to giggle and whisper and while Emma could hardly go around telling them to shut up, she hoped they would calm down before Elise arrived.

The one notable absence, Emma observed with a mixture of sadness, disappointment and anger, was her boyfriend Dougie. She didn't even know why she was sad about it; she ought to have been used to being let down by him. When she thought about their relationship, her memory often played tricks, so that, in her mind, the slide into indifference was never quite as fast as it had been in reality.

In the early days he'd been so attentive, but the change had begun pretty soon after he'd hooked her. It had started with little things like being late to a date for no apparent reason, or making arrangements and changing them to suit him (despite the fact it really put her out), and then moved on to cancelling them altogether at the last minute. That had progressed further until he was missing events he was supposed to be attending with her entirely. He'd had a job in the beginning, a decent one at the council, but then he'd been made redundant. That had been followed by a bust-up with his parents that had seen him thrown out of the family home, and Emma had felt sorry for him. She'd moved him into her house and he'd promised to pull his weight as she was paying the mortgage, but it hadn't taken him long to start going out when he was supposed to be waiting in for workmen or to conveniently 'forget' chores Emma had asked him to do while she was at work and he was home.

In short, he'd started to take her for granted and today proved it was only getting worse. Though now was hardly the time to pose the question, Emma had to ask herself again why she continued to hope he might once again become the man she'd fallen for. They were engaged too, and she wanted to believe that their eventual marriage might change things for the better – but when she really forced herself to face the cold hard facts, why would it?

Yet, despite all this, the thought of being without Dougie scared her. For reasons she didn't even understand, she loved him. At least, she was fairly certain she did. But it was about more than love; he was her constant, her anchor, the one person in her life who was always there (except when he wasn't). With Dougie she at least knew where she was, even if that was quite low on his list of priorities.

It wasn't always bad either. During the good times he made her laugh and he brightened her days. He was cute and good-looking and they liked the same things – same TV, same radio stations, same takeaways on a Friday night. If only she could get him to understand that when he let her down it cut deeper than him just missing a date or leaving workmen scratching their heads on the doorstep, things with Dougie could be perfect. And if not perfect, good enough to make her content with the life she had. She wasn't like Elise – she didn't need to chase a dream or adventure. She only wanted to feel safe and valued – she just needed to feel solid ground beneath her feet.

But there was no time to dwell on any of this now, because if Elise took one thing seriously it was timekeeping, and, true to form, she arrived at the allotted hour almost to the second.

Emma went to meet her and their dad at the gate. Elise was asking why they were going straight to the garden instead of knocking at the front door to be let in, and her dad was struggling to give a convincing excuse.

'Emma… Hi!'

Elise greeted her sister and then her gaze was drawn to the garden as they walked in. She took a moment to note the tables set for food, the bunting and balloons, and, as understanding began to change her frown into a look of illumination, everyone leapt out.

'Surprise!'

Elise let her mouth fall open, and then her eyes began to fill with tears.

Emma laughed. 'Oh my God. You're not supposed to cry.'

Elise looked round at everyone. 'This is for me?'

Dominic put an arm around Patricia, who stood next to him. 'Well the sign does say "Good luck Elise", so I think your clue might be there.'

Elise wiped a hand across her eyes. 'I don't know what to say!'

She didn't have to find anything either, because a second later friends and family began to crowd round to offer hugs and kisses and words of congratulations and warm wishes for her new venture. Emma stepped back and went to stand with Patricia and Dominic to give them all time. Patricia smiled fondly as she watched.

'Well,' she said. 'Phase one went as smoothly as could be expected.'

Emma nodded. 'Didn't it? I think it's going to be a lovely evening.'

'Me too.'

It was going to be more than lovely, Emma thought. Perhaps it would be close to perfect, if only it hadn't meant she was shortly about to say goodbye to her little sister.

*

By 8 p.m. almost everyone in the garden was well on their way to drunkenness, even Emma, who, despite getting more annoyed at Dougie's absence as every hour went by, had decided that it wasn't going to ruin her afternoon.

She'd just looked at her phone again, thinking about leaving another angry message for him, before deciding against it, when Elise came up behind her and flung her arms around her neck. Emma whipped round and smiled when she saw who it was.

'I've hardly had a chance to talk to you all afternoon,' Elise slurred. She was looking bleary and very much like someone who'd had a drink pressed into her hand by everyone she'd spoken to that day.

'You've been a bit busy,' Emma said, smiling. 'I'll forgive you this once.'

Elise waved her arms around with about as much control as a streamer in the breeze. 'I can't believe how many people you managed to get here without me knowing a thing about it!'

'It wasn't easy – but it was worth it.'

'Thank you for making the effort…' Elise stumbled slightly over her own foot and Emma caught her with a laugh. It was hard to imagine how she'd managed to trip over without actually walking anywhere, but perhaps it said a lot about just how drunk she was.

'And you're supposed to be climbing up mountains – you can't even stay on your feet on flat ground.'

'No… no…' Elise landed a barrage of heavy pats on Emma's arm. 'Listen… I love this party. I couldn't love you any more for doing it.'

'I can't take all the credit – though I do appreciate the sentiment. Patricia and Dom did a lot, and Dad was in on it, of course.'

'You're all too good… I don't deserve all this fuss.'

'Of course you do!'

Emma regarded her sister with a swell of love. Though she was closer to thirty and Elise only twenty-two, they didn't look so different. Elise's cheeks were perhaps a little plumper and the faint beginnings of crow's feet tellingly absent, but the sisters shared the same eyes, a shade of green closer to grey, and the same willowy figure. Where Emma dyed her hair blonde, Elise had opted for a bright copper to cover her mousey locks. Not knowing that there was a party planned in her honour, Elise had turned up in a pair of black jeans and a fitted T-shirt but she still looked incredible. Around her neck she wore a pendant fashioned from a piece of volcanic rock – her favourite thing ever, she often said – that Emma had given to her on her twenty-first birthday. Emma had never seen her without it since that day, which made her happier than she could say.

Elise kissed her lightly. 'I'm going to miss you so much. You'll come and visit, won't you?'

'Come to Iceland? Why ever would I do that?'

Elise laughed. 'It's not always cold, you know.'

Emma smiled. 'Of course I'll visit. You just try keeping me away.'

'Good,' Elise said with a violently wobbly nod. She glanced around again. 'Where's Dougie, by the way?'

'He's… running late,' Emma said. She could have launched into a rant about the truth of his absence but that was hardly going to improve her mood and would put a damper on things to boot.

The fact was, Dougie let her down a lot and there was no way Elise wouldn't have noticed that, but perhaps out of respect, or perhaps because she thought her opinions about him might not be welcome, she'd never made a big deal about it to Emma. She'd comment and then Emma would make an excuse and they'd both let the moment pass without further discussion. Their dad, Noel, was a different matter – he had many words to say about Dougie and hardly any of them were complimentary. But then again, he had many scathing words to say about a lot of things so it wasn't all that surprising.

Elise opened her mouth, looked as if she was struggling for a moment to get her brain in gear, and then was about to say what was on her mind when their dad joined them.

'Where is he?' he asked gruffly.

'Running late,' Emma repeated, having no need to ask who her dad meant.

'Very late. Anyone would think he's avoiding us.'

'He's not, Dad… why would he? He just got held up somewhere.'

Noel raised his eyebrows in disbelief. 'Hmm, I can see how it might be murder at the fishing lake at this time of day – fish throwing themselves at your rod left, right and centre…'

'Dad…' Elise, even in her drunken state, seemed to sense the sudden increase of tension. 'I'm sure he'll be here when he can get here.'

'Maybe,' Noel said, though his tone made it clear he didn't believe that for a second. 'Although, it's not like anyone's missing him anyway.'

'Dad, don't,' Emma said. 'Not today please.'

'I'm not going to start anything, but I'm your dad and you can't expect me to say nothing because I care too much to do that.'

'I know – but just not now, eh?'

As if he'd known he was being talked about, the garden gate now opened and Dougie strolled in. He was in grubby jeans and still wearing the jacket Emma knew he fished in, his shoulder-length hair pulled back low at his neck and tied with a band. The sight of him here, clearly not even having gone to clean himself up first, made Emma bristle. Ordinarily it didn't bother her, and she'd once even liked that he had no airs and graces, but he knew what this party meant to her and she'd specifically asked him to make an effort. She'd asked him not to go fishing, but she'd suspected he would anyway. That was really OK too – as long as he was there when he'd promised he would be and arrived at her uncle and aunt's house clean, she couldn't really dictate his movements before then.

'I'm just...'

Emma made a vague excuse and went to meet Dougie, intercepting him before there'd been time for anyone else to see he'd arrived. She shoved him towards the gate. 'Back out – now!'

'I know what you're going to say, babes, and I'm sorry, I—'

'Don't!' Emma put her hand up to halt the barrage of excuses that were coming. 'Out – now!'

'Look...' He placed his hands on her shoulders and tried to move her aside, but she stood firm and glared at him. 'If you're going to roast me for this then I get it, feel free, but at least wait until the party is over, yeah?'

She wanted nothing more than to let rip, to tell him exactly how furious she was – if nothing else it would make her feel better. But galling as it was, she couldn't deny that he had a point. Now wasn't the time or place to make a scene.

'Only because this is Elise's special day,' she said in a low voice, 'I'm letting it go for now. But you'd better mingle and you'd better be charming. You also need to apologise to my aunt and uncle for all the work you were supposed to do that they had to do because you weren't here. And to Elise for not being here earlier, and to my dad because right now he's the only person here now who hates you more than I do...'

'Babes…' he began, but Emma didn't wait to hear whatever pathetic excuse was coming. She didn't want to know where he'd been or why he was late because it would probably only make her more furious than she already was.

Instead, making sure nobody was looking, she hurried into the house and took refuge in the spare room so she could cry in private and let all her frustration out. Then she went back to the party as if nothing had happened.

Chapter Two

As Elise wasn't actually leaving until later that week, Emma bid her a brief farewell as the party wound up and promised to catch up with her before she left. She'd worn her smile well all afternoon, but it disappeared as soon as she and Dougie got into the taxi to go home. They sat side by side, stony-faced and silent the whole journey. Emma was desperate to vent her frustration but aware that the back of a cab probably wasn't the place to do so.

But as soon as the front door had closed and they were safely in, she let rip.

'How could you do that to me? To Elise? She's leaving the country and you couldn't even be bothered to come and say goodbye!'

'I did come.'

Emma threw her bag onto the sofa and followed Dougie into the kitchen. 'Hardly! How do you think it looked to everyone that you weren't there?'

'I'm sure they told you,' he said carelessly.

'They bloody well did! Doesn't that bother you one bit?'

'Why should it? I can't do anything about what they think of me.'

'Of course you can! Do you know what they say?'

'I'm sure you're going to tell me,' he sighed as he sat on a chair.

'They think you're a waster who lives off me.'

'We know that's not true.'

'That's hardly the point – it makes me look foolish that I defend you all the time, that I'm giving my life to someone who gives nothing back! You may not care that they think you're a waster but I do. You may not care that they think I'm an idiot to have you but I do—'

'You care way too much about what other people think – that's your problem.'

'And you don't worry enough about how other people feel! You might think it shouldn't bother me or that it's my problem that I let it, but the fact remains that it *does* and you're supposed to love me, which means it should matter to you how I feel about it. But you don't give a shit, and what am I supposed to make of that?'

She stood next to the table, too wired to sit down with him, and he got up and pushed past her to fetch a beer from the fridge.

'I suppose you're about to tell me,' he said.

'I shouldn't have to tell you! I've told you so many times now you ought to know! If you cared one jot about me, Dougie, you'd get it!'

'You know I care; I just don't take things as seriously as you do. It's not like Elise is going forever.'

'That's not the point! I asked you to be there and that should have been enough. I'd have done it for you. It's not about Elise or how long she'll be gone; it's about you and me, how we treat each other…' Emma's voice faltered. 'It's about making each other happy and taking seriously the things the other thinks are important. You clearly don't think I'm worth the effort at all.'

'Jesus, I was late! You're overreacting, as usual! OK – get this rant out of your system and then please let us get back to normal!'

'That's the problem, Dougie… I don't know if our normal is enough for me anymore.'

'What?'

'I think... I don't think I have the energy to carry this on.'

'Good, because I'm sick of this argument.'

'I don't mean the argument. I mean us – I don't think I can keep it up. I'm tired, and I'm sick of being the only one who makes an effort. I don't think I can do it anymore and I don't think I ought to.'

'You can't mean that?'

'Why not?'

He slammed his beer onto the table and glared at her. 'This is stupid!'

'No, for once this is sense. Where has the past two years got us, Dougie?'

'We live together.'

'It's my mortgage – that's hardly commitment.'

'We're engaged – what more commitment do you want?'

'We're only engaged because you were drunk enough one night to ask. We haven't even set a date for the wedding.'

'We said in a couple of years.'

'No, *you* said in a couple of years. *A couple of years* – what does that even mean? It means nothing – there's no real intention in it.'

'Alright then, pick a date right now if that's how you feel.'

Emma sighed and ran a hand through her hair. 'It doesn't work like that.'

'Of course it does.'

'No it doesn't. Planning a wedding is supposed to be a joyous thing, full of anticipation and hope. It's not supposed to be a solution just to get you off the hook after a row that you caused.'

Dougie moved towards her now and tried to take her in his arms but she shifted out of range.

'You know me, babes,' he said, his voice dropping to a more persuasive lilt. 'I want to marry you, I do, but I need pushing along from time to time or I'll never do anything.'

'Dragging is more like it. And how do you think that feels?'

'I have no idea,' he said, the gentleness of his tone falling away again.

'Like I'm forcing you to love me.'

'Don't be stupid.'

'Well,' Emma demanded, 'how would it make you feel?'

'I could say the same to you. You're forcing me to change for you.'

'I'm not asking you to change! Unless taking a second to consider someone else's feelings is asking for change. Go fishing, go out with your mates, forget arrangements from time to time... I accepted those things about you a long time ago. I don't want a lot; I just want to be able to count on you for the stuff that really matters. When the chips are down I only ask that you're with me. Surely that's not too much for someone you're supposed to love?'

Dougie grabbed his beer again with a sigh. 'It was just a party. I'll see Elise again before she goes if that's what you want.'

Emma pressed her lips together, but the sting had gone from the tail of her anger. She had no more energy left to feel anything but defeated.

'Maybe you won't.'

'Won't what?'

'Maybe you won't be here by then. If I can't count on you for something like this then what can I count on you for? And if I can't count on you for anything then what's the point of any of it?'

'God, it was just a party, Em! She's only going for a year!'

'She's my sister! And you know what she means to me. It was more than just a party to me. I wanted to say goodbye properly to my best friend, to the girl I watched grow up without a mother and yet still achieve amazing things. It was supposed to be a celebration of all she's overcome, of recognising that the tragedies of life don't have to define you and that there's always hope. That party meant things that I can't put into words, and you know that.'

'I didn't know that. If you'd put it like that to me before—'

'What?' Emma folded her arms across her chest. Every muscle was taut. 'You'd have made more of an effort? No you wouldn't have, and even if you had that's not the point. You shouldn't have needed to hear it like that to do the decent thing; you should have been there because I'd asked you to, because you'd promised – it shouldn't have to be anything bigger than that.'

'What do you want me to do? I said I was sorry, I said you could pick a wedding date. I can't do any more. I can't turn back time and change it.'

'No, and more's the pity neither can I.'

'What does that mean?'

'It means if I could go back to that day in the park where we met, maybe I wouldn't have sat on that bench to tie my shoe. Or maybe, when you'd started to talk to me, I would have walked away instead of giving you my number.'

'Yeah? Well maybe that goes for both of us. It hasn't been easy street for me either. I've lost count of the times you've flipped out on me over nothing.'

'I don't flip out over nothing! Yes, sometimes I ask you to put yourself out for me but isn't that what couples do? I do things for you all the time.'

'I don't ask you to.'

'You don't need to ask when you please yourself either way.'

'So I can't have a life of my own now?'

'I'm not saying we ought to be joined at the hip, just that there are some things we should pull together for.'

'Well I'm sorry. It won't happen again.'

Dougie grabbed his beer and stalked out of the room. A moment later, Emma heard the bedroom door slam shut and the sound of his games console being switched on.

She let out a long breath. Every time they had one of these arguments he said the same thing – *It won't happen again* – but it always did. She had to wonder why she kept letting it.

Emma woke the next morning on the sofa, where she'd spent the night. The sound of the front door slamming had dragged her from a sleep she wasn't sorry to see the back of because it had hardly been sleep at all. She'd tossed and turned for most of the night and the odd hour when she'd settled into something deeper had done nothing more than give her a nice crick in the neck.

She pushed herself up and off the sofa and padded through to the kitchen in bare feet. The kettle was cold, but Dougie's Wellingtons were gone from their usual spot by the back door. An inspection of the lean-to revealed his fishing gear had gone from there too. So much for having a grown-up discussion once they'd both sobered up. He must have woken early and gone straight out. To avoid her? It was quite possible and she didn't know whether to feel frustrated or sad about that. She could have phoned him but she suspected he wouldn't pick up, and the way she felt she wasn't altogether sure she wanted to talk to him anyway. It was certainly too early to call anyone else to get things off her chest, so she set about making a cup of tea.

She stared out of the window at a citrus-hued dawn, sunlight just beginning to slide across the rooftops of her street. Her head felt woolly, her thoughts sluggish, her eyes swollen from lack of sleep and the tears she'd shed the night before as she'd lain on the sofa and tried to drop off, knowing she was in for a bad night.

The hangover she had now was hardly helping. Before Dougie turned up she'd been determined to enjoy the party, and as the drink flowed she'd gladly taken her share. Then Dougie had arrived and, far from making things better, he'd made them worse, so she'd drunk to deaden the anger and frustration that had threatened to explode from her. At home after the party she'd carried on, unable to get any decent resolution from her argument with him. She'd decided to stop only when she'd realised she was so numb and dizzy she was likely to pass out with one more anyway. And, far from making her feel better, it seemed every glass was making her more miserable, so what was the point?

She was certainly paying for it this morning.

Once she'd made tea and a slice of toast she sat in the silent kitchen, her gaze once again drawn to the window. It was a beautiful morning now the frost had melted, the kind that would send waves of sunlight across sleepy fields where the hollows were still hidden by blankets of mist, through newly budding trees, vibrant green and bursting into life.

Dougie had probably gone to his usual spot to fish at a nearby pool. Even though he called it the fishing lake, in reality it was slap bang in the city centre and barely big enough to qualify as a lake at all, but it had everything he said he needed for a lazy day by the water. Usually he'd meet friends there; some of them worked and some – like Dougie who'd been made redundant the previous Christmas – didn't. There was always someone for him to catch up with and it didn't seem to matter to Dougie who it was.

Sometimes he'd smell suspicious when he came home but he would always reassure Emma that even though his friends might indulge in a little 'herbal roll-up' he didn't. She was never sure she believed him but didn't see the point in airing her doubts. To her, the idea of sitting by a lake all day – and not even a particularly pretty or peaceful one as the sound of the traffic on the nearby road roared past, while just over the treetops you could see apartment buildings rising into the sky – was so dull she imagined the only way you could get through it was with the aid of a 'herbal roll-up', so she wouldn't have been surprised to discover that Dougie did partake.

Taking a sip of her tea she grimaced, realising she'd been staring out of the window so long it had gone cold. Her toast hadn't fared much better, but she forced herself to eat it anyway, washed it down with the last of her cold tea and went to get dressed.

The morning was cool but the sun was bright as Emma walked to Dougie's fishing spot, certain she'd find him there. It was still spring and though they'd been blessed with unseasonably warm weather recently – prompting them to change Elise's party from an indoor to outdoor event – the chill of the morning took a little time to burn away.

She hadn't decided yet what she was going to do or say if she found Dougie there; it just seemed to her that activity of any sort was better than the dreadful inertia of sitting, pointlessly fuming alone in an empty house while he carried on as if nothing had happened. Something *had* happened. Something was broken – at least, it was for Emma – and she wasn't even sure she wanted to fix it. Whether she did or didn't, it still needed addressing. She'd been so afraid of life alone she'd indulged Dougie for far too long now, but when all was said and done, would life alone be worse than this? Their relationship was filled with uncertainty and a lack of real commitment or promise. Was it really worth fighting for when the battle was so exhausting and thankless?

Totally absorbed by her thoughts, she barely registered that there was a woman out for an early morning run, head down with EarPods in, making straight for her. At the last moment she looked up and stopped dead feet away, and, as their eyes met, she broke into a smile.

'Emma?' she asked uncertainly, wiping sweat from her brow. Then she repeated it. 'Emma… Emma Cotton… It is, isn't it?'

Emma tried not to frown. She hated situations like this, where someone recognised her and she didn't recognise them – it was all sorts of awkward. But then the features suddenly registered and a memory clicked into place.

'Tia?'

Emma paused, taking in the trim figure, cropped hair, flawless olive skin and huge dark eyes. Tia Capaldi – she'd been wildly jealous of this girl at high school, who'd always seemed so perfect, so blessed and popular. Seeing her now, even all these years later, that pang of envy caught her again, but this time entirely by surprise. She shook away the ridiculous notion. They were grown women now and the time for that sort of insecurity ought to be long gone.

'It's me!' Tia said. She nodded approvingly at Emma. 'You look great! Have you coloured your hair?'

'For many years now,' Emma said. 'And I was just thinking the same about you. I mean, you always had a great figure but now – well, you're ripped!'

Tia laughed lightly. 'Thanks! It takes a lot of work, let me tell you, and some mornings I wonder whether I ought to trade some of my muscle mass for a nice lie-in.' She put her hands to her hips and swayed from side to side; Emma presumed it was to keep her muscles from tightening up as she stood and chatted. 'So, what are you doing with yourself these days?'

Emma took a breath to reply, but then paused. What *was* she doing with herself these days? If she was perfectly honest, not much. A relationship that was going nowhere, a job pretty much the same, a distinctly underwhelming salary, a tiny, unassuming house, and not much in the way of prospects to change any of that.

'Oh, you know,' she said, 'mostly working.'

'Yeah? Must be something clever – you were always the brainbox of the class. I remember you used to help me out with my maths questions when the teacher wasn't looking – you were always such a sweetie. I don't think I would have got through those classes without you.'

Emma didn't remember it quite like that. She recalled Tia leaning over from the table in front to catch a quick look at Emma's answers, grinning and putting a finger to her nose and then copying them down on her own sheet. That was how it had been pretty much every week in the run-up to their exams. It didn't seem important now, though, and wasn't really worth bringing up.

'I think you might be confusing me with my sister,' Emma said. 'She was the clever one.'

'No… I seem to recall you were clever too.'

'Well… anyway…' Emma wasn't sure what she was supposed to say to that, 'what are you up to now?'

'Right now I'm in between jobs,' Tia said. 'If I'm honest life is a bit crap at the moment. I've just gone through a horrible divorce – a huge relief but messy as they always are. We sold the gym we'd been running together and I get half of that…'

'I'm so sorry to hear that. So what are you planning to do?'

'I have some plans… Well, I'm sure you don't want to hear about all that.'

Emma sensed that despite Tia's words, she wanted to tell Emma her plans. Perhaps they were the sorts of plans that were more dreams, dreams that only came true if you spoke them out loud, and maybe she hadn't yet been able to tell them to anyone. Emma could be that person, and if she couldn't help herself maybe she'd be able to help someone else. After all, it took no effort to listen.

'If they're things you can tell me about I'd love to.'

Tia's face lit up. 'I've seen a business opportunity. It's a crazy one, but I'm really thinking about giving it a go.'

'Oh? What's that? Is it fitness-related?'

'No, a million miles away from the gym, but I think that's what I like about it. It's in Dorset.'

'So a million miles away from here too,' Emma said with a smile.

'Oh, I suppose so,' Tia said. 'But I think a clean break is what I need. You know, new scenery, new people… I think it will do me good.'

'I understand that,' Emma said, longing to add that she understood better than Tia could imagine. 'So what kind of business is it?'

'A boutique hotel,' Tia said. 'I'm looking for a partner at the moment, someone to come on board with me. My funds will only cover half of what I need to get things off the ground… at least my dodgy maths is saying as much. I don't suppose you know anyone who might be willing to take a chance on a hotel in Dorset…?'

Emma gave a sympathetic smile. Maybe Tia's dream needed more than speaking out loud after all. 'Sorry,' she said. 'I can't say I do.'

'So you're not in the market for an exciting new venture in the Dorset countryside yourself?'

'I wish!'

'I suppose you wouldn't want to give up your job for something that wacky,' Tia said ruefully. 'That's the thing – it's finding someone who would. Most people I know are either in good jobs or are settled here and don't want to move all the way to Dorset. Still, I'll keep looking and I'm sure something will turn up eventually…' She gave a smile that felt to Emma like it had taken a little effort to conjure. 'It usually does.'

My job's not that great, Emma wanted to say. *I work as an assistant to the HR manager at a haulage company in a tiny Portakabin. They treat me like crap. There are no prospects of promotion at all because that would mean I'd have to stop skivvying for the manager, while the owner looks at the women in ways he shouldn't and thinks it's OK to pinch your bum as he walks past…*

But she didn't.

'Well,' Emma said. 'It was lovely to see you again but I expect you want to get on with your run.'

'Oh, yes, I'll go off the boil if I stop for too long. It was lovely to see you too. Listen, look me up on Insta or Facebook; don't be a stranger. I'd love to hear more about what you've been up to.'

Emma wasn't sure she believed that. Unless Tia was very desperate to fall into a coma from sheer boredom, in which case Emma could provide plenty of material to assist with that. She gave her brightest smile-that-wasn't-really-a-smile.

'I will,' she said. 'Are you on there as Tia Capaldi or did you change when you got married?'

'I'm changing my name back, so you'll find me as Capaldi easily enough. Or I could find you... Don't worry, we can work it out somehow.'

Working it out somehow was something Emma was already beginning to recognise as one of Tia's mantras. Perhaps it wasn't a bad one to have. Now that she thought about it, Tia had always been carefree and chilled at school and that had been one of the reasons everyone had liked her so much.

'It was great to catch up,' Tia added, starting to run on the spot to warm up again. 'Don't forget to look me up!'

'I won't!' Emma called after her as she began to jog off. A moment passed while Emma watched her go, and then she turned to her path again. She put one foot in front of the other and stopped.

Now that she thought about it, she didn't know whether she liked the look of this path after all.

Chapter Three

She didn't go to the pond in the end. After bumping into Tia, it suddenly felt like an unproductive, pointless waste of energy to confront Dougie, a negative experience that would only set her up for more misery. Instead Emma decided it would wait and that she'd be better off getting ready for work, collecting her thoughts before she went.

By the time she got to the office it felt as if she'd been up for half the day already. Technically, she had, having woken at the crack of dawn and arriving at work four hours later. At this rate she'd be ready for bed just after lunch.

Margot, the woman who purported to be the HR manager but who, in reality, held the title, collected the salary and let Emma do all the actual managing, was tucking into her usual 9 a.m. toast and jam when Emma finally sat at her desk. Emma could never quite understand why Margot didn't just eat breakfast at home like everyone else rather than as soon as she got to work, but she'd given up trying to understand Margot a long time ago.

Margot looked up, toast halfway to her mouth. 'Good morning, Emma,' she said, spraying crumbs across her desk and wiping them onto the floor before cramming in another mouthful to replace the toast she'd just spat out.

'Morning...'

Emma's gaze was drawn to a pile of folders on her desk. Personnel files – at least they looked like it. Burnbury's Haulage had yet to enter the computer age so it wasn't a surprise to see paper folders, but she did wonder why they'd been left there.

'They need warnings,' Margot said.

Emma looked up. 'What kind of warnings?'

'They've all had too many absences this year.'

Emma picked up one of the files and frowned at it. 'All of them?'

'I know… shocking, isn't it?'

'If there are so many how come it's only just come to light? Surely we ought to have been picking those up as they happened.'

By which Emma meant Margot ought to have been picking them up, as she was the manager and it was her job. Margot simply shrugged.

'Who's got to issue these warnings?' Emma asked with a horrible sinking feeling. They had been left on her desk, after all; there wasn't a lot of working out to it.

'I had thought you could write the letters,' Margot said, shoving the last corner of toast into her mouth and wiping her hands on her skirt.

'That's all? I just write letters and that's it?'

'I think so for now.'

'And you're signing the letters?'

'Of course, but your name will have to go on there too. After all, you're my assistant and when I'm not here they'll need to know who else to contact if they want to discuss them.'

And when the complaints came in – as they would – Emma would be picking them up whether Margot was there or not, because Margot always did her damnedest to avoid answering her phone at all times, and especially when she was expecting trouble. Come to think of it, she avoided actual work as much as she could at all times. For someone with the title of HR manager she did precious little managing, unless you counted managing a slab of cake an hour after the 9 a.m. toast. And then managing her lunch at eleven thirty. And then a second lunch at one because she'd already eaten her first one but she was hungry now because it was actually lunchtime. Then the mid-afternoon pick-me-up at 2 p.m., then the snack at four thirty to keep her going until she got home. She managed all those things bloody brilliantly.

Emma shoved the files to one side with a barely contained sigh. 'I'm going to make a drink before I start this lot,' she said, getting up.

'Oh, you couldn't just pour an extra one?' Margot scooted over on her wheeled office chair and dumped her mug onto Emma's desk before scooting back again. 'I'm absolutely snowed here.'

Doing what, exactly, was a mystery, but Emma took the cup in silence and went to the tiny Portakabin next to theirs that doubled as a reception area to see drivers. It was where Burnbury's kept their kitchen equipment, and when Emma got there she found Leonard Burnbury, the managing director, in there reading a paper.

'Morning, Leonard,' Emma said. 'Don't mind me, I was just making—'

'Making a brew, are you?' Leonard looked up from his paper. 'Couldn't just manage another one, could you? There's a good girl; I'm parched.'

Would it be slightly hysterical, Emma wondered, to throw the mugs she'd collected at Leonard Burnbury's head and tell him to stick his job? In a better mood she might have given a wry smile – some brilliant career for the school brainbox. If only Tia Capaldi could see her now.

*

Dougie was asleep on the armchair when she got home, looking like an old man who'd had a miraculous facelift. Emma was struck by a startling flash-forward of the kind of scene she might be treated to in fifty years' time if they were still together, and it wasn't a vision that cheered her. In fact, it was just about the rotten cherry on her miserable, rancid cake of a day.

She'd typed half the warning letters, having had no choice but to do otherwise, when she'd happened to notice one of the staff members the letters were intended for didn't qualify for a warning at all. So then she'd gone through the rest of the files to double-check, only to discover that Margot's calculations had been as lazy as Margot and were way out. In fact, nobody had broken the sickness and absence rules at all. At least Emma hadn't sent any of the letters – she could only imagine what kind of hell would have broken loose if she had – but it was still deeply irritating that the job had been given to her at all and she'd wasted hours on it. She'd confronted Margot, who'd just laughed it off and gone to the shop to buy some crisps, leaving Emma to silently fume at her desk.

'Dougie...'

He opened his eyes and pushed himself up in the chair. 'Sorry, babes... only closed my eyes for a minute. Knackered.'

'I'm sure,' she said dryly. 'Where did you go at the crack of dawn?'

'Thought I'd get a few hours in at the lake. Nothing else to do.'

Emma went through to the kitchen to put the kettle on. Dougie followed her.

'So you haven't heard back from any of those jobs yet? I'd have thought you'd have plenty to do today applying for some more. Unless you can do that and fish at the same time—'

'Actually, I've got an interview Friday,' he said indignantly.

Emma turned to him, suddenly feeling guilty. Perhaps she was being harsh on him. Maybe she'd forgotten how hard job-hunting could be; after all, it was a long time since she'd had to do it. 'That's brilliant!'

'Yeah.'

'Where is it?'

'That warehouse on the trading estate that does wholesale trade.'

Emma looked blank.

'Next to the garage,' Dougie added.

Emma nodded. 'Oh, I think I know where you mean. That's good. The job looks good, does it?'

'It's a job, innit? It's a bit beneath my qualifications if anything, and if I take it I'll be selling myself short, but as you keep insisting I take the first thing—'

She held a hand up. 'Dougie, I don't insist you take the first thing, but it's been months and you haven't taken anything. We can't manage for much longer with just me earning; we need the money, and I think whether it's beneath you or not is a moot point right now. Do you think I love my job? I do it to put food on the table.'

'You could get another job if you don't like it – I don't make you stay.'

'What? Just flounce out and spend months unemployed?' She planted her hands on her hips. 'I can't see that working out, unless your long-term couple goals are for us to be homeless.'

'Babes…'

Dougie gave her a pleading look. She knew it well and it was hard to stay angry in the face of it. At this point she'd usually give in, but she'd had a shitty day and she still hadn't forgiven him for the debacle that was Elise's party.

'Please tell me you're going to take this job if they offer it.'

'It depends what the pay is like and the—'

'You know what,' she cut in, grabbing her jacket from the back of the chair where she'd put it only moments before, 'I can't deal with this right now. Find something in the fridge and feed yourself.'

'Where are you going?'

'I have absolutely no idea, except that it will be away from you.'

Emma didn't plan it, but her walk took her to her aunt's house. She'd briefly considered texting Elise to see if she was home, but she'd probably be busy with last-minute packing. Besides, Emma needed to offload and she didn't want to worry her sister, who really didn't deserve to have the shine stripped from her impending adventure. Not only that, but there was an awkward truth to acknowledge here: Emma felt like a failure when she compared herself to her little sister, and to go and admit all her troubles to Elise would somehow only make it all worse.

Patricia opened the door with a faint look of surprise.

'I know you weren't expecting me,' Emma said. 'But I was just passing. You don't mind me calling, do you?'

'Just passing?' Patricia raised her eyebrows but opened the door wider to admit her niece. 'It's not often you're just passing anywhere but of course I don't mind. Come in – Dominic's just bottling up, but it doesn't all have to go into a bottle.'

Emma smiled. She and her uncle's home brew had been intimately acquainted before. It was potent stuff and the last time she'd had three or four glasses she'd been off her proverbial trolley. While the prospect of that was quite appealing right now, it was a week night and work the following day promised to be busy; probably best not to take another hangover in with her.

'That does sound lovely but maybe another time? Tea would be good, if you don't mind.'

'Tea it is.'

Emma followed her aunt down the hall and into the kitchen. Through the window she could see her uncle tinkering with a strange-looking arrangement of pipes and bell jars at the open doors of his garden shed.

'What's he making?' Emma asked.

'Hmm?' Patricia hunted in the cupboards for the mug she always gave to Emma on her visits. She had one for Emma with a letter E wrapped in rambling roses, and one that Elise always used, also with a large, cursive letter E on it, the difference being that the flowers were long chains of daisies.

'The wine,' Emma said. 'Is it wine he's making or something else?'

'Oh, yes… wine. Peach. There was a big crate of damaged fruit going cheap outside the greengrocers and he thought they might make a nice drink.'

'I think they would,' Emma agreed. 'Summery.'

Patricia nodded vaguely. 'Are you hungry?'

'I could eat – haven't had tea yet.'

'Neither have we. There's plenty if you want to stay.'

Emma gave a weak smile. She felt as if she owed her aunt better but she just couldn't muster it. 'Sounds nice – if it's no bother.'

'Not a bit. It's nothing fancy; mostly salad.'

'Better than I was planning.'

'What were you planning?'

'Nothing. I was just going to see which tin leapt into my hand first and heat up the contents.'

Patricia gave a soft chuckle. 'One of those sorts of days, eh?'

'A bit.'

'Anything you want to talk about? I'm all ears and not exactly pushed for time.'

'I would, but I don't know where to start.'

Her aunt turned to her. 'Is this about Elise leaving?'

'It's about everything, and Elise leaving is just making me look at all the things that are wrong when I've been so used to ignoring them for all these years. Quite successfully too.'

'I don't think you've ignored them,' Patricia said gently. 'I think you simply put them out of your mind so you could concentrate on caring for everyone else. It's so very typical of you. And it seems to me that everyone who needed you needs you a little less these days and you might have more time very soon to think about yourself and what you might want. Why not take that time to look at all the things you feel are wrong; maybe even kick a few out of your life…'

Emma's smile was a little wider now, but still as rueful. 'You mean Dougie?'

'Did I mention Dougie? No – but his is the first name that popped into your head. Doesn't that tell you something?'

'It tells me that right now I'm annoyed as hell with him, but surely that's no reason to call the whole thing off.'

'If you think that, why are you even posing the question?'

'I'm not – you did.'

'I did nothing of the sort.'

Patricia placed two mugs of tea on the table and took a seat. Emma shrugged off her jacket and joined her.

'Do you think I'm a doormat?'

Patricia reached for her drink. 'Of course I don't. I do think you could be more assertive at times but I'd never call you a doormat.'

'Do you think I'm boring?'

'God no!'

'Unambitious?'

Patricia was more thoughtful when she answered this one. 'I think,' she began slowly, 'you're capable of more than you give yourself credit for.'

'Do you think I've underachieved?'

'I think you've been given fewer opportunities... Emma, where on earth has all this come from?'

Emma dragged her mug across the table and gave a vague shrug as she studied her tea.

'Something must have started it,' Patricia insisted.

Emma looked up from her drink. 'Do you remember Tia Capaldi from when I was at school?'

'Goodness... now you're asking! It's some years... I don't recall. Was she one of your friends? I don't remember you talking about her much and it's quite a distinctive name.'

'She wasn't one of my very close friends really, so by rights I shouldn't have been on her radar at all. She was one of the popular girls; a bit spoilt and entitled to be honest, family had a bit of money. I pretended not to care but I envied her perfect life. I could never really hate her as much as I wanted to, though, because she was actually quite nice and always kind to me whenever our paths crossed.'

'OK...'

'Well, I ran into her this morning. Actually, she ran into me – she was jogging.'

Patricia raised her eyebrows. 'Jogging? Now that sounds like an overachiever to me.'

Emma laughed lightly. 'I know what you mean. We had a chat. It was quite good actually. She was telling me what a horrible time she'd been having going through a divorce, and she ought to have been moping but she wasn't – she was so upbeat. She was looking forward, planning, doing things to make it better.'

'That sounds commendable.'

'It does, doesn't it?'

'But everyone deals with life differently. If you're comparing yourself to her, you shouldn't.'

Emma sipped her tea, her thoughts returning to the conversation with Tia that morning. It felt like a lifetime ago already – perhaps because it had been such a very long day and she was tired now.

'But I don't know how people do that,' Emma continued. 'Get up and dust themselves down and just carry on.'

'Maybe she only has herself to worry about. It's much easier to face forward when there's nobody else to take along. Does she have children from this marriage?'

'She didn't say, but I got the impression there aren't any.'

'There you go then – easier to move past something when there's nobody else to carry.'

'But I don't have anyone to carry.'

'Emma… your cart is so full of passengers it's a wonder the wheels don't fall off! You have your dad, Elise, Dougie…'

'Dad doesn't really need me – I think maybe I pretend he does but it's really the other way around. Elise is leaving. And Dougie…' She let out a brief sigh. 'I don't know what's going on with Dougie anymore.'

Patricia gave her a tender look. 'Your mother should have been here for conversations like this,' she said softly.

Emma did her best to look brave and as if it didn't matter that her mother wasn't around for this stuff, but she couldn't deny she'd often thought that herself.

'I know,' she said. 'I wish every day I could talk to her. But I can't. I have you instead, and she'd be glad to know it.'

'You're allowed to say you miss her. I do, all the time.'

'I do too,' Emma said.

They became silent. There was nothing else to say about how they both missed Emma's mum that hadn't been said many times before. To remind themselves that she'd always be in their thoughts no matter how many years passed without her was enough.

After a minute or so, Patricia got up from the table. 'I'm going to get our meal started or we'll be eating at midnight.'

'Want me to help?'

'There's honestly not much for you to do. I made the salad earlier so there's just a few things to go in the oven. Why don't you go out and say hello to Dom?'

Emma nodded. It might be a welcome distraction to listen to her affable uncle wax lyrical about his latest batch of home-made wine. But as Patricia went to the fridge to look for what she was going to cook, Emma was sidetracked by her phone. She noted a text from Dougie, though she certainly wasn't in the mood to read it. She also noted a new Facebook notification. As she'd promised, Tia had tracked her down and sent a friend request. Emma opened it up and accepted, and was then immediately consumed by curiosity, so rather than going out to her uncle, she took a moment to scroll through Tia's timeline.

There were lots of photos of perfect-looking people in perfect homes and perfect gardens. There were shots of Tia in exotic locations, of her training and taking part in sporting events. Some of the other people in the photos Emma recognised: Tia's parents were familiar from the few times they'd been into school with her for report evenings and celebrations – as were girls Tia had hung around with at school, all grown-up and glamorous now. And though they were interesting in their own way, what really caught Emma's eye was a picture of a tumbledown old railway station building overlooking a weed-choked track.

Isn't this the cutest thing? the caption read. *It's called Honeymoon Station in a village called Honeymoon. It's ripe for development and I'd love to be the person who brings it back to life but I need a partner. Please DM me if you're interested and have some capital to spare!*

There were a few comments below the post, mostly to the effect that it was a lovely place and the writer hoped Tia was able to find the right person to help her take it on. From what Tia had said to Emma earlier that day, it didn't look as if anyone had messaged her to offer their help or, if they had, things hadn't worked out.

Honeymoon Station. The name itself was so ridiculously adorable, so hopelessly romantic, it couldn't possibly be a real place. Although, as Emma took a closer look at the photo, she couldn't help but feel that it was going to take a lot of work to make it look as romantic as it sounded. Even so, there was something about it…

Whiteboard cladding (probably hadn't been white for a long time), a low grey roof with yawning chasms of missing slates, old signage just about visible beneath decades of moss and dirt, grimy windows running the length of the single-storey building, plant pots now filled with weeds… despite all this it was still beautiful.

Emma could almost hear the whistle of the trains as she let the sight of it soak into her soul; could almost imagine the scene of a bustling station perhaps sixty, seventy, maybe even more years ago, the platform wreathed in steam as a gleaming red engine pulled majestically in. Lovers and families and friends – all walks of life would be waiting, watching with expectant eyes for the train to come to a halt. Some would be boarding for adventure, and some would be bidding a tearful farewell to a loved one, old leather suitcases resting at their feet, while train guards in starched uniforms and caps gilded with gold braid hurried everyone along. The station would be freshly painted; spick and span and running like clockwork, looking like something from a black-and-white film.

Restored to that former glory, Honeymoon Station could be achingly beautiful, an evocative reminder of a gentler age. Emma could see why Tia was so taken with it, but she was also a little surprised. She'd never had Tia down as the sentimental type. Now that she thought about it, she'd never really had herself down as the sentimental type either, but something about Honeymoon Station called to her. Perhaps it was special. Perhaps there was some kind of magic, and it had called to Tia too, as if it had chosen who should save it from rotting into history.

Emma was suddenly aware of eyes on her, and looked up to see Patricia regarding her with a quizzical look.

'Are you alright?'

'Yes,' Emma said brightly, 'of course.'

'You looked as if you were well away with the fairies.'

'Did I?' Emma gave a self-conscious laugh.

'You were certainly somewhere, and it looked as if it must have been nice.'

Emma got up and slipped her phone into her trouser pocket. 'I'll go and see if Dom needs any help out there if you don't need me in here.'

'He'd like that,' Patricia said. 'In fact, he'll just be glad someone's taking an interest in his brewing.'

'You do that.'

Patricia smiled. 'Someone other than me. I'm sort of a hostage audience so I don't count.'

Emma returned the smile. 'I'm interested… just more interested in that point where all the work is done and I can drink it.'

Patricia's smile turned into a chuckle. 'Oh, we're all interested then!'

Chapter Four

Elise's flatmate, Cindy, opened the door to let Emma in. It was obvious she'd been crying and Emma guessed there had been a few tears from her and Elise that morning. Originally, Cindy and Elise had met each other through a convenient flat-share arrangement, but during the time they'd been living together they'd actually become genuinely close. Emma could see how it had happened: Cindy was easy-going and pleasant, and anyone who met Elise fell instantly in love with her sweet, unassuming nature.

'She's having a last check round her room,' Cindy said. 'Go through.'

'Thanks,' Emma said. 'Have you found a new flatmate yet?'

'Why, do you want to move in?'

'That does sound tempting right now,' Emma said with a smile. 'But I think my boyfriend might have something to say about it.'

'Well it was worth a try – next best thing to Elise would be her sister and all that. I've got a few people coming to view next week and I think one of them will take it if nobody else does; she's friends with my cousin and she seems nice, so I hope she does to be honest. Although, I don't suppose I can be picky as long as they help me pay the rent.'

'Good luck with it,' Emma said. 'It seems like new beginnings all round.'

'It really does. End of an era.'

Cindy's eyes watered again. It was probably time to leave this conversation, so Emma made her way down the narrow corridor to Elise's room. She found her sister wrestling with the zip on an overfilled suitcase.

'How many pairs of shoes do you have in there?' she asked.

Elise looked up with a bleary grin. 'Too many, I think.'

'I'm pretty sure you won't need your diamanté mules on that volcano.'

'Ah, but I might need them if a hot Icelander asks me out on a date.'

'I'm not sure they're even practical for downtown Reykjavik. Doesn't everyone in Iceland wear huge woolly jumpers and boots all year round?'

'Apparently it's quite pleasant in the summer,' Elise said mildly. 'Though their summers probably only last for about three hours or something.'

'Probably,' Emma agreed. 'There must be a reason it's called Iceland.' She looked at the suitcase. 'Do you need any help with anything?'

'I think I'm pretty much done.'

Emma nodded. 'I just talked to Cindy. I don't think she's coping well with your last day, is she?'

'Oh, we've both been in floods of tears all morning. It's a good job I did most of my packing earlier this week because I'm good for nothing today really.'

'She'll get used to things being different soon enough.'

'She will. I think it's a little easier to bear knowing she'll be able to come and spend some time with me in Iceland once I've settled in.'

'That is a bit of a sweetener, I suppose.'

'Although I know you won't,' Elise added wryly.

'I will do my best – you know I will because I really want to – but not straight away. I can't spare the money for the air fare just yet.'

'Tell Dougie to hurry up and get a job and then you might be able to.'

'Hmm…'

Emma thought back to the passive-aggressive text message she'd opened the night she'd had dinner with her aunt and uncle after the row she'd had with Dougie.

I'll take that stupid job if it means that much to you.

Whether it meant anything to her or not was irrelevant. She'd told him as much when they'd discussed things on her return. It wasn't about what she wanted; it was about fairness and equity in their relationship, and even more than that it was about the simple need to keep a roof over their heads. She pulled her weight to support their lifestyle (though at times it felt more like simply life with no style) and to pay for the home they shared, and he should want to do his bit regardless of what Emma said about it. That was how successful relationships were supposed to work, wasn't it?

She was suspicious too – though she didn't want to be. A bit of her wondered whether Dougie would make a show of going along to the interview only to sabotage his chances deliberately so he didn't get the job, and thinking such things surely indicated that something wasn't right in their relationship; having so little trust didn't bode well for their future. To Emma it felt like a no-win situation: if he got the job he'd resent her for the fact he'd feel forced to take it, and if he didn't she would resent that, even if it ultimately wasn't his fault.

'He's trying,' she said, wondering why she was bothering to defend him. She supposed she was so used to doing it by now she didn't really know how to stop.

'I suppose he must be,' Elise said. 'It must be tough managing in the meantime.'

'I'm sure it won't be for much longer. Anyway, I don't want you to worry about that. I want you to concentrate on being ready when Dad comes to pick you up.'

'I can't believe the day's actually here! I'm excited but also bereft all at the same time… I can't tell you how weird that feels.'

'Bereft? Why?'

'I'll miss everyone here like mad. I'll even miss this silly little town that I always said I couldn't wait to leave.'

Emma smiled. 'You did used to say that a lot. Sometimes you have to be careful what you wish for.'

'I won't miss it for long,' Elise replied with a grin.

'And it won't be forever anyway,' Emma said.

'That's the thing…' Elise's smile faded now into something less certain. 'In one way or another I think it will. If I come back home it means I've somehow cocked everything up. If I'm as successful as I hope to be then I'll get other projects and postings in other places. So I'm torn – I'll miss home but I don't want to come back because of what that will mean.'

'But you'll come to visit?'

Elise's smile returned. 'I suppose I can do that. You'll be alright, won't you? When I'm gone, I mean. You'll be OK?'

'You're the one going to live next to a volcano – I ought to be asking you that.'

'I'm sure everyone thinks I'm a bit mad. It hasn't erupted for years, so fingers crossed it doesn't start feeling frisky any time soon, eh?'

Emma chuckled. 'That's an understatement if ever I heard one.'

'But, Em… promise me you won't let everything get on top of you here. And remember I'm only a phone call away if you need to talk.'

'You'll have enough going on in Iceland and I've got plenty of people here if things do get a bit tricky, so you shouldn't be worrying about that. You go and have your amazing adventure and don't even look back, not for a second. Life is for living and I'm so happy you're getting to live your dream.'

'I still can't quite believe it myself. How many people can say they've landed their dream job and actually mean it?'

'Not many,' Emma agreed. 'But my clever little sister can.'

'You only have a clever little sister because I have a clever big sister.'

Emma looked incredulous. 'You're the one with a degree.'

'And you're the one who taught me so much before I'd even set foot in a school. The teachers thought they were dealing with some genius child prodigy when I arrived.'

'Dad used to tell me how they'd gush at parents' evenings,' Emma said with a fond smile.

'And that was thanks to you.' Elise looked suddenly serious. 'I did wonder sometimes if you might hate me a little bit for being born because then Mum died. I remember whenever I asked you that, you'd hug me and tell me something lovely to make me feel better and I'd wonder then how I ever doubted you. You might laugh, and you might not see it, but you made me who I am today, Em. All this is down to you.'

'I think Dad had a hand in it too…'

'Yes, but it wasn't the same. Dad provided but he worked so hard he never really had time to sit with me. That was all you.'

Emma sniffed back tears. 'It works both ways. You were the best little sister I could have asked for and only mildly annoying some of the time.'

Elise laughed through her own new tears. 'That's good to hear.' She pulled Emma into a brief hug. 'I wish you could have come to the airport with us.'

'Me too, but perhaps it's for the best. We'd both be wrecks by the time the plane was ready for boarding. Besides, I'm pushing my luck getting an hour off to come and see you as it is.'

'They take advantage of you at that company,' Elise said with a frown.

'They do. But if I wasn't there they'd only have Margot… Imagine that.'

'That's bad management on the part of the company. If it was anywhere else Margot would have been fired years ago. It's not sensible to carry someone like that and it's not fair to expect you to prop up the department because she can't do her job. They should think about what would happen if you left; it's silly not to.'

'They probably know that will never happen; I'm like part of the furniture.'

'One day you will.'

'I doubt it.'

'You should think about it, though. You're wasted there – I've always said it.'

'It suits me.'

'It can't make you happy to be there.'

'Well…' Emma gave her a brave smile. 'Those dreams that come true for some aren't out there for everyone. Some of us are content to have a job we don't hate if we can't have one we love.'

'See, now that makes me sad.'

'I don't want you to be sad, not over this. Today is about you, not me, and I want you to catch that flight full of confidence and positive thoughts. If I know you have, then that will be enough to make me very happy.'

Elise reached to hug her again. As she pulled her close, Emma squeezed her eyes against fresh tears.

'That's not to say I won't miss you like crazy,' she whispered.

Elise hugged her tighter still. 'Not as much as I'll miss you.'

'You want to put a bet on that?'

Emma heard now the muffled sound of Elise laugh-crying into her shoulder. She wished dearly she could have spent her sister's final hours in England with her, that she could have gone to the airport with her dad to see Elise off properly but, as usual, life had decided not to indulge Emma. She wasn't bitter; she felt only a little guilty and the keen loss of those extra moments with the sister she loved more than anyone else in the world.

'What am I going to do without you?' Elise asked, suddenly sounding like a young girl again and hurtling Emma into a barrage of memories of them growing up together, when Emma had been more a mother than a sister.

'You're going to do what you always do,' Emma said with such fierce love it almost burned. 'You're going to shine.'

Chapter Five

Emma didn't really know why she was here.

Actually, she knew why she was supposed to be here – she'd suggested meeting up. Tia had been delighted and proposed that they meet at the ice-cream parlour by the park instead of a stuffy chain coffee shop. Emma had been surprised that Tia even knew what the inside of an ice-cream parlour looked like, because she had the figure of someone who lived on soya milk and nuts. In a way, it was quite comforting to know that Tia liked a sugary treat as much as everyone else.

What Emma really didn't know was quite what she was expecting from her afternoon with Tia. It got her out of the house, which had delighted Dougie because it meant he'd been able to spend Saturday afternoon fishing rather than half-heartedly doing the sorts of couple things Emma could tell he had little interest in. Apart from that, she had wondered whether she might end up leaving the meet-up feeling distinctly more useless than when she'd arrived, but she'd still wanted to come. She wanted to hear more about Tia and her life since school, and about the plans she had for the future. More than anything, she wanted to hear about those wonderful, impossible, impractical dreams of restoring Honeymoon Station, though it was hard to understand why. A bit of her hoped Tia still hadn't found her business partner.

And a bit of her wondered what mad thing she might do or say in the heat of the moment if she learned that Tia was still looking.

When she got there Tia was already sitting at a pink table. Most of the other tables contained parents or grandparents with their young charges; the parlour overlooked a popular play park and Emma imagined most of them had been to play first or were heading there after they'd had their ice cream. The day was bright, if a little brisk, but probably perfect weather for racing about from swing to slide.

'It's lovely to see you again,' Tia said, standing to greet her. 'If you don't mind me saying, quite unexpected too.'

'We didn't have a lot of time to catch up the other day when I saw you out, but I really enjoyed our chat and thought it might be nice to set more time aside to do it properly.'

They sat down and Tia handed Emma a menu. 'I've already chosen.'

'What are you having?'

'Banana split – that way I can kid myself I've had fruit and nuts and conveniently forget about the ice cream bit.'

Emma smiled as she briefly scanned the list. It all looked wonderful but she wasn't all that hungry.

'I might get a scoop of strawberry,' she decided.

'*One* scoop? Seriously?'

Emma looked up.

'Come on.' Tia laughed. 'You can do better than that.'

'OK,' Emma said, her smile spreading. 'Maybe I could be persuaded to have two.'

A young girl wearing a pink apron (Emma was beginning to notice that everything in here was pink) over jeans and a white T-shirt came to their table.

'Do you know what you're having?'

'Yes,' Tia said. 'Can we get a banana split and two scoops of strawberry in a bowl please?'

The girl jotted it down on a pad and went again.

'I've been saving myself,' Tia said. 'I love it in here.'

Emma raised her eyebrows slightly. She hadn't meant to, but Tia laughed.

'I know, I'm such a pig.'

'I was thinking the opposite,' Emma said. 'You have such an amazing figure I'm surprised you even know what ice cream is.'

'Well I work hard at the gym and I figure I deserve a treat for it every now and again.'

'I suppose that's true. I do the treat bit but I skip the gym. I've joined more than one but I get so bored I never stick it longer than a month and then end up saddled with a contract until I can cancel my membership.'

'I'd say you look in pretty good shape to me.'

'That's clever dressing – it's a whole different story under these clothes.'

'I'm sure it's not.'

Emma moved the menu to one side and rested her elbows on the table. 'So… how have you been since I last saw you? Any update on your plans?'

'Plans?'

'You said you had a business plan… Is that anything to do with Honeymoon Station?'

'Ah!' Tia grinned. 'You saw my photos on Facebook? It's a bit pie in the sky really. Unless someone who's as mad as me joins me I'll probably have to forget about it. Back in the real world I'll probably start up as a fitness coach again – as a freelancer this time – advertise for some new clients and build up a customer base.'

'I'm sure you must be brilliant at that.'

'It should be straightforward enough when I get a few on the books. Not exactly rocket science, as they say.'

'If you don't mind me saying, you don't look as excited about that as I would expect you to be.'

Tia shrugged. 'It's a great job… flexible, easy to set up, something I know well…'

'But?'

'I fancied a change.'

'Why don't you do something else then?'

'I don't know what else to do. I could keep my eyes peeled for something a bit like Honeymoon that requires a bit less capital. It might take a while but I bet it's out there.'

'I'm sure there must be loads of properties like that.'

Tia twiddled with the corner of a menu. 'I'd just sort of fallen in love with that one. Daft, I know. It's just an old building. My mum's family are originally from that area of Dorset and I can only think that's why I'm so stuck on that particular place. They always said how lovely the villages were around there.'

'You've never visited?'

'No, more's the pity. Never seemed to get the time.'

The waitress came back and placed their orders on the table with the bill.

'Blimey,' Emma said as she marched away again, 'they don't want us to hang around, do they?'

Tia laughed. 'I don't suppose it's often anyone comes in and eats more than one so they're probably used to us shipping out pretty quick.'

'I had a good look at the station,' Emma said. 'I can see why you're so keen to have a go; it could be beautiful. You still haven't got anyone interested at all?'

'It's a risky venture halfway across the country and a lot of money to stump up…' Tia dug a spoon into her dessert. 'Hardly surprising when you look at it that way.'

'I must admit that thought crossed my mind,' Emma said. 'A lot of money for not a lot of actual building when you look at what's still standing.'

'Very true,' Tia said, licking her spoon. 'Still, I think it could have been fun.'

'Wouldn't your parents… I don't know… Would they be interested in it? Or could you borrow from them if they don't want to get involved?'

Tia gave a rueful smile. 'We used to be quite rich, didn't we? I suppose it must have been very obvious at school. Daddy's business went under a couple of years ago. They managed to keep the house but not much else – I wouldn't even contemplate asking them to get involved in something like this; it would be far too stressful for them now.'

'Oh, Tia… I'm *so* sorry; I didn't mean—'

'Don't be. It's not your fault, and really, it's only what everyone thinks. Never mind that now – tell me about how you're doing. You're married?'

'Almost.'

'No kids?'

'Not yet.'

'Me neither. I didn't really want any – I suppose that sounds a bit selfish?'

'God, no!'

'And actually, I'm glad now because that was one less thing to worry about when the divorce was going through.'

'Here's me, not even married yet and you've been married and divorced. I'm a bit slow off the blocks, aren't I?'

'I married too young. Mum said it was a rebellion thing and I'm beginning to think she might have been right, though I'd never tell her; I couldn't stand the crowing.'

'We all do daft things when we're young…' Emma swirled her ice cream to mix the melted edges in. 'Some of us carry on doing them when we're old enough to know better too.'

'Yes.' Tia smiled. 'Like trying to buy knackered old railway stations.'

'So remind me what you're planning to do with that. That's your hotel project?'

'I had thought it would make a lovely little hotel – something cosy and boutique. Quirky accommodation is all the rage; I'm certain guests would be queuing up to stay somewhere like that in such a gorgeous location.'

'From what I saw it would take a huge amount of work to get it ready for paying customers.'

'It would, but I've costed it all taking that into account. Although, Daddy says it's bound to go way over my budget. I'm quite sure he's right too.'

Emma sucked on her spoon, her gaze on the park beyond a field of breeze-blown grass. The children playing there were little more than squealing coloured blobs, hurtling up and down while their adults looked protectively on.

Honeymoon Station… The more she thought about what Tia had told her, the more she could see Tia's vision, but it *was* a lot of money. Even half the auction guide was a lot of money and that was before they started to think about renovation funds. And, of course, auction guide prices were rarely the price the item fetched – it was just the minimum the seller was hoping for.

Still...

A few years back, just before Elise had embarked on her degree, their dad had offered to help them both out by releasing equity from the family home and gifting them both a sizeable chunk of money. It would see Elise through her course, he'd said, and enable Emma to pay off a chunk of her own mortgage, or spend it on anything else she thought would make her life better. Emma had refused her share. She hadn't really needed it and hadn't felt right accepting such a generous offer. Elise had done the same, insisting she'd work her way through university. Both sisters had agreed that their dad needed to keep his home safe and they weren't certain this was the way to do it.

Emma wondered vaguely if the offer would still stand. If she went to her dad now, would he still be willing to help? Circumstances had changed and he'd see that. Sitting here, listening to Tia, Emma couldn't help but be swept up in the promise of a new start, of an adventure, and a chunk of money like the one her dad had offered those years ago would help her and Tia realise all that potential locked away in Honeymoon Station's crumbling ruins. It wouldn't cover it all, and Emma would have to find another way to raise the rest, but still...

When she looked back, Tia was digging happily into her banana split. Emma watched her. This was madness, wasn't it? She hardly knew this woman – she hadn't even known her that well in school. It was a huge amount of money to throw at a wreck of a building neither of them had seen in the flesh. They had no experience whatsoever and absolutely no guarantees their enterprise wouldn't ultimately fail. They could well lose everything.

Perhaps, painful as it was, Emma had to face the notion that the draw of Tia and her mad project was more about being left behind by her high-flying little sister, stuck back home in their small town with the same old people in her modest house and modest job, and a boyfriend who would 'just do', than about a burning passion for the heritage of the Dorset countryside. And anyway, if Emma told her dad what she wanted the money for he'd rightly never agree to it because he'd see the folly of the thing.

'Excuse me…'

Two young boys of perhaps seven or eight approached their table.

'Hello,' Tia said brightly. 'What can we do for you?'

'We're selling tickets,' one of the boys said.

'Tickets for a car,' the other said. 'And some money.'

Tia smiled. 'I like the sound of those tickets. We just buy a ticket and you give us a car? How much do they cost?'

'One pound,' the first boy said, looking pleased.

A woman rushed over to them. 'I'm sorry… I hope we're not bothering you but we're selling raffle tickets for the children's ward of the hospital and the boys have taken it upon themselves to be chief salesmen.'

'They're doing a good job,' Emma said.

'I was certainly hooked by the sales pitch,' Tia agreed.

'The first prize is ten thousand pounds,' the woman said. 'Second is a Mini Cooper.'

'Wow!' Emma glanced at Tia. 'That certainly beats the second-hand potpourri you normally get!'

'Yes, I'd take either of those right now,' Tia said.

'There are a lot of very good prizes,' the woman said. 'The consultants at the hospital pulled a few strings with local businesses.'

'I could do with them pulling some strings for me if they can get donations like that,' Tia said. She took some coins from her purse. 'I'll take a couple of tickets.'

Emma looked in her own purse. She had only a ten-pound note. 'I don't suppose you have change for a ten?' she asked the boys. They looked up at their guardian.

'Now you're asking,' the woman said. 'We've only just started selling and I'm not sure…' She began to rummage in a very limp-looking money bag. 'Maybe I could come back to you…'

'Do you know what?' Emma said, fired by a sudden rush of optimism. 'I'm feeling lucky. I'll have ten tickets so you needn't worry about the change.'

'Oh, thank you!' the woman said. 'I hope you win for being so kind.'

She collected the money from them both and the boys took another minute to carefully tear all the tickets from the book, and then another five minutes to painstakingly write Emma and Tia's phone numbers on the back of every ticket they'd bought. By the time they'd finished Emma felt as if she'd done a full day at work.

'The draw's on Monday actually,' the woman said. 'Today is our last big push to sell tickets.'

'So we'll be on top of the pile,' Tia said. 'Nice and easy to pick us out.'

The woman laughed. 'Oh yes. We'll leave you in peace – thank you so much, ladies!'

With that, she ushered the boys away to try their luck at another table.

'Cute kids,' Tia said.

'Yes,' Emma agreed. 'Although that's a tenner I'll never see again.'

'Ah, but you have to speculate to accumulate. That's ten chances in the bag for you. And you've helped a good cause.'

'Well I'm glad about the good-cause bit,' Emma said with a wry smile, 'because I've never yet won a raffle in my life.'

When Emma got home a few hours later she was smiling. Properly smiling, like she felt she hadn't done for months, like she might never be able to stop. Tia had been surprisingly good company: funny, lively, interesting, with an enthusiasm for everything that was irresistibly infectious. At school she'd been the party girl – if it had been an American teen movie she'd have been the glamorous and blessed cheerleader with a pristine house in the suburbs, a quarterback boyfriend and an invite to every soiree going – and though that girl was still in evidence, this older Tia no longer seemed as spoilt and entitled as Emma had often considered her. But since high school Tia's family had lost their business and perhaps that had been a humbling experience, or perhaps the life lessons had been closer to home, courtesy of her difficult divorce. Whatever the reasons, Emma liked this Tia much more than she'd imagined she would.

The house was empty, even though it was gone six, and Emma supposed Dougie must have run into friends at the fishing pool and decided to stay and share a few beers. While the idea irked her slightly, there was a part of her that was relieved too. Lately, every day around Dougie felt like a battle zone, a silent, simmering, resentful sort of conflict where she found herself constantly biting her lip, holding back on the things she really wanted to say in order to keep some kind of peace. But that peace was hard-won and wasn't healthy – not for her or the relationship – and it was exhausting. It had started to feel like a boil that needed lancing, and if she didn't do something about it soon the poison would spread into everything else in her life.

She'd ended up eating a second bowl of ice cream at the parlour with Tia, feeling like a naughty toddler sneaking cheeky seconds, and the sugar had gone to her head. Now she had the beginnings of a headache and she certainly wasn't in the mood for the evening meal she'd planned. With Dougie out and likely to be for some time, there really didn't seem much point in cooking for one anyway. Instead, she made a cup of green tea in an attempt to cleanse her system and curled up on the sofa with a book she'd been trying to get through. Less than an hour later, she was fast asleep.

The sound of the front door slamming woke her. The tea she'd made was on the side table, barely touched and stone cold. Her book had fallen onto the floor, pages splayed and creased, the bookmark lying nearby so that her place had been lost; she cursed herself for being so careless with it. But what demanded her attention most of all was looking at the clock, seeing it had gone eleven, and noting that she now had a crick in her neck from sleeping in an awkward position, and that Dougie's vague eyes and slurred greeting meant he was very definitely drunk.

She hated this. She didn't want to nag. She didn't want to start a row either, but she had a right to know where he'd been and she had a right to expect him to spend time willingly with her occasionally… didn't she? However, she pushed all that from her mind and made an effort to be bright and neutral. It was late, and she was too tired and groggy to start any kind of meaningful discussion, and Dougie wouldn't be able to recall it in the morning anyway; he never did, so what was the point?

'Good day?' she asked casually.

'Yeah.'

'Catch anything?'

'A bit, yeah.'

'Who did you see?'

'Chas and Willard.'

'Oh. They stayed out with you then?'

'Yeah, they got some cans.'

'Right...'

Either he'd forgotten her afternoon plans to meet Tia or he didn't really care. He didn't ask about it and Emma didn't feel like volunteering any information now anyway.

'I'm going up,' Dougie announced, staggering towards the stairs.

She listened to his heavy steps as he lumbered up to bed. It was strange how you could live with someone and yet still feel like the loneliest person in the world.

Chapter Six

Margot was on the warpath. Ostensibly it was because someone had moved her pile of magazines (she claimed), but mainly it was because she'd been forced to do some actual work. One of the drivers had asked to take extended paternity leave and Margot had smiled serenely and told him she'd sort it, before asking Emma to do it once he'd left the office. But now she was apoplectic with rage because Emma had then been nabbed by Mr Burnbury to do something more urgent and the job had been left to Margot after all. Emma had secretly been glad about the intervention. Even though the new task would probably be a much shittier one, it was worth it just to see Margot pull her weight for a change.

'Damn... Where's the number for the... I know it's here... Why is there no proper filing in this office... Now I'm in a bloody virtual queue, whatever one of those is... This information makes absolutely no sense...'

As Margot became more and more frustrated and a little frantic, Emma almost felt sorry for her. Almost. But Margot got paid more than her and most of the time did very little to deserve that money other than delegate all her tasks to her assistant. Emma probably could have sorted it in ten minutes too, but she really would deserve her doormat status if she gave in and took on the task. Instead, she worked steadily through a list of permits that needed to be renewed and kept her head down so as not to attract Margot's irked attention.

When Emma's mobile started to ring, she hurried to retrieve it from her desk drawer and was surprised to see that the caller was Tia. If it had been anyone else she might have left the phone to ring out and then called back when the office was less fraught, but she was intrigued that Tia was calling during office hours.

'Oh, Emma!' Tia squeaked. 'I had to phone you first because you were there!'

'Hi,' Emma said in a low voice, giving the phone a slightly bewildered smile.

'I won the bloody car!' Tia cried. 'Can you believe it?'

Emma's mouth fell open. 'You mean the raffle prize?'

'Isn't it completely mad? You must be my lucky charm! If I enter a competition from now on you have to be there!'

'Wow!' Emma said, trying very hard not to think about how many more tickets than Tia she'd bought and how it was typical of her lousy luck that it hadn't made a scrap of difference. 'That's amazing. Did they just call you?'

'Yes! I still can't believe it!'

'Neither can I,' Emma said, perhaps a little too frankly. 'It's a lovely car.'

'I know. But does it sound very ungrateful if I say I don't think I'll keep it?'

'What are you going to do with it?'

'Sell it, I expect. If I'm allowed to – sometimes you don't know with these prizes, do you? Do you want to buy it? Knockdown price for lucky charms,' she added with a laugh.

'Even at knockdown it would probably still be too pricey for me.'

'It was just a thought. You bought tickets too.'

'Oh, I wasn't bothered about the car – it was just to support a good cause, you know.'

'Well this car's going to support a good cause when I sell it; I'm going to put the money in my pot for Honeymoon Station. It'll make a huge difference towards my target, and as I can't find a partner I could do with winning a few more to raise the rest... Fancy entering some more raffles with me?'

'I'm not sure I'm the lucky charm you think I am. I suspect it might have been all you.' Emma smiled. It was hard to be resentful when Tia was so excited and, really, when she thought about it, more deserving too. She'd had a tough time lately and she'd do a lot of good with that money. If Emma had won the car it would have been nice but it wouldn't have made a huge difference to her life. Tia, on the other hand... it had the potential to take her a step closer to her dreams and that had to be worth cheering for.

'It feels like a sign,' Tia said, 'it really does. First I bump into you and we get on so well and then this raffle... I think my luck is about to change and everything is going to come good. Thank you!'

'What are you thanking me for?' Emma said with a little laugh.

'For bringing my change of luck.'

'I think you've done it all by yourself. Being determined, having a goal – it makes your luck eventually, just like it did for my sister. Whatever you're working towards will come good because you'll make it happen, whatever tries to get in your way.'

'It's sweet of you to say it like that. There are plenty of others with less faith in me.'

'You don't have to listen to them. Anyway, it has nothing to do with faith. Anyone who talks to you for five minutes can see you're destined to do amazing things.'

'Oh, Emma…'

Tia started to reply but a grunt from the desk across the room distracted Emma. She looked up to see Margot glowering at her.

'I'm so sorry to cut you off, Tia,' Emma said, 'but can I phone you later? I'm kind of busy at work right now.'

'Oh God, you should have said!'

'No… I'm glad you called. It's lovely to hear your news and I'm happy you phoned to tell me first. It's brilliant, honestly, and I'm thrilled for you. We'll talk more later if you like.'

'That sounds lovely. I'll speak to you soon then.'

'You will. Bye, Tia.'

'Bye, lucky charm!'

Emma was still grinning as she ended the call. Margot definitely wasn't.

Let her frown, Emma thought, *miserable old trout*. One personal call during work hours wouldn't trouble Margot's daily record and Emma wasn't about to apologise for it.

Once a week Emma took her dad shopping. He didn't need taking but she liked to see that he was buying the right things to eat, and, strangely, they really only ever had easy conversation when engaged in another activity at the same time, so it was always a good time to chat. Her dad didn't cope well with soul-baring and any talk of emotions made him uncomfortable, unless he was so engrossed in something else that he didn't realise any soul-baring was going on.

'Did Elise call yesterday?' Emma pulled a trolley from the line and followed him into the store. 'She phoned me and said she was going to speak to you afterwards.'

'She did. Sounds like she's settling in alright.'

'She sounds really happy – made loads of friends already.'

Her dad nodded. 'She's always been good at making friends. Folks are drawn to her like ducks to water.'

'She sounds like she loves the place she's living in. What's it called again?'

'Don't ask me to pronounce it! Icelandic is worse than Welsh, and that's saying something!'

Emma nodded vaguely as they made their way to the fresh fruit and vegetables. 'I know. She says all these names to me and I can't repeat them to anyone who asks because I can't get my tongue around them. Makes me a bit embarrassed – English people really are rubbish at other languages.'

'That's because most of the time we don't need them – especially ones so complicated.'

'I suppose English seems complicated to people in other countries.'

'Ah, but a good many of them can speak it.'

'That's worse, Dad,' Emma said with a wry smile. 'That means we're just too lazy to make any effort.'

'Probably. Lucky for us we don't need to.'

'You need carrots?'

Her dad nodded and Emma tossed a bag into the trolley.

'So what have you been doing this week?' he asked. 'Managing to keep your mind off Elise going? You two were always thick as thieves; you must be missing her.'

'Like mad, but I'm OK. She's happy – that's all I'm bothered about. I've just been keeping busy with the usual... work and home.'

Her dad sniffed. 'Kicked that waster out yet?'

'Dad...'

He held up his hand as a gesture of surrender. 'OK, I won't talk about him.'

'Good... Actually, I did meet up with a girl from school.'

'Oh yes?' he asked vaguely, inspecting a savoy cabbage.

'Tia Capaldi... I bet you don't remember her.'

'Her dad owned that motorcycle showroom; flash bugger. How could I forget them?'

'Tia's not flash – not now anyway. She's actually lovely; we got on really well. She's had a tough time going through a divorce and her dad went bankrupt.'

'Hmm. I did wonder why the showroom had gone – thought it had moved out of town. Not so flash now then.'

'I expect bankruptcy humbles you a bit,' Emma agreed.

'So what's she doing now?'

'That's just it. She's looking for a new start and – you'll never guess – we bought raffle tickets when we were together and she won a car!'

Her dad looked unimpressed as he chose a head of broccoli. 'Lucky always makes luck,' he said flatly.

Emma held up a bag of parsnips and he nodded that they were acceptable before she put them into the trolley. 'What does that mean?'

'Luck's like magnets. If you have it you always attract more.'

'Don't magnets repel each other?'

'Alright, magnets and metal then,' he said tartly. 'You know what I mean.'

'Maybe luck just goes to the people who deserve it.'

He huffed. 'Not in my experience. You deserve it but you don't win cars. How do you explain that? Like I said, lucky makes luck. The likes of you and me have never had any – that's why we don't ever get any.'

'So what you're saying is you're born lucky or you're not, and you can't do anything to change that?'

'This conversation is getting daft…' He wandered off to a refrigerated shelf and Emma followed with the trolley. 'Where are those grapes I like…?'

'Here.' Emma pulled a box from the shelves and handed them to him. He peered over his glasses to check the label. 'Anyway,' she continued, 'Tia's selling the car to get money for this property she wants to turn into a hotel. It's in Dorset. It looks like it could be beautiful if it gets done.'

'So she's lucky and daft then.'

'I don't think it's daft.'

'You wouldn't; too much like your mum. It's the sort of thing she would have tried to talk me into doing if she'd still been with us. Retirement project, she'd have said. Like retirement is for speeding up, not slowing down.'

'Is it?' Emma asked doubtfully.

She'd been eight years old when they'd lost her mum, but she didn't recall that side of her at all. She'd been kind and sweet and caring and all the other things a young girl wanted from her mother, but a dreamer, a schemer and planner…? Emma hadn't seen that. To Emma she was just the woman who tucked her in at night, who laughed with her at playtime and fed her lovely dinners and comforted her when she was sad. Perhaps she just hadn't been old enough to know her mother in a way that revealed that other part of her nature.

'So you don't think it's a good idea?' Emma asked, not even knowing why she suddenly needed her father's approval for a plan that wasn't even hers.

'I didn't say that. I don't know anything about it so I can't say either way.' He looked askance at her over a bag of Granny Smith apples. 'Why are you asking me? What does it matter what I think?'

'I'm just curious, that's all.'

'I'm sure it's a winner for the person who knows what they're doing. Hotel in Dorset… goldmine, I should imagine. How much is it costing her?'

'I'm not sure. The building's going up for auction soon. The guide price isn't bad, but Tia thinks it will go for a lot more than that.'

'I'm sure it will. Sounds like she's thinking on her feet when it comes to money. Perhaps she's got her dad's business head – although, if she does plough on with it, I hope it's better than her dad's.'

'I think her dad was just a victim of unfortunate circumstances.'

'It does sound like a better bet than his motorbikes.'

Emma put a bag of baby spinach in the trolley.

'I don't want spinach,' he said.

'Yes you do.'

'I don't like it.'

'You said that last time, but you ate it on sandwiches and said you preferred it to lettuce.'

'Did I? Was that spinach?'

'Yes, Dad.'

'Oh, shows what I know.'

'What did you think you were eating?'

He shrugged. 'Some leaves.'

She laughed. 'Spinach *is* some leaves!'

He flashed her a sheepish grin.

'How's work?' he asked a moment later.

'Horrible, as usual.'

'You say that every week. Why don't you get something else?'

'I don't know… I feel like everything else will be just as bad. I think I'm bored working in HR but I don't know what else I'm qualified to do.'

'You could retrain; you're still young enough.'

'I could but I don't know what I want to retrain in. Nothing I see appeals to me.'

'So you don't fancy volcano-chasing like your sister?'

Emma smiled. 'Can you even chase a volcano? Where's it going?'

'You know what I mean.'

'No… I'll let Elise take that one – there's only room for one nutter in any family.'

'Something more down to earth then?'

'Hmm. I suppose I'll know the right thing when it comes along and bops me on the nose.'

'That's exactly why it won't. You need to take charge. Letting things drift… that's how you ended up where you are now.'

'Thanks, Dad,' she said wryly. 'I'm not on the streets; just in a job I'm a bit fed up of. It's better than some.'

'It is, but if it's not what you want to do… I think that's enough fresh stuff. I liked those sausages last week… I wonder if they're still on offer.'

Emma followed as he began to push the trolley again. 'We could look. If not, I'm sure they'll have some just as nice a bit cheaper. So what do you think I should do?'

'About what?'

'The future… my job…'

'I can't tell you.'

'But you must have thoughts.'

'If I air them we're likely to have cross words.'

'Why?'

Her dad looked at her with raised eyebrows. 'Because it always ends that way.'

'Only when you're telling me to get rid of Dougie.'

'Since you're asking me I'll tell you again that he's a big part of your problem as far as I can see. Your future would be a lot brighter without him in it; everyone but you can see that.'

She was silent for a moment as he raked the shelves for his sausages, and then she replied. 'Maybe I'm beginning to see it,' she said in a small voice.

'About time,' was all her dad said, though she couldn't help but notice he looked pleased.

'I haven't said I'm leaving him,' she warned. 'There's no need to be smug about it.'

'I'm not being smug. I only said I'm glad you're starting to see sense. I don't know what hold that boy has over you but I know he's not good for you; he takes advantage of your good nature. You're like your mum in that respect too, but even she wouldn't have let someone like him walk all over her.'

'He doesn't,' Emma said, knowing that he did, but that old unshakeable impulse to defend him had taken hold again.

'See… there's no talking to you where he's concerned. I told you it would get ugly if we started this conversation.'

'It isn't getting ugly.'

'Hmm. Sausages are full price again…' Her dad held up another pack. 'These look alright, don't they?'

'Yes.'

'Right.' He put them in the trolley. 'I'll give them a whirl tomorrow with a bit of mash.'

Emma watched the sausages go in. Here she was, trying to get to grips with a future that seemed nebulous, unknowable, bigger than she was capable of comprehending, pondering a crossroads in her life… and her dad was deciding what to have for tomorrow's supper. It was no wonder she couldn't figure anything out – there were always too many distractions, too much else to think about. She could never see her future because her present was full of cleaning and cooking and bailing out Margot and making sure her dad ate spinach.

Though she barely knew her, she was finding herself increasingly envious of Tia's choices, of her clarity and focus. Tia knew what she wanted and, even if she didn't get it, it meant she was one up on Emma, who didn't even know where to start. Emma had always refused to be bitter about her circumstances or to begrudge anyone more fortunate ones, but sometimes she found it hard.

'Maybe you should start your own business,' her dad said suddenly.

Emma looked at him. 'What on earth would I do? Ironing lady… that's about my skill set.'

'People do set up ironing services,' he said practically. 'I've seen them. They must do OK or nobody would bother.'

'Imagine ironing all day. I don't mind doing a bit but that would make me go mad.'

'You get people to help, don't you?'

'I don't think so, Dad.'

'Well, what's this woman doing?'

'Who?'

'This girl from school.'

'Tia?'

'Yes, you said she needed a partner.'

'I must admit I've thought about it, but she needs them to have a lot of money and I don't have a lot of money.'

'Dorset, you say…'

'Yes.'

'I like Dorset. Your mum used to like Dorset too. It's a long time since I've been there.'

'I can just about remember going to Weymouth on holiday one year when I was a kid.'

'That'll be the last time I was there, I expect. I can't think I've been since that trip. If you want to go and have a look at this place I'd go with you.'

'Look at it?' Emma handed him the pack of butter she knew he bought every week without fail. He dropped it in with the rest of his shopping.

'Why not? What have you got to lose? It's clear it's caught your imagination.'

'Is it?'

'Look at it. If you get there and it's obvious it's too big to tackle then you can put it out of your mind and move on.'

'What if I like it?'

'Then you could tell this woman you're in.'

'But I don't have the money to be in.'

'I have some. You know I've told you before I can get at it if you need help.'

'It's your house!'

'The house won't be going anywhere. When I die it'll go to you and Elise anyway, so have your share before I die or after – makes no difference to me. As long as I can live there until I snuff it I don't care how much of it I own.'

'Of course you'd be able to live in it! Regardless, I still don't feel comfortable about taking money from your house, and even then I don't know if it would be enough.'

'This is all just talk until you find out more. See your friend and put it to her. Ask her what she'd need to cut you in.'

Emma shook her head slowly as she stared at the yogurts. He made it sound like a poker game rather than a huge, life-changing risk.

'This is crazy,' she said. 'I'd probably have to sell my house too. What would Dougie do?'

'Wouldn't he go to Dorset with you?'

'I've never thought about it. I suppose I'd have to put it to him, but I doubt very much he'd want to. All his friends are here.'

'In that case, all the more reason for you to go, as far as I can tell.'

'Dad…' Emma warned, but a bit of her thought that he might have a point.

Emma looked across to the sofa where Dougie was slouched watching an old James Bond movie. They'd had a surprisingly pleasant evening – civil and good-natured – and they'd even shared the sort of sparring banter that Emma had loved as part of their relationship in the early days. Dougie's humour had been one of his biggest attractions and she'd missed it of late.

He swiped to take a call that had just come through on his phone.

'Yep…' He was frowning slightly, but then the confusion cleared from his features as the call went on. 'Oh yeah,' he said, 'I remember. Of course… Yeah, I'm still interested…' He glanced at Emma, who was pretending not to listen but absolutely was. He'd have known it too. 'Yeah,' he continued, 'I can be there Monday no probs.' He winked at Emma now and she couldn't help a grin.

Sometimes it was hard to remember why she'd fallen for Dougie, but on occasions like this he'd remind her and she'd wonder why she'd ever doubted their future together. Perhaps this was all normal, she told herself now – not for the first time. Perhaps it was supposed to get a little harder; perhaps you were supposed to work a little more at love when the shine of the new had worn off. Maybe that was the way you earned happiness – or at least, if not total happiness, then contentment. And maybe that was OK.

'Eight on Monday… Report to the foreman's hut. Got it, yep… See you then. Cheers.'

Dougie put his phone away and lay back on the sofa, hands behind his head, looking pleased with himself.

'You got a job?' Emma asked.

'Of course I did,' he said with a grin. 'Did you doubt me?'

'No,' she said.

'Liar!'

'Well maybe a little bit. I was wrong, wasn't I?'

'Yep.'

'It's brilliant, Dougie. I'm glad to be wrong.'

'Sometimes you could have a bit more faith in me.'

'You're right – I should have more faith.'

'So you'll never doubt me again?'

'Never,' she said, going over to kiss him. 'Let's hope you can keep this one, eh?'

Chapter Seven

Monday morning came around quickly, as it always did. Dougie had left for work by the time Emma went off to Burnbury's to start her own week. He'd kissed her sleepy mouth, told her he'd see her later, and she'd groggily wished him good luck.

'I'll hardly need that,' he said as he left. 'It's only warehouse work; I could do it with my eyes shut.'

'Please don't – it might not go down very well.'

Margot was in a better mood than she'd been the week before. A distant aunt had left her a pot of money and she was already spending it, starting with booking a fortnight in Antigua. Emma couldn't help but think back to her dad's remark – lucky makes luck. If that were true, Margot was proof of it; one of those blessed people who sailed through life doing as little as she could get away with and yet still having everything she needed and more just falling into her lap. Maybe, Emma reflected wryly as she listened to Margot phone just about everyone she knew to tell them about her good fortune, she needed to change tack. Perhaps if she stopped caring about everyone and everything, a bit of luck would come her way too.

But then, later at home, she forgot about all that. Dougie had got in just before her and on the way had picked up beers and a Chinese takeaway. He'd told her it was an indulgence to celebrate his new job, and they had the most relaxed evening they'd had in ages. Maybe Lady Luck was treating Emma just fine after all; she had a nice house, a good man, they were both working again, and surely things would start looking up from now on.

Tuesday began in much the same way as Monday, only Dougie had left the house with a touch less enthusiasm and when Emma arrived at work Margot was back to her cynically lazy self. She was utterly brassed off because she'd discovered that some illegitimate cousin had laid claim to half the distant aunt's money and 'wasn't it a bloody liberty'. She'd dealt with the disappointment by giving Emma a woefully out-of-date spreadsheet of overtime payments that were now two months overdue and had disgruntled employees chasing them. Of course, this was Margot's job, Margot's mess, but Emma's to clear up.

Tuesday ended with Dougie making beans on toast for her and letting her choose what they watched on TV.

Wednesday morning came and went without incident. At work, Margot had a pretend migraine and so had to divert all her incoming calls to Emma's phone. While she had a five-hour lie-down in the Portakabin they sometimes lent out to exhausted drivers for a sleep, Emma quietly got on with everything in the office and secretly enjoyed her absence.

At home Dougie went out to buy them a portion of fish and chips to share, and it was at this point that Emma started to get suspicious.

'Work's still going well?' she asked as they buttered bread to go with their meal.

'Good, yeah. Boss says at this rate I'll be taking his job, I'm picking it up so quick.'

'Well you have the qualifications to progress and they know that,' Emma replied. 'They must have all that info on your CV after all. They're probably realising they've stumbled across a little gem.'

'That's the first time I've been called a little gem,' Dougie said with a laugh.

Emma began to unwrap the chips. 'Oh dear; I hope it hasn't put too much of a dent in your masculinity.'

'I can cope.' He took some bread and butter from the pile she'd just placed between them on the table.

'So…' She sat down and tried to maintain the air of a casual chat. 'Anything else happened?'

He looked up sharply from his plate. 'Like what?'

'Oh, nothing in particular. It's just that you haven't said much about work since Monday. What are your colleagues like? There's a canteen, right? The food's good? Are you rushed off your feet or is it OK?'

'It's fine,' he said. 'Canteen's alright. Workmates are pretty much your typical warehouse crowd and it gets busy but it's OK. Makes the day go quicker when it's busy.'

'I suppose it does,' Emma said before she decided to eat her food and say no more about it.

On Thursday Dougie didn't come to kiss her before he left for work. Though it troubled her slightly, she had to assume he was in a rush. She was happy to forgo a kiss if it meant not making him late.

Margot's migraine had gone but she now had 'women's problems' and kept disappearing for hours on end. On another occasion Emma might have found it annoying but instead she just savoured the peace in the office; if all her days could be like this she might not mind working in HR so much.

When she got home Dougie was out. She sent him a text to ask when he'd be back so she could cook, and he replied saying he was doing overtime and didn't know when he'd be in so not to bother. So she warmed up a curry from the freezer and ate in silent contemplation of a universe in which Dougie willingly stayed behind to work extra hours. Maybe he liked this job after all. Maybe he'd realised it was time he brought more money into the house. Maybe he'd finally grown up. Whatever the reason, Emma appreciated that he was making the effort. Over the past few months she'd grown sick of nagging about his unemployment, and he must have been sick of hearing it. If they could finally start pulling together as a team domestically as well as as a couple, it would be nice to see some tranquillity descend on the house as a result.

Emma fell asleep on the sofa and was woken by Dougie coming in around nine.

'You worked all that time?' she asked, bleary-eyed and confused.

'Yeah, babes, I'm knackered. Going to bed.'

'I'm not surprised. You don't want to eat first?'

'I'm alright, just tired. See you tomorrow, yeah?'

'I'll be up shortly,' she called after him.

'I'll be asleep by then, babes,' he called back.

By the time she'd tidied and checked the house before going up she was wide awake again. Typical, she thought, as she made another cup of tea.

*

Friday morning. Emma woke when Dougie's alarm went off and decided she might as well get up too so she could see something of him this morning before he left.

'End of the week already,' she said, rolling over to face him as he pulled on a pair of joggers in the half light of the dawn.

'Yeah.'

'It's been OK, though? At the warehouse, I mean? This one might be a keeper?'

'It's alright,' he said. 'It'll do for now.'

'That's OK then. You can do it for a bit and if you still feel it's not challenging enough you can look for something else at the same company or elsewhere. The main thing is you're working now. I can't tell you how much stress it takes off me knowing we're both bringing a wage in.'

He nodded briefly and pulled a T-shirt over his head. Then he dragged his shoulder-length hair into a band at the nape of his neck.

'You're not working overtime tonight?' Emma asked.

'Don't know. Why?'

'I thought I might cook something nice – celebrate the end of your first week.'

'You don't need to; it's not that big a deal.'

'But I want to.'

'Well… whatever.'

'Want me to make some breakfast?'

'I'm alright… not hungry.'

'But you'll be hungry in an hour and lugging stuff around on an empty stomach in that warehouse will do you no good. At least take a slice of toast to eat on the go so you'll have something—'

'Babes, I'm fine. Go back to sleep.'

'I can't; I'm awake now.'

She was about to say something else when Dougie grabbed his trainers and dashed from the bedroom.

'See you later!' he shouted as he went.

Emma lay back on her pillow and stared up at the ceiling. He really was taking this job seriously.

When she got into work herself, Margot was eating her second (or maybe even third) breakfast and reading the paper. That took her until 10 a.m., by which time Emma had processed all that week's driver expenses. Then Margot went outside to take a private call – which lasted another hour and must have been very private indeed because she usually didn't care about taking personal calls in the office. When she came back in she announced that her blood sugar was low and she needed tea and biscuits or she'd faint. Emma let out a sigh as Margot left the office again to go to the kitchen, and for the first time that week she allowed herself a moment to imagine running off to Dorset with Tia to rescue a beautiful old railway station.

She hadn't spoken to Tia since the day of her raffle win, and she supposed her new friend was now busy, boosted by the welcome advantage of the extra cash and trying to raise the remainder of what she needed. After the conversation with her dad about it at the supermarket, Emma had decided once again that it was a reckless endangerment of the money her dad had worked so hard all his life for and she wouldn't risk it, no matter what he said about inheritances and fresh starts or being captain of her own ship or any other such wisdom he sometimes liked to spout. If she lost that money – and there was every chance she might on such a risky venture – she'd never be able to face him again for the shame and guilt. Still, she could daydream about what that life might be like…

The week with Dougie so far had been calm, even promising, and at least that was one thing to cling to when her own day in the office wasn't going so well. She tried to shake thoughts of Dorset and focus on making her relationship with Dougie a success, which was a far more realistic prospect.

Margot managed to make it through to twelve thirty before she decided she had to eat lunch. Her break took them to 2 p.m. Emma ate her sandwiches at her desk while she processed some holiday requests. Then Margot needed a hot chocolate from the drive-through coffee house down the road (to her credit she offered to get Emma one too) which got them to 3 p.m. At four thirty, after messing around with the printer for an hour trying to change the toner cartridge, Margot announced she was taking half an hour of time owed to her (for what, Emma had no idea) so she could make a hair appointment and rushed off, leaving Emma wrapping up the week's work.

'I thought we might go out for the day tomorrow,' Emma said as she put their meal out. She'd told Dougie he could have anything he wanted as a reward for completing his first week at his new job and, rather predictably, he'd asked for steak and chips. 'As it's Saturday and we're both off,' she continued. 'We deserve a bit of downtime, right?'

'I was going to meet Willard and get a few hours in at the lake.'

'But you do that every weekend. I thought we could drive out – shopping, countryside, the coast… I don't mind, you choose.'

'I've already arranged it with Willard now. Can we do it next weekend, babes? I'm shattered; I just want to chill this weekend.'

'Oh... well I suppose we can if you're really set on fishing this weekend. I suppose I could go and see Patricia. She mentioned shopping. She'd probably like that.'

'Got any ketchup, babes?'

'Sorry, we've run out.'

Dougie frowned.

'We've got barbeque,' Emma said. 'Would that do?'

'It's not the same.' He took the plate she'd just handed him and slumped onto his chair at the table like a primary schooler who'd just been told playtime was cancelled.

'I could go and pick some up at the shop on the corner,' she said. It was the end of the week and having a couple of days' rest to look forward to gave her more patience than she usually had. Dougie had worked hard all week, and she supposed she could indulge him this once...

'It's alright,' he said, clearly meaning that it wasn't. 'I can eat it – it just won't be the same as it is with ketchup.'

Emma hesitated. If she went out to the shop their dinner would be cold when she got back. She could stay home and eat, but he'd whine and fuss and make little comments about how much better the meal would be with his ketchup, and in the end she decided that tepid food was the lesser of the two evils.

'I'll be as fast as I can,' she said, grabbing her purse on the way through to the front door before rushing out.

Clive was behind the counter. He looked up from his newspaper as Emma dashed in.

'Where's your ketchup, Clive?'

'Third row down, love. You want me to come and show you?'

'No, got it!' Emma called, racing back to the counter with some in record time.

'How are you, love?' he asked as he checked the bottle for a price.

'Good.'

'Dougie still looking for a job?'

He found the price and rang it through the till, Emma wishing he'd be a bit quicker about it.

'No,' she said. 'He's got one, his first week this week. He's enjoying it too and by all accounts picking it up quickly.'

She took the change from the five-pound note she'd just handed Clive and smiled brightly before she turned to leave.

'Oh, I almost forgot!' Clive called. Emma turned back. 'Hang on…' He reached beneath the counter and pulled out a small pack. 'Jeanette was on this afternoon – she said Dougie forgot to pick up his Rizlas when he left the shop. They're all paid for. Want to take them home for him now?'

'Oh, right…' Emma held up her hand for the cigarette papers. Cogs were slowly cranking into gear, but too slowly yet to make any sense. 'He came in this afternoon?' she asked.

'Yes, love,' Clive said cheerily. 'Must have been on a break.'

'Yes,' Emma agreed, though it was a heck of a drive from his warehouse just to come to Clive's shop on his break. 'Thanks, Clive.'

She left the shop far more slowly than she'd arrived, taking the corner that led back to her own street deep in thought.

It wasn't odd for Dougie to buy cigarette papers – though he didn't smoke. He'd often pick them up for his friend Willard when they were going fishing together because Clive's shop was close to home and there wasn't one as handy to Willard that sold them. Did that mean Dougie had seen Willard today? But how, if he'd been at work?

Still, there was probably a perfectly good explanation.

Dougie rubbed his hands together as Emma passed the ketchup, though for a man who couldn't countenance chips without it, he'd eaten quite a few while she'd been out.

'Money couldn't buy a diamond like you,' he said.

'Oh, and Clive said you left your Rizlas behind when you were in there earlier today,' she said casually, placing the pack of papers down in front of him.

'Oh...'

Emma watched closely. Was it her imagination or did Dougie look flustered?

'Thanks,' he said.

'It's a bit of a way out, isn't it?' she said. 'Clive's shop, I mean.'

'Well, you know... that's the only place that sells the papers Willard uses.'

'But you didn't see Willard today, did you?'

'I'm going to see him tomorrow, aren't I?'

'I suppose so,' Emma said slowly, and she had to admit that much was true. 'It still doesn't explain why you had to drive all the way from work today to get them. Clive would have been open early enough in the morning to pick them up before you met Willard.'

Dougie stuffed a forkful of chips into his mouth and chewed rapidly. Without another word, Emma went to get his car key from his jacket pocket and headed outside. Marching to his car, she unlocked it and started the engine to check the petrol gauge. Unless he'd filled it (and he never filled it), he hadn't made enough of a dent in the fuel to have travelled far at all through the week. But if he'd been driving across town every day, he really ought to have done.

Dougie came to the front door and, to his credit, lost some of the colour in his face as she relocked the car – the very car Elise had been kind enough to loan him while she was away so he'd find it easier to work. The car he wasn't using at all to get to work as far as Emma could see. Had he made this whole job thing up? Had he been anywhere this week? Surely he'd never sink that low.

'I filled it,' he said.

Emma walked to the step and looked up at him. 'How do you know that's what I was looking at?'

'Just a guess.'

'OK… So have a guess what I'm thinking now.'

'I don't know. This is stupid. Are you coming in to finish your steak?'

'I'm not hungry anymore. Dougie… tell me the truth. Are you even going to work? Did you make the whole job thing up to shut me up?'

'God, no! Of course not!'

'Then why do I feel like a mug right now?'

'Call the warehouse if you don't believe me!'

Dougie glared at her. She wanted to believe him but, even as he issued his challenge, she still didn't and she couldn't even explain why. Something was wrong; she felt it deep in her gut, and even if he was telling the truth about the job he was keeping something from her.

One thing was certain: she couldn't call the warehouse to check right now – it was too late to get an answer and it would tell Dougie that she doubted him, and maybe he really didn't deserve that after all.

It was a hell of a thing to spend a weekend stewing over. It could be that she'd been let down so many times before it was easy to disbelieve him this time, but she'd felt like he'd really been trying this week and she'd liked that – she wanted it to be true. She wanted to believe that he was finally making an effort for the sake of her – for the sake of *them*.

'It doesn't matter,' she said. 'Let's forget it.'

'I don't know if I can,' he said sullenly.

'Look, it's been a good week and I'm sorry, I don't want to ruin it. Honestly, I was just confused why you drove out to the shop, but if you say it was to get Willard's papers then that's fine.'

'We'll say no more about it?'

Emma forced a smile and nodded, even as that little voice of doubt whispered to her again.

She felt horrible doing it. Like some sneaky, unreasonable, distrustful wife, and it wasn't even like Dougie was having an affair. Perhaps that would have been a far easier lie to unpick and she'd have certainly felt more justified in snooping around.

But Dougie had gone out to the lake early, as he so often did, and Emma had jumped in her car to drive to the warehouse where he'd spent his last week working, if only to silence that voice of doubt with proof. The best way to do that was to hear it straight from the horse's mouth.

Her heart was thumping as she pulled up in the car park. It was strange, but it almost felt as if her entire future hinged on this one event. They'd either move on together, or Emma would have to make a call, one way or the other, and live with it. She only knew that if Dougie was lying to her and she let him get away with it, she'd never deserve any respect from him, whether she got it or not.

The building looked quiet. It was Saturday, but she thought she'd heard Dougie say weekend work might be an option once he was trained properly, so it stood to reason there would be staff around somewhere today. A moment later a door opened and a couple of men wandered out, lighting cigarettes. She leapt out of her car.

'Excuse me…' she called, hurrying over. 'Do you know where I have to go to ask about a lost thing?'

'A what, love?'

'My boyfriend works here; he lost his AirPods and he asked me to come and see if anyone had found them here. He can't remember, but he might even have left them in his locker. Could I look there? I wouldn't be a minute.'

'What's his name?'

'Dougie Prince.'

The first one shot a puzzled look at the other. Then he turned back to Emma. 'Are you sure he works here? I don't know anyone named Dougie.'

Emma smiled. 'Maybe that's because he only started Monday.'

The second man suddenly looked enlightened. 'Brown hair? Wears it in a ponytail?'

'That's him,' Emma said.

'I don't know if anyone found anything Monday morning but I would have thought it would have made its way to lost property in the office by now if they had. He doesn't have a locker so I wouldn't know about that.'

'Oh, you don't have lockers? But I thought—'

'We have lockers, sugar,' the first man said. 'That's because we work here. He's not going to have one – we don't keep them empty for people who aren't coming back, do we?'

Emma looked from one to the other, her stomach lurching. 'What?'

'He doesn't work here, love.'

'But he…' Emma faltered. This was the one response she'd been afraid of, and now it was the one she wished she could unhear.

'Walked out Monday lunch and never came back. Don't you talk to each other if you're his girlfriend?'

'Oh, right… of course we do,' she said. 'I mean… never mind. Thanks anyway.'

She walked back to the car. She could feel the eyes of the two men on her back as she went and goodness knew what they made of her. They probably thought she was an idiot.

And, apparently, so did her boyfriend.

Chapter Eight

She was strangely calm as she drove to the fishing pool. Part of her had been expecting something like this and, had the situation come as more of a shock, she might have crumbled. Instead, she was gripped by a controlled rage. She wasn't going to rant and make herself look like a hysterical woman; she was calmly and assertively going to tell Dougie what she knew and what she was going to do about it. That was the important bit, the bit that was going to be different this time. It wasn't going to be about what he did next because she'd seen and heard it all before – but about what *she* did.

And she *was* going to do something about it.

The sky had darkened and it was drizzling as Emma spotted Dougie and his friend Willard at the lakeside. They'd set up a canvas shelter and were passing a roll-up cigarette back and forth, laughing hysterically at something, rods propped up on stands and dangling idly in the water. As Emma drew nearer, Dougie saw her and shoved the cigarette at his friend before shooting up off his seat and coming to meet her. Emma could smell it on him as he got close – not the normal cigarette smell – and it did nothing to quell her rage.

'I thought you didn't have any of Willard's dope?'

'Babes, what are you doing here? I can—'

'Forget it,' she said. 'It's not why I'm here.' She paused. Dougie really had taken her for a mug and now that she was here, the stench of marijuana clinging to him, she wondered if he even deserved the explanation she'd prepared so he'd be able to accept her next actions. Maybe she ought to be more like him: do whatever the hell she wanted and screw the consequences for anyone else. After all, it had worked pretty well for him all his life as far as she could see.

She took a breath. 'Willard's got a spare room, right?'

'I don't know…'

He looked worried. *Good*, she thought savagely.

'He'll have a couch, at least,' she continued. 'As you like spending time with him so much you'll be happy to use it tonight. In fact, you can use it the night after that too, and the one after that and the one after that…'

'Babes?'

'I want you out. If you're not over to collect your stuff by sundown you'll find it on the street – rain or not.'

'But what have I done?'

'Do I really have to tell you?'

'You're kicking me out over that?'

'It's my house and I don't want you there – that's why I'm kicking you out.'

Emma began to walk away, a curious triumph building in her. She suddenly felt lighter and freer than she had in months – perhaps even years.

His hand closed around her arm to pull her back and she shook him off.

'I said sundown!' she hissed.

'But I haven't done anything!'

'Exactly!'

'But, babes… I love you!'

Emma turned once more and began to stride towards her car.

'You know what, Dougie…?' she called, never looking back. 'I don't love you.'

Knowing that Dougie would likely head straight back to the house to try to talk her out of her decision, Emma didn't go home. Instead, she drove to her dad's house.

He opened the front door to her looking faintly confused. 'Hello… have we…?'

'Don't worry, Dad, you haven't forgotten anything. I know you're not expecting me, but is it alright if I come in?'

'It's always alright, love.' He stepped back and Emma followed him into the house.

'It smells good in here,' she said.

'I've just had an omelette,' he said. 'You could have had… I can make you one if you're hungry? It wouldn't take me a tick.'

'No, thanks, Dad, I'm not hungry. I wanted to…'

Even now, desperate to ask for the help he'd offered freely so many times before, the words stuck in her throat. She wanted this new start – she *needed* it – but to take this from her dad went against every principle she had.

'I'm going to sell my house,' she said, sitting on the sofa across from his favourite armchair, where he now settled.

'What's brought this on? I didn't know you were thinking of moving house. Is this something to do with Dougie's new job?'

'Sort of,' she said. 'But we're not moving, not as such. Well I'm planning to, I suppose. Dougie is too, in a fashion… just not with me.'

'I don't follow, love.'

'We're splitting up. I suppose I could have put that more succinctly, but there it is.'

Her dad let out a long, sad sigh, and the fact that he looked at her with such pain now, and with no pleasure at the news at all – when she knew a bit of him must be pleased – made her love him more than she'd ever loved him before. No crowing, no 'I told you so', no 'Good riddance' – and he'd have had every right to all of those sentiments. He only saw her unhappiness and he wanted to be there to make it better.

'Well,' he said finally. 'I can't say it's unexpected and I can't say I think it's a mistake – you know my feelings on that boy well enough. Are you alright? That's all I need to know.'

'Strangely, I am. At least, right now I am. It's all a bit new to me. In fact, I only decided about an hour ago.'

'You've told him?'

'Yes, he knows.'

'And he's accepted your decision?'

'He doesn't have a choice.'

'So you're selling up. What are you doing that for? It's only your name on the mortgage, isn't it? I thought Dougie wasn't able to get credit.'

'He couldn't. And I pay the mortgage too, along with pretty much everything else, so it's really my house.'

'In that case, is there really any need to sell up? Can't you just kick him out?'

'I want a fresh start, Dad. That includes the house... There just feels like too much about it that would drag me down if I stayed.'

'Fair enough. You know there's always space for you here if you need it.'

'I know, Dad.' She gave him a grateful smile. 'But...' She drew a long breath, a sudden courage filling her. She didn't even know where it had come from, but it was all she needed; it was now or never. 'I was thinking... if that offer of help is still there, I might go a little further afield. I was thinking Dorset maybe...'

Chapter Nine

The weeks between Emma's decision to leave Dougie and her arrival in Dorset had been a mad blur.

When Emma had approached Tia with her proposition to come on board as a business partner so they could buy Honeymoon Station, she'd been thrilled. They'd talked into the night, making plans and lists, researching and working out the maths, and had spent many evenings after that doing the same. Along the way they'd found out a lot about each other, about their lives since school, their heartbreaks and their triumphs, about what each valued, and Emma was reasonably confident that Tia was a woman she could trust with the next phase of her life. As her dad and Elise and Aunt Patricia had reminded her, she had to be, because everything now depended on it.

The sale of Emma's house had raised a little money – though not nearly as much as she'd hoped for. That might have been down to the quick sale of course, but she'd needed it to go through swiftly in case she got cold feet and changed her mind, not to mention the risk of Dougie putting a spanner in the works. Although he hadn't given her as much trouble as she'd imagined he might.

At first he'd done his utmost to change her mind, motivated, no doubt, by the shock of suddenly losing his ever-dependable meal ticket. He'd hung around the house like a cloud of gnats round the head of an evening jogger, until the house had changed hands and he'd been forced to start phoning. He hadn't dared come to her dad's house, where she'd stayed for a few weeks while everything in Dorset was finalised, and she had to be thankful for small mercies.

Once Dougie had finally got the message, contact had dwindled – just a few pathetic text messages and unanswered phone calls until there was nothing. The last she'd heard of him he'd moved in with Willard permanently, where they were both enjoying their evenings smoking themselves into oblivion. At least that was one less thing for Emma to worry about.

Handing her notice in at Burnbury's and seeing the look on Margot's face was a particular highlight of the final weeks of her old life. There were many things she'd wanted to say to Margot, about all the times she'd used Emma as a skivvy and left her to take the rap for a mess that was her fault, about the endless breakfasts and never-ending lunch breaks, the hours of personal calls and sneaky late starts and early finishes. But in the end Emma just wished her good luck in finding another mug who would be stupid enough to do all Margot's work for a fraction of her pay and strode out of the building feeling like the triumphant heroine from a romantic comedy.

To make up the financial shortfall, Emma had sold all her furniture, her car, most of her jewellery apart from one of her mother's rings, a large portion of her clothes (she wouldn't have much call for evening dresses working on a building site) and had even cashed in some ancient savings bonds. What she'd still needed after that her dad had provided, though she'd done her absolute best to make sure the amount he had to put in was as small as possible. It was still a lot.

Now the moment had finally arrived. Tia killed the engine in a little parking bay that was as close to the station house as the weeds and rubble would allow, and in silence they both looked up at the building. A large section was obscured by trees and ranging shrubs, but Emma could see the faded wood of the eaves which had once been painted pristine white, and the shingles of the roof now dotted with holes, and the flutter of excitement within her fought with the sudden sinking feeling that she'd just done the most stupid thing of her entire life. She looked across at Tia and wondered if she was thinking the same.

'Well,' Tia said finally, 'we'd better go and see what we've bought.'

They'd looked before, of course, but it had been via a virtual online tour, aided by the information from various surveys, which was how the auctioneer had deemed it best to accommodate a large number of viewings in a quick window of time for the sale. Emma's dad had offered to drive down with her to sneak a look round, but Tia had convinced her that there was no need. Perhaps, secretly, she'd been afraid seeing it in the flesh would give Emma cold feet, and perhaps, if Emma was honest, she'd been a little afraid of the same thing herself. If she'd been to visit before the sale, would she have wanted to back out? A small part of her hadn't wanted the escape route, because that part of her knew her life needed a new direction. Often the leap that would offer you freedom needed to become a push or it would never happen. And the fact that nobody could see it officially in person, Tia had reasoned, would put some off bidding and meant the selling price would eventually be lower as a result.

Emma had been encouraged by that, and they'd been so swept up in the excitement of the moment that they'd bid with confidence and kept going until they'd won. Looking back, if she was perfectly honest, the excitement at the prospect of owning Honeymoon Station had been so intoxicating that in the heat of the moment they'd have carried on bidding, despite not feeling armed with enough information to know exactly what they were buying. It represented so much more than a building or even a business for both of them. Two women who needed fresh starts and big changes – it was a powerful force.

Emma's mouth was dry and her heart thumped as they walked around to the front of the building. The iron of the tracks was long gone, but the scars of their existence still ran the length of the platform and out towards the tunnel of overgrown trees in either direction. A butterfly bush almost as wide as the roof clawed at the sky straight from a hole on the left side. Whenever Emma saw shrubs growing from an abandoned building like that, she was always astonished at their hardiness. Various trees and shrubs and thick-stemmed weeds crowded the platform and obscured the columns holding up the canopy that must have once sheltered the waiting passengers, some which Emma recognised and some she didn't. A squirrel darted up one of them and disappeared into the foliage.

'They always say that nature would reclaim the planet if we died out,' Tia said wryly. 'This lot certainly proves that theory.'

'I suppose it's been empty a long time. I mean, it would have been nice to have less to do, but I guess it's to be expected.'

'Hmm.'

Tia was quiet for a moment, but then she turned to Emma with a manic grin and pulled her into a violent hug.

'We're here!' she cried. 'We've done it!'

'Steady on!' Emma laughed. 'We've done nothing yet; this is only the beginning.'

But despite her words of caution, she felt the emotion too, a curious mix of fear and ecstasy, of hope and optimism and doubt. It was a heady cocktail.

'Of an amazing journey!' Tia insisted. Her eyes were shining and she had a grin that looked like it would never end. She made her way towards the building and stood outside the boarded-up entrance, gazing up at it. 'Isn't it beautiful?'

It had certainly filled Emma's head with romantic notions when she'd viewed it online but, now she was here, she wasn't sure beautiful was the word she'd use. Tragic was what came to mind now. Lost, ruined, hopeless… maybe potential was the most positive word she could summon.

Tia pulled an iron key from her shoulder bag and handed it to Emma.

'Want to be the first one over the threshold?'

'Really?'

'Why not?' Tia smiled. 'You're half owner after all.'

'You're half owner too.'

'I'd have been none owner if not for you riding to my rescue. Come on, this is your moment and you've earned it. Get that door open and let's have a proper look inside.'

Emma took the key. Her palms were suddenly clammy. This was crazy – why was she so nervous? It was just an old building.

The door was heavy and stiff, and Emma had to check she'd unlocked it properly twice because she struggled to get it moving at first. But eventually it yielded and groaned open.

The first thing that struck her was the smell. While outside the overgrown vegetation had been strongest in her nostrils, now the faint dampness she'd detected from behind the locked door hit her with full force. It was the damp and mould and rot of years of abandonment, and if a scent could have an emotion attached then it was about the saddest thing she'd ever smelled.

The second thing was how dark it was. The windows had been boarded up and even the bright sun outside struggled to find a way in. Never mind an old station house, Emma thought, the melancholy of the place seeping into every fibre of her being, this was more like a crypt.

'Oh, isn't it amazing!' Tia gasped. 'Look at the wood! And the ticket window! And these gorgeous seats!'

Emma cocked an eyebrow at her. 'You mean those seats covered in bird poo?'

Tia grinned. 'But there's bound to be gorgeous old craftsmanship beneath that bird poo!'

Emma's eyes raked the gloom. After a moment, the shape and features of the space began to emerge. Crafted in the glory days of steam, in its heyday this would have been a beautiful place. The rosewood of the counters and ticket-booth walls would have been sailed in directly from Africa or India and would have gleamed, glossy and freshly varnished, and the leather upholstery of the benches would have been soft and rich with the smell furniture wax, while the polished floor would have echoed with the footsteps of travellers, the air of the tea room humming with chat and vibrant with the scents of freshly baked cake and gusts of fresh air as the doors of the waiting room opened and closed. Art deco posters, bold with colour and geometric designs would have adorned the walls, advertising trips to the seaside or the mountains of the Scottish Highlands or the majestic Lakes, alongside painted enamel plaques selling chocolate or cigarettes. Officials in gold-trimmed caps would have hurried here and there, all polished shoes and shining whistles. The air would have been rent by a shrill blow that told everyone the next train was about to leave and there'd have been a flurry of activity and goodbye kisses.

Looking at it now, though it had all once happened in this very spot, it was hard to see those glory days. All Emma could think about was how much there was to do.

'I think it's all going to have to come out,' she said. 'I don't see how anything in here is salvageable – it all looks rotten to the core.'

'It might not be as bad as it looks. It's hard to tell when it's so dirty. First thing we should do is clean the place and get a proper look.' Tia wandered over to a window and yanked at a plank of wood. 'If we could just get a bit of light on the matter…'

She pulled, and then tore her hand away with a squeak. 'Ow! Bloody splinter!'

'That's a good start,' Emma said. 'Let's go outside where I can see properly and I'll get it out for you.'

'Could you? I can never do it.'

'I've pulled enough splinters in my time to be an expert.'

'Lucky for me then.' Tia followed her outside. 'How come?'

'Elise,' Emma said, getting her handbag from Tia's car and retrieving a pair of tweezers. As Emma had sold her car to raise money and Elise's car had been confiscated from Dougie and was being stored at her dad's, Tia's car was essentially the business car now, which meant in a strange way it was also Emma's, but it still felt odd and impertinent to have her own keys for it. 'She was always picking them up from somewhere or other, and Dad was hopeless at getting them out because he said his hands weren't steady enough. It wasn't that at all – he just had no patience.'

'Must have been hard.' Tia turned her face away so she wouldn't see Emma work at the wood lodged in her fingertip.

'What?'

'Growing up without your mum.'

'I suppose it was but I got used to it very quickly. You do at that age. We were alright really. We managed the best we could, because we didn't have any other choice.'

'I suppose not...' Tia winced as Emma got purchase on the end of the splinter.

'Hold still... almost... there!'

Emma held up the offending object for Tia to see.

'It felt a lot bigger than that,' Tia said, eyeing it with a look of deepest offence.

'They always do,' Emma said. 'Like grit in your eye – feels like a bloody house brick but when it's out you can hardly see it at all.'

'Well at least I know I can rely on you to keep me safe while we're working on this place.'

'Or maybe we should make the DIY store our first stop to get safety equipment. I might be able to patch you up but there's no point in ruining our nails and hands if we don't need to.'

Tia looked back at the building. 'Well now we've seen it in the flesh, I suppose there's a lot more to talk about.'

'You can say that again.'

'We should take some photos so we can study them later. Might be handy to get some advice on what we could salvage and what we'd have to ditch too.'

'OK, we can do that. And then what?'

'I vote we drive to the village and find our rental cottage. We'll probably need to get some supplies too and I suppose it wouldn't hurt to get chatting to one or two of the locals... You never know when their knowledge of the area might come in handy.'

'And then?'

'Lunch,' Tia said. 'I'm starving already.'

'Do you think we'll get to start any work on this place today?'

'Depends how sleepy lunch makes me,' Tia said with a grin. 'Kidding!' she added in reply to the frown forming on Emma's forehead. 'Let's get lunch, pick up a few bits of equipment and food, and see if we still have time to make a start this afternoon.'

Chapter Ten

Their rental cottage was tiny, a little two-up two-down with a pocket square of garden at the back and a front door that opened directly out onto a higgledy-piggledy high street. In fact, it wasn't just the high street, it was more or less the only street of note in the village. The house was small, but it was big enough as Emma and Tia weren't planning to spend a lot of time there – which was lucky, because otherwise, in such a small space, they'd have been ready to kill each other very quickly.

Outside on the street the paving slabs weren't made of concrete as they were in most towns, but an older stone, worn smooth by generations of footfall and pleasingly uneven. The wrought-iron lamp posts were adorned with baskets of flowers, and tiny stone cottages, some with thatched roofs and some with grey slate, jostled for position along either side of the street like a crowd of children trying to get to the front of a queue for ice cream. The road that wound between them was barely wide enough to let two cars pass. Emma reflected that, in the age of horse power, there wouldn't have been much more room for two carts either.

At the far end there was a market cross raised up on a small roundabout, surrounded by flower beds of pink and lilac and peachy blooms. There was an old stone sign within the flowers, engraved with arrows and mileage for Dorchester and London and other places Emma wasn't familiar with but which must once have been important locally. There was another signpost made from iron – still old – rust-bitten and weathered and patched up with years of paint to make the directions legible. This one indicated the way to nearby villages and towns. There were a couple of shops, a tiny post office that nobody ever seemed to go into, the obligatory country pub (charmingly named the Randy Shepherd), a café (the rather more conservatively named Honeymoon Café) and not a lot else. It was all perfectly adorable and perfectly quaint and would undoubtedly be a lovely stop-off for holidaymakers on their way to the coast or the New Forest, but there wasn't a lot to make them stay.

As they made their way to the cottage and took it all in, Emma was plagued by worries that now, not only did they have a hotel to build, but they also had to find reasons for their guests to come. She aired these doubts to Tia, who seemed unconcerned. Emma couldn't decide if this was a comfort or not, but she did decide that they probably should have found out more about the village before going to such lengths to win the auction.

The cottage owner, June, was waiting for them with the keys when they arrived. She'd explained over the phone that she usually let it out to weekenders and at that point Emma had wondered whether she'd be happy to hear that they wanted to live in it for the next few months while they worked on a hotel that would be in direct competition with her once it was open. But June had cheerily told them that she'd been thinking of retiring after the summer anyway and so, if anything, their arrival had done her a favour by giving her the push she needed to put the cottage up for sale once they'd finished with it. She'd even asked if they wanted to buy it instead of their long-term rental arrangement, but, lovely as the offer was, Tia explained that, financially, it was totally out of the question. After the call, Tia had told Emma it was a sign, an omen of good fortune that they'd bought Honeymoon Station at exactly the right time. Emma smiled and nodded but had silently doubted life was always so simple.

'You must be Tia and Emma!' June said as she came out to greet them. 'Do you have a car, my darlings?'

'Oh, we had to park it on a bit of ground near the shop,' Tia said. 'We thought it might get in the way in front of the house with the road being so narrow.'

'You'll be alright – people will just drive around and we hardly have that much traffic anyway,' June said. 'Bring it round when you want to unload.'

'Thank you,' Tia said.

'Well...' June swept a hand towards the cottage. 'Here's home for you now.'

'It's lovely,' Emma said.

'I'm sure it's smaller than you're used to,' June replied. 'They used to build small back in the day, but I think you'll have everything you need.'

'As we won't be in a lot, I don't think we'll need that much to begin with,' Tia said. 'A couple of beds, a bath and a kettle – that ought to do it.'

'Well we definitely have those,' June said cheerily. 'Now, I know I said over the phone, but I must remind you of the bats in the loft—'

'Bats?' Tia asked sharply, glancing at Emma. Emma didn't recall any mention of bats and, judging by her reaction, she guessed Tia didn't either.

'Didn't I tell you?' June asked vaguely.

'You might have done,' Emma said. 'I don't remember for sure. Will they be alright?'

'They'll be just fine – they don't mind you being there at all, and you might hear a bit of scratching and flapping every now and again when the house is quiet, but you won't notice after a couple of days.'

'Oh,' Tia said, looking as if she thought she might notice.

'That's alright,' Emma said. 'We don't mind them at all.' Whether they did or didn't, there was no use complaining because the bats were there and nothing was going to change that. Really they didn't have a lot of choice, as June's cottage was the only one available to rent in Honeymoon.

'I suppose bats are protected too,' Tia said.

'Oh yes.' June nodded vigorously. 'Some folks love them but knowing they're there puts some off so I always mention it. Whether I like them or not they're there and I can't move them, so guests can take it or leave it.'

'We're fine with them,' Emma said.

'You're staying a good while too,' June said. 'You'd be surprised how quickly you'll get used to hearing them up there and forget they even exist.'

Tia and Emma both smiled, though Emma doubted they'd forget the existence of a roof full of bats if they were that noisy.

'I should mention that there's also a little family of field mice in the shed in the garden,' June added, 'but they're doing no harm and as long as you keep the back door closed they shouldn't trouble you in the house. I haven't the heart to get rid of them.'

'Oh, right,' Emma said. Bats and mice now – rather than open a hotel, they ought to be thinking about a zoo.

'I'm a few doors down,' June continued. 'Knock if there's anything you need. In the morning the chickens sometimes give me more eggs than I can eat – when they do I'll pop a few over for you.'

'That sounds lovely,' Emma said.

'Have you always lived in Honeymoon?' Tia asked.

June nodded. 'Born and raised here. Wouldn't thank you for a mansion anywhere else. My mother was born here and her mother before her. In fact, the house you're staying in was my mother's. She left it to me when she died, and as I rather liked the one I'm in now I thought I could get a nice little income from it to save for my twilight years.'

'And has it?' Tia asked.

'Oh yes!' June said. 'I could have rented it twenty times over for everyone who's stayed here. Such a lovely little spot and close to the New Forest for your walkers. That's mostly who I get, ramblers and birdwatchers. Suits me just fine that way.'

'That's good,' Tia said. Emma could tell by the way her face had lit up that she was doing little mental calculations and deciding that it boded well for their venture that they at least had some ready custom once the hotel was open for business. Emma shared her optimism to a certain extent, but she had to temper it by reminding herself they had a long way to go to get it up and running before they could even think about guests.

'Would you like me to show you where everything is?' June asked.

'Oh, don't worry,' Emma said, glancing at Tia who nodded agreement, 'I'm sure we'll manage, and you're only down the street if we can't. I think we're just going to unload the car for now and then head out to get some lunch.'

'Ah, well, if you're after a hearty one, then the pub does a nice steak that's really local. In fact, you can probably see the cows from the window.'

Emma wasn't sure she was completely OK with watching a cow wander around the field while she ate its best mate but she smiled. 'Maybe something lighter for now – is there anywhere else?'

'If you're after a quicker bite then Honeymoon Café does salads and sandwiches and that sort of thing.'

'Thanks,' Emma said.

June held out the keys and Emma let Tia take them. She was bouncing around like an excited toddler and it seemed a shame to deprive her of the grand opening of their new home – at least, what would be their home for the next few months.

'Don't forget, I'm only a hop away,' June called as she started to walk back to her own cottage.

'We won't!' Tia called after her. She turned to Emma with that manic grin Emma was already beginning to recognise well. 'We're here! This is actually happening and I still can't actually believe it!'

'Neither can I,' Emma said with a smile. 'I'm sure I'm going to wake to find it's all been a crazy dream.'

'You got the crazy bit right,' Tia replied. 'But then, what life is worth living without a bit of crazy in it?'

They settled on a lighter lunch in consideration of a busy afternoon. A sleep-inducing mound of chips and half a chicken or steak might sound good but it wouldn't exactly keep them nimble. So they followed June's recommendation and sought out Honeymoon Café. Not that it took a lot of seeking in a village as small as Honeymoon – across the main street and set back a little on a tiny cul-de-sac (which was essentially half a dozen houses in a little semicircle) was about as far as they needed to go.

'It's very cute,' Tia said.

'It's very seventies,' Emma replied, and Tia grinned before pushing the door open. Emma followed her in and they were greeted by a very pretty, petite girl with dark hair and a starched white apron over a calf-length dress. She looked about twelve, but from her demeanour Emma guessed straight away that she was one of those baby-faced women who looked a lot younger than they actually were.

'Hi!' the girl called as she rushed over. 'Would you like a table or is it takeaway?'

'A table please,' Tia said.

'No problem,' the girl said, and she gestured around the empty dining room. 'Sit where you like and I'll bring some menus over.'

They settled at a table by a window dressed in lacy curtains.

'It's so quaint,' Tia said in a whisper that was a bit too loud for Emma to be comfortable about it.

'I wonder when it was last decorated,' Emma replied, her voice lower still, but then she blushed as she looked up to see the girl was already back at their table, fumbling with their menus and blushing herself.

'I know it looks a bit dated,' she said apologetically. 'You'll have to excuse that – we only bought it this year and we're still working on getting it done. I've made a few changes…' She pointed to a brightly tiled floor. 'That's ours.'

'It's lovely,' Emma said, feeling awful for her overheard comment and deciding to keep her mouth shut for evermore after today.

'We had to do structural repairs too,' the girl said. 'A new roof and chimney.'

Tia smiled at her. 'I can see how that might hold up other things. Do I detect a northern accent?'

'Oh yes,' the girl said. 'Though I've been in Dorset for a few years now. I lived with my cousin for a while in another village down the road. She has a bakery and a café there; taught me the whole business, and then I got married and we wanted something of our own. This place went on the market at just the right time. We bought it earlier this year but my husband has only just been able to join me because he had to wait for his army discharge.'

She flushed with obvious pride at the mention of her husband, and Emma had to wonder if she'd ever meet a man who was so clearly all the stars in her sky.

'That's another reason why we've been a bit slow with the renovations,' the girl added. 'Are you both on holiday?'

'Actually, we're starting a business here too,' Tia said. 'Don't worry, though, it's not going to be a café and it's a couple of miles out.'

'Oh,' the girl said, 'I didn't mean… It's just we're not exactly rushed off our feet here. We knew it would be a small place but we'd hoped for passing trade and holidaymakers… I suppose it's quite early in the season yet,' she concluded lamely.

The comment left Emma troubled again by how quiet the village seemed. A lack of passing trade didn't sound good. In fact, the only person they'd met so far who seemed to get on OK was June.

'Maybe we'll make things better for you,' Tia said. 'We're opening a hotel.'

'A hotel!' the girl said. 'Where?'

'At the old railway station.'

The girl's eyes widened. 'Honeymoon Station?'

'Actually, we're renovating the old station building; we're going to convert it into guest rooms, maybe even have a gym and spa, that sort of thing.'

'Wow, that would certainly attract visitors,' the girl said. 'But won't you have a restaurant on site?'

'We might,' Tia said. 'But people don't always eat every meal in their accommodation, do they? I know I don't – I'd rather try out places in the local area. And with a lot more accommodation near the village you should get more holidaymakers passing through and so more trade. I think everyone wins.'

'Oh,' the girl said. 'Tariq will be so pleased. He's been so worried about this decision ever since we got here. I don't mind admitting to you it hasn't been as easy as we'd imagined.'

Emma tried to look sympathetic but her stomach was sinking. This really wasn't what she needed to hear right now.

'I'm Darcie by the way,' the girl said. 'I'm so pleased you came in today – I feel like it was such a stroke of luck.'

'Tia… and this is my friend Emma. Old school friend actually. So Tariq is…'

'My husband. We got married last year. I met him while I was working at my cousin's bakery. He's such a sweetie – if you met him you wouldn't imagine him being a tough, burly soldier at all.'

'I hope we get to meet him soon then,' Tia said. 'It'll be nice knowing there's someone else in the village a little bit in the same boat as us, you know what I mean?'

'Oh absolutely!' Darcie beamed. 'It'll be so nice! Any way we can help, you must let us know. I mean, it might not be a lot in the end but we've at least been here a few months so we are a little bit more familiar with the village. Where are you living? You can't be staying at the station?'

'Oh no,' Emma said. 'God no! We're renting a cottage.'

'From June?' Darcie asked. 'She's lovely.'

'She seems very nice,' Emma said.

'Everyone is very sweet here,' Darcie said. 'Well mostly, but you get that everywhere, don't you? I was a bit worried when we first arrived, how people would take us, you know. I think the lady who owned the café before was very well loved and everyone was apparently very sad when she died suddenly, and Tariq and I are outsiders, and... well, I don't want to be negative. We needn't have worried, though. We love being here; we just wish there was a bit more trade because that's our biggest worry now and we don't want to lose this place just as we get it right.' Darcie drew a breath. 'But you're here now, and that's very exciting.' She bounced on the balls of her feet as if trying to contain that excitement. 'I have such a good feeling about this.'

'Me too,' Tia said.

Emma wanted so badly to be swept up by that same optimism. She was envious of how quickly Tia and Darcie had decided their futures suddenly looked much rosier than they had a moment before, just because they'd met. But life had taught her that optimism was often misplaced and what looked rosy didn't always turn out to be. Nonetheless, she put on her bravest smile and agreed that she had a good feeling about things too.

'Oh, I almost forgot,' Darcie said with a sweet little tinkle of a laugh, 'menus! Here you go! I'll just be cleaning the counter – give me a whistle when you've decided what you're having.'

'Thanks,' Emma said, taking her menu.

Darcie left them.

'She's adorable,' Tia said in a low voice.

'She's lovely,' Emma agreed, putting the menu up to her face.

'Are you alright?'

Emma lowered it again to look at her friend. 'Why wouldn't I be?'

'I don't know. Since we got here you just seem a bit… subdued. Not got cold feet already, have you? I hope not, but if you have we need to talk about it.'

'I'm just tired,' she said, looking at her menu again.

'Emma…'

Emma let out a sigh and looked up at Tia once more. 'It just seems so daunting, doesn't it? Now that we're here, I mean. I can't help but wonder if we've bitten off more than we can chew. And the village is so small, much smaller than I thought it would be, and it's so quiet, and then Darcie just told us there was a lack of trade—'

'She said there was a lack of *passing* trade. That's because there's no reason for people to visit here yet – at least, anyone who doesn't want to walk or look at wildlife. But you heard June: the cottage is never empty and she could rent it out twenty times over to those people. The custom is there, I just know it is. We have to find the means to bring it to us. Honeymoon could thrive once we're open.'

'Do you think the people of Honeymoon are ready for it to be thriving?'

'We own the station now,' Tia said, though looking more doubtful. 'People round here must have known it was for sale and that the buyer would want to do something commercial with it. Us converting it into a hotel shouldn't be a surprise to anyone.'

'It might not be a surprise but that doesn't mean they have to like it.'

Tia sat back in her chair. 'Come on, Em, it's not like it's going to be The Ivy. It's just a little guest house of twenty or so rooms – at least it will be. I think they'll be fine. I mean, June didn't seem concerned and we already know Darcie is going to be happy about it.'

The door to the café opened and two men walked in. They looked remarkably alike, both tall and dark-haired, with a cheeky twinkle in their brown eyes. One was broader-shouldered than the other and looked as if he might be very familiar with the inside of a gym, whereas the other had more of an athletic build, indicating he might be a runner rather than a lifter.

'Oh hi!' Darcie said, glancing up from a spot on the counter she'd been scrubbing at. 'Are you looking for Tariq?'

'Are we early?' the broader man asked.

'Oh no, he's in the back. Go through – he'll show you what needs doing.'

The two men glanced at Emma and Tia, gave a good-natured nod and smile, then followed Darcie through a door behind the counter.

'Well,' Tia said approvingly, 'if those are some of the locals we have to persuade, then I think I might find a way to make the process very enjoyable.'

Emma laughed, despite her anxieties still being very much on her mind. 'You go for it. I'm off men so you won't get any competition from me.'

Tia grinned. A moment later Darcie came back through. 'Friends of yours?' Tia asked her.

'They're doing some work on the café,' Darcie said.

'They're builders?'

'Sort of everything. Name a trade, they can probably do it. Everyone in the village goes to them; they're really good at what they do.'

'I'll bet they are,' Tia almost purred. 'So if we wanted their assistance, who would we ask for?'

'Blake and Aidan,' Darcie said. 'They're brothers. I think their surname is Ronson, but if you just said Blake and Aidan to anyone they'd know who you meant.'

Emma looked at Tia. 'We already have builders coming.'

'Oh yes,' Tia said, 'but you never know when you might need other little jobs doing. It's good to have a backup plan, isn't it? And when our contractors leave we'll need help with maintenance too.'

'I suppose we will,' Emma said.

'You could do a lot worse than those two,' Darcie put in.

'Just what I was thinking,' Tia said, and Emma got the distinct impression she wasn't talking about building work.

Chapter Eleven

After a fresh salad served with crusty bread and a succulent breast of chicken, Emma felt brighter. Perhaps her low mood as they'd come away from Honeymoon Station earlier that day had been down to fatigue after all, and with a good plate of food inside her, a rest and a chat to Darcie and her husband Tariq – who'd come out to join her and meet them after Darcie had excitedly told him of their plans – she felt a lot better. Tariq had been every bit as pleased by their arrival as Darcie, and as a bonus the distractions of Blake and Aidan hadn't materialised again, meaning Tia's thoughts were back on track too. They had a lot to do and even more riding on the station house's success – the last thing they needed was for one of them to get involved in an ill-advised fling, and it might not help their cause with the locals either. That was assuming either of the men were even single.

'We'd better get a few bits to tide us over,' Tia said as they left Honeymoon Café and stepped back onto the high street. 'What about that little convenience store along the road?'

'Wouldn't it be easier to drive straight out to the supermarket?' Emma asked. 'We passed one on the way in, didn't we? It was only about ten miles out – wouldn't take long in the car and there'll be more choice than the local shop.'

'There might be,' Tia said, 'but there won't be locals in there. At least, we wouldn't know it if there were. We need to spend our money here for a while, get people used to seeing us around and let them see we want to support the village by shopping here.'

'Ah.' Emma smiled. 'Hearts and minds.'

'Exactly.'

'You're good at this.'

'I know.'

'At least it's not far away,' Emma added.

'Nothing's far away in Honeymoon.'

'I'm still deciding if that's a good thing,' Emma said.

'Well it's a thing so we'll have to make the best of it.'

In the time it had taken to have this brief discussion they'd arrived at the door of the shop. It was a converted cottage with a parking bay barely big enough for two cars that had been cut into the pavement. The smaller windows that graced the residential cottages along the row had been removed and replaced by one larger window, which displayed goods, ads for special offers, plus a corkboard covered in cards and posters to publicise local events, lost pets and found items that wanted returning.

'Oh, hello,' the lady at the counter said as they came in. She was small and perhaps about sixty, and if someone had wanted to print a photographic definition of the word jolly in the dictionary, they could have done a lot worse than insert a picture of her face. She smiled at them from beneath quite generous greying eyebrows, her hair similarly unruly, a crocodile clip struggling to contain it. But she was very welcoming and pleased to see them, and it seemed like a good sign.

There was one other customer in the store, a balding man who looked around seventy or so, dressed in a tailored suit and tie and highly polished shoes. He had a neat, slender white moustache the likes of which was now only ever seen in black-and-white films about the Second World War. He had turned at their entrance, having just been reading the back of a cornflakes box, and was regarding them with rather more suspicion than the shopkeeper.

Emma looked for a basket and, as she did, Tia strode up to the counter.

'Hello,' she said. 'Lovely day, isn't it?'

'Nice enough this morning,' the shopkeeper replied. 'Given out rain for later. Hope it's not going to ruin your plans. On holiday, are you?'

'Oh no, we've just moved here. Like, literally today.'

'Oh,' the woman said, looking confused. 'I don't recall a house for sale in the village. I know June has been talking about it but...'

'We're renting June's cottage,' Emma said as she joined them now, basket in hand. 'We've got it for the summer.'

'We're hoping to have our own place ready by the end of the season,' Tia added. Emma glanced to see the old man, who had briefly resumed his perusal of the cornflakes box, look sharply at them now.

'Your own place?' the shopkeeper asked. 'Where would that be?'

'Honeymoon Station.'

The woman stared at them and the old man put down his box of cornflakes to give them his full attention.

'You've bought that old wreck?' the woman asked incredulously. 'We knew it had gone for auction but we never imagined anyone would buy it!'

'We had to beat a lot of bidders actually,' Emma said.

'Really? Goodness! Who would have thought? And you're... I mean, I wouldn't have thought it would be someone like...'

'Two women?' Tia raised her eyebrows slightly.

'No, no… It's not that,' the woman said. 'It's just… well, well… And you're turning it into a house? You're going to live there? Together?'

'No,' Tia said. 'We're turning it into a guest house. And we're not a couple, in case you're wondering. We're just friends.'

'A guest house, well I…'

At this point there was a loud sniff from the old man. Emma turned to see him looking sourer than he had when they'd walked in, if that were possible.

'That's all we need,' he snapped. 'A load of tourists tramping up and down the high street all day and night. I suppose amusement arcades and nightclubs will follow and then we won't be able to afford to live in our own houses and then they'll be knocked down to make way for some horrible theme park.'

'Sid!' the woman behind the counter chastised.

'It's alright,' Emma cut in. 'Honestly, sir, that's not what we're planning at all. The sorts of guests we'll get might bring a little extra trade to the village, yes, but I would imagine most of them will come for the sort of tranquillity they can only get in a place like this. They won't want amusement arcades and theme parks.'

'The resorts that have all those things already do it well, and people who want that kind of holiday will still go to them no matter what we do,' Tia added. 'We want to offer a peaceful alternative. It's going to be classy.'

'And I suppose there'll be bulldozers and all sorts driving up and down all day,' Sid continued as if he hadn't heard a word either Emma or Tia had just said.

'We can't lie,' Emma said. 'There'll be noise and dust for a while, but we hope it won't be for long.'

'This is where it starts,' Sid said, his face getting redder and his posture stiffening. 'The beginning of the end. The end of Honeymoon!' He turned to the woman behind the counter. 'You mark my words – I said it here first! This hotel will be the end of our village!' He jutted out his chin and turned with a loud huff. 'And I'll be buying my cornflakes elsewhere!' he shouted as he marched out.

'I don't know where,' the shopkeeper said wryly. 'There are no other shops in Honeymoon and he hates everywhere else.'

'I hope we didn't upset him too much,' Emma said, feeling mortified. It wasn't their fault but she still felt responsible.

'Don't mind Sid,' the woman said. 'He'll have a moan about anything – sort of a hobby of his.'

'But you don't mind the hotel?' Emma asked. 'When we first mentioned it you seemed a bit shocked.'

'Well I was. Honestly I never imagined it would sell. I'm glad it has, though, and to such nice people.'

'We don't intend to make the village change,' Tia said.

'If you ask me,' the woman said with a wink, 'the village wouldn't suffer from a bit of change, even if the likes of Sid don't know it yet. For my part, I wouldn't say no to a bit of extra trade so I don't mind. Not that there won't be a bit of opposition to what you're doing – it's only fair to warn you.'

'We expected that,' Tia said. 'But so far most people we've met have been very nice about it.'

'My grandfather was stationmaster there, you know,' the woman said proudly. 'And my aunt worked the ticket booth before she got married. Everyone born and bred here has some connection to that old station. It felt like a hand had been cut off when that line closed, and plenty of people felt it cut the village off too. Folks moved away – that's how come the village is so small now. It used to be much bigger, but nobody wanted to live in a place that was so hard to get to. Of course, plenty of roads now and you can be here as quick as a wink, but by the time decent roads came the damage had been done. It'll be nice to see new faces round here again, even if they only stay a week or two in your hotel. Now… have you got your tradesmen?'

'We have someone lined up,' Emma said.

'That's a shame,' the woman replied. 'Could have pointed you in the direction of two very reliable boys.'

'Blake and Aidan?' Tia asked.

'Oh yes! You've already met them?'

'Just – in the café,' Emma said. 'Only briefly though.'

Tia nodded. 'If we'd known about them before now we'd have certainly got them on board.'

'Well,' the woman said, 'I expect you didn't know of them because they don't advertise. Don't need to, see – they have more work than they can shake a stick at round here.'

'I can imagine,' Tia said.

'I'm Emma, by the way,' Emma said, stepping forward to shake the woman's hand. Tia followed suit.

'Emma and Tia…' The woman smiled. 'Lovely names. I'm Nell.'

'Have you lived in the village all your life?' Emma asked.

'For my sins,' Nell said. 'Took this place on from my dad when he retired. Gets a bit boring, truth be told, but it suits me well enough.'

'But you must be happy here,' Emma said.

'Oh, I wouldn't live anywhere else. For the most part everyone is welcoming and we all look out for one another. You don't want to mind the odd bad apple like Sid; he's in the minority. There'll always be some who feel the need to oppose any kind of change, even when the fool can see it's good change.'

'As long as he doesn't persuade everyone else to oppose it,' Emma said, and then immediately wondered if she'd overstepped the mark. But Nell just shook her head and didn't seem offended at all.

'Sid would oppose a lottery win, but his bark's worse than his bite. He'll come round soon enough, and if he doesn't he'll find something else to complain about and forget he was supposed to be angry about your hotel.'

'Has Sid always lived here too?'

Nell gave a solemn nod. 'And he's always been a miserable old sod too.'

They were all laughing when the bell of the shop door tinkled and one of the brothers they'd seen at Darcie's café walked in. It was the broader, more muscular one of the two.

'Blake!' Nell greeted him. 'I was just telling Emma and Tia about you and your brother.'

'I thought my ears were hot,' he said, scratching lazily at his six-pack through his T-shirt. 'I hope you haven't given them the wrong impression.'

'I was telling them that if they need any building work you're the boys to call.'

Blake was regarding them both with more interest now, though his gaze very obviously rested on Tia a little bit longer, and it was all Emma could do not to groan. 'I just heard you bought the old station.'

Tia gave him a brilliant smile and ran a hand through her hair. 'News travels fast then – we only arrived this morning.'

'And you've also just been telling Darcie your life story,' he said glibly, 'where we've been working.'

'Oh, yeah,' Tia said.

'Not such a mystery then,' Emma put in, if only to break the unbearable sexual tension that was already sizzling in the air between Blake and Tia.

Blake leaned against the doorway and lowered his voice. 'Why… was it supposed to be a secret?'

'No,' Tia whispered back and he started to laugh.

'You've got your builders,' he stated rather than asked, and Emma supposed Darcie had told him that too.

'We would have asked you if we'd known about you,' Tia said.

'That's alright,' Blake said, folding his broad arms across his chest and regarding Tia with an indulgent look. 'We're quite busy anyway. Who've you got in?'

'Someone called Purcell and Sons… know of them?'

'Can't say I do.'

'That's a shame,' Emma said. 'You could have told us in advance if they were any good.'

'Sorry.' Blake shrugged. 'Not a clue. But if they don't work out for you feel free to give us a call and we can check our schedules.'

'I'd definitely give you a call,' Tia said.

He grinned, and the way they both looked showed they understood each other perfectly. Emma took a moment to get a closer look. Blake was very hot, but he also gave the impression that he knew it. From what she could recall of his brother earlier, Blake also seemed the more groomed of the two and clearly worried about his appearance.

He was undoubtedly a hunk, but if Emma had been forced to choose (and thank God she wasn't), she'd have gone for the subtler charms of his brother. Aidan had given the impression that you could take him as he was or leave him, and seemed a lot less high-maintenance. She wondered who was the oldest. It was hard to tell, but they were almost certainly close in age – not more than a couple of years between them – and perhaps in their late twenties to early thirties.

Blake bounced himself off the door frame and sauntered to the counter where he picked up a packet of gum from the display, holding it up to Nell.

'Would you put it on the tab for us, Nell? I'll be in to settle up later when I'm done at the café.'

'Right you are,' the shopkeeper said, taking a notebook from beneath the counter and flicking through the pages before jotting a figure down at the bottom of a list headed with Blake's name. As she did, Blake winked at Emma and Tia.

'I'll be seeing a lot more of you girls around then?'

'You can be sure of it,' Tia said.

With a lazy flick of the hand to bid them farewell, he left the shop.

'He's a one, that Blake,' Nell said as she watched him leave. 'Him and his brother are lovely boys but that one… he's got a wild side. Aidan's as steady as they come, but Blake…'

She didn't finish her sentence, but she didn't really need to.

'He seems very charming,' Tia said.

'Oh, he could charm the birds from the trees,' Nell agreed. 'Just ask Missy Baxter, or Lisa Pendle, or Holly Edwards, or—'

'Hmm, I think we get the picture,' Emma said, laughing. She had to laugh because Nell's summary was quite funny, but also because she was so uneasy about Tia's obvious attraction to Blake. The idea of her getting into a fling so soon after they'd arrived in the village was bad enough, but it was even worse to hear that the man was such a well-known Casanova. It was obvious Tia's recent divorce had left her with a thirst for adventure that involved more than just moving across the country; Emma just hoped it didn't involve Blake Ronson. Perhaps Nell's veiled warning would do the trick.

'Anyway,' Emma continued, glancing up at the clock over the counter, 'I suppose we ought to get this shopping done before the rest of the day gets away from us.'

'That's me, keeping you talking,' Nell said. 'I'm terrible once you get me going… so bored in this shop for most of the day.'

'Oh, don't think that,' Emma said. 'We love that you want to chat.'

'Don't tell me that,' Nell said with a light laugh. 'I'll think you mean it and you'll never be able to pop in quickly ever again!'

Chapter Twelve

Emma was woken the next morning by the sound of rain beating against the windowpane. Groggy, she lay in bed for a moment in the half light of the dawn, taking in the details of the tiny bedroom that still felt so new and strange and not like home at all. It was an odd, in-between kind of home, somewhere they were certain to spend a good many months but not forever, somewhere that was homely and comfortable enough but with no expression of her own tastes or personality in the way home usually was. It was like a nice hotel that she'd be staying in for a very long time; she'd get used to the way it looked, but she would never have designed it that way.

Her thoughts turned to breakfast. There hadn't been a huge choice at Nell's shop, but she and Tia had got the basics so at least there was cereal. June had promised to drop off eggs if there were any spare from her chickens too, so they wouldn't go hungry. Emma had never been a big breakfast-eater anyway, though she'd vowed to force as much down as she could this morning because they had a lot of heavy jobs to do and fainting wasn't going to help. Once they'd driven out to the nearest DIY store and picked up all the things on their list (and some they hadn't realised they needed until they saw them) the previous day, and then got unpacked at the cottage, there'd barely been any of the day left, so they'd decided to start work at the station today instead.

There was a light tap at her bedroom door.

'I'm awake,' she said, sitting up. Tia came in with a cup. She looked bright and fresh and as if she'd been awake for hours, even though Emma had thought it early enough when she woke.

'I've made a pot of tea,' she said. 'Want one?'

'I'd love one.'

'Here…' Tia put her cup down on the cabinet next to Emma's bed. 'Have this; I've just made it and not drunk any yet. You don't have sugar, do you?'

'Well remembered.' Emma took the cup. 'Thanks.'

Tia sat on the edge of the bed. She looked full of barely contained excitement and flashed Emma one of her manic grins.

'Today's the day!'

Emma smiled. 'It is.'

'How do you feel?'

'Ready to run home.'

'Really?'

Emma gave a light laugh. 'No, I'm kidding. I'm perhaps not as excited as you at the prospect of trying to pull up thistles that are taller than me, but I'm raring to go.'

'I still can't believe we're actually here and this is actually happening.'

'Well it is, and I think that's mostly down to your tenacity.'

'I couldn't have done it without you.'

'You'd have found a way; I'm certain of that. I've never met anyone in my life who is so determined… Apart from my sister, and she got what she wanted too.'

'You will,' Tia said gently. 'Are you still feeling OK about what happened between you and your boyfriend? You don't talk much about it.'

'Ex-boyfriend,' Emma said. 'And no, I'm not sure I am alright, which is why I don't talk about it. I'm never going back, that much I do know.'

'Has he called you recently?'

'No, so I suppose that means he's given up and he was never really as into me as I was him.'

'Or maybe he just knows a lost cause when he sees one. Does he know you've moved here?'

'I think my dad took great delight in telling him when he saw him out a few days ago,' Emma said. 'He never did care much for him.'

'My parents loved Jerome,' Tia said, her mood flatter now. 'I think it was because he was from a well-heeled family. I think they were more gutted when my divorce came through than I was.' She smiled at Emma. 'What a pair we are. I think that old man in the shop yesterday thought we were a couple and maybe that's actually not such a bad idea. We certainly can't rely on blokes.'

'He actually looked a bit horrified about that too,' Emma said. 'Despite us telling him we weren't a couple I don't think he believed it. And I hope you don't mind if I don't put anyone right, because if the men of the world leave me alone from now on that will suit me just fine.'

'Really?' Tia poked her playfully. 'Because even you have to admit those builder brothers are very attractive. You're telling me if one of them asked you wouldn't be a teensy bit tempted?'

'No, you're OK. You take your pick with my blessing.'

'I don't actually know if either of them are single.'

Emma put her tea down and stretched. 'There's only one way to find out. Just promise me one thing, would you? I don't want to be a party pooper, but if you get involved please promise it won't interfere with our renovations.'

'Of course not!' Tia said. 'Absolutely not! That has to come first – it's the only reason we're here after all.'

Emma saw how earnest her expression was and the worries of the previous day melted now. Perhaps she'd been overtired and anxious about nothing much at all.

'Then go and get yourself some fun,' she said. 'If anyone deserves some fun it's you.'

'It's both of us.'

Emma shook her head with a wry smile. 'I'll get my fun pulling up the weeds and knocking old tiles off the station roof – it's far less likely to break my heart.'

Tia had already eaten so finished getting dressed before making a packed lunch for them while Emma ate and got dressed herself. Then they headed to the station to meet the builders they'd contracted. The plan was for Purcell's to spend the first day on site making preparations to start work – erecting scaffolding, etc. – while Tia and Emma saved money by doing the kinds of labouring that didn't require much in the way of skills, like clearing the ground of weeds, carting old furniture and rubble away, and general fetching and carrying.

With a new day and the overwhelming strangeness of their arrival in Honeymoon behind them, although the place still looked as neglected and forlorn as it had the day before, somehow the prospect of tackling the work needed to restore the station didn't seem so daunting.

Tia checked the time on her phone as they walked the area again to take stock and work out what to tackle first.

'Purcell's said they'd be here by eight thirty,' she said. 'It's almost nine.'

'Hmm. What builder has ever been on time?'

'True,' Tia said. 'But it's annoying. We can't really get stuck into anything until they're here.'

'We could do a bit.'

'But we'd just get into it and then have to stop again, and that's a pain.'

'We'd probably be in the middle of pulling a weed… I'm not sure that's a time-sensitive task.'

Tia burst out laughing. 'See – I said you were the brains of the outfit.'

'Well you're definitely the muscles,' Emma said.

'At least I won't miss the gym – there's plenty enough working out to be had here, that's for sure.'

'And it's free.'

'Apart from the thousands we had to pay to buy the place?'

'Ah, well, yes… apart from all those thousands. Let's not think about that too often.'

Tia checked the time again. 'I'm going to call them,' she said. Before Emma could offer an opinion either way she had dialled the number and put her phone to her ear.

'Nothing,' she said a moment later. 'Not picking up.'

'Maybe they're en route.'

'And they don't have hands-free in the van? Purcell is running a business – that's the least he should have.'

'You think that because you're very good. Maybe he's not quite as efficient as you are.'

'That on its own isn't a good sign. If he's not here by nine thirty, which is an hour late, I vote we fire him and find someone more reliable.'

'We can't do that! Who are we going to find at such short notice? There might be a perfectly reasonable explanation for them being late – roadworks or anything.'

'Yes, there may be, but most people would call ahead to warn us.'

'Perhaps they weren't able to for some reason.'

'Well I think it's poor. If this is the first day I don't hold out much hope for the days after this.'

Emma looked askance at her friend. This new ruthless Tia was someone she hadn't seen before. It was probably a good thing – one of them needed a ruthless business head – but she wasn't sure she was a fan.

'I still say we can't just fire them without giving them a chance,' she insisted, and she felt she was right. Tia might have had a point about professional courtesy, but Emma believed in fairness and giving the benefit of the doubt. Not to mention the time and effort they'd have to expend finding someone else – time they didn't have and effort they'd be better putting into the renovation work.

Unless...

Emma's thought processes paused momentarily as she struck on perhaps the real reason Tia was so keen to get rid of the company they'd booked already. She quickly dismissed it – surely Tia wasn't that shallow, and surely she wouldn't play so fast and loose with this project, the thing that was about to change both their lives forever. Whether that would be for better or for worse it was impossible to tell right now, but a lot was riding on the decisions they made about it.

'Why don't we at least mark out what we want to get cleared today,' Emma said. 'The skip will be here soon and we're paying by the day – we might as well make full use of it.'

Tia looked at her phone again and then relented. 'Alright,' she said. 'Let's get started.'

An hour later Emma was covered in sweat. Her arms and back ached, her hands were blistered, despite the heavy gardening gloves, and she was covered in tiny scratches. She was fairly sure she had a few bug bites too, and it would be fun trying to sleep with those itching like mad later. But she was happy now, fulfilled, doing a task that felt like something more worthwhile than any poxy overtime spreadsheet she'd filled in at Burnbury's.

Taking a moment to stretch her arms and back, she took off a glove to wipe her brow and looked across at Tia, who was now stripped down to leggings and sports bra and looked like the sort of goddess you saw on the athletics track at the Olympics. She was currently wrestling with a thick-stemmed weed that was taller than her. Emma had no idea what it was but it wouldn't have looked look out of place in an old *Star Trek* episode, planted on the landscape of an alien planet.

Seeming to sense Emma's gaze on her, Tia stopped what she was doing and looked across.

'What time is it?' Emma asked.

'Time Purcell was here,' Tia said shortly.

'Should we try phoning again?' Now even Emma couldn't deny that their contractors had had plenty of opportunity to let her and Tia know they were going to be delayed and what time they planned to get there. And if they couldn't predict a time, they could at least offer an explanation for it.

Tia yanked off her own gloves and took her phone from a thigh pocket in her leggings. Emma watched as she made the call and saw her forehead begin to wrinkle into another exasperated frown as it rang out again. It wasn't the most auspicious start to their venture – Emma only hoped it wasn't a bad sign.

Tia put her phone away with a thunderous expression that needed no commentary.

'OK,' Emma sighed. 'I suppose if we don't hear anything today we're going to have to do something about it.'

'It's not a great start, is it?'

'Just what I was thinking.'

'Still' – Tia put her gloves back on and faced her towering weed-foe once more – 'I suppose it'll all work out eventually.'

Emma couldn't help a smile. Her friend had already stopped worrying about it, and Emma was beginning to feel that Tia's faith in nothing in particular was infectious, because as she turned back to her own toil she decided not to let it bother her either. After all, getting angry wasn't going to bring those contractors over any quicker.

By the time lunch arrived Emma had completely forgotten she wasn't going to worry or get angry and was now very concerned about their contractors' no-show.

'What are we going to do?' she asked. 'We need some kind of contact from them and nobody is picking up on that number you have. Is there another one you can try?'

'I tried it,' Tia said. 'First thing I did.'

'You did?' Emma asked, wondering when Tia had called it because she hadn't noticed.

'Yes, and they didn't answer that one either.'

'What kind of terrible management is that?'

'I know.' Tia opened a pack of crisps and shovelled a handful into her mouth. 'God, I'm starving!'

Emma perched on an upturned wheelbarrow. 'Me too. What flavour crisps do we have?'

'I put ready salted and chicken in.'

'Bit of a random selection.'

'First ones I grabbed this morning. Which ones do you want?'

'I'll have chicken.'

Tia tossed a pack over from her hamper. 'I suppose we could ask the Ronson brothers if they could fit us in,' she said carelessly.

Emma looked up from her crisps. 'I still think we ought to find out what happened to Purcell's first. It's going to be very awkward if we employ someone else and then they turn up to do the job after all.'

'They should have turned up when they said they were going to and then we wouldn't have to get anyone else. Besides, they won't turn up if we tell them to stick it.'

'Still...' Emma said lamely, though she knew she was already losing this battle. She also had to agree privately that Tia had a point, though the force with which she was driving it home made her suspect an ulterior motive.

'And I only said we could ask if they could fit us in,' Tia continued. 'Nell at the shop said they're busy all the time so they might say they can't, in which case we're back to plan A.'

'Whatever the hell that is now,' Emma said.

'Something will turn up.'

Emma raised her eyebrows in mild disbelief. 'I wish I could share your optimism.'

'I think the boys will find a way to fit us in. After all, it's months of steady work right on their doorstep – that's got to be an attractive prospect.'

'That's probably not the only attractive prospect,' Emma said wryly.

'Well,' Tia said with a grin, 'I'd be lying if I said our original builders letting us down wasn't a bit serendipitous.'

'Look at you with the fancy words!'

'Just trying to keep up with you.' Tia got up and dusted down the back of her leggings before folding her empty crisp packet and stuffing it into the pocket of their cool bag. 'I'm going into the village – want me to get anything for you while I'm there?'

'You're going now?'

'Yeah, I want to go to the shop.'

'What for? You've brought loads of stuff.'

'I could murder a cola.'

Emma frowned. 'How are you such a toned goddess? I've seen you eat crisps and cake and now fizzy drinks… I thought people like you lived on nuts and the rarefied air of gym-cooling systems.'

'I used to,' Tia said with a grin. 'But that was all Jerome's doing. Now I'm going to let myself go, and I'm going to enjoy it.'

'Really? Undo all that work it took to get your amazing body?'

'I'll let you into a secret,' Tia said carelessly, 'it was Jerome's idea to be at the gym every day. He was the one measuring obsessively and nagging me to do more. I like a workout as much as the next reasonably healthy person, but I hated being there so often. I hated the protein shakes and the detox diets and the macronutrient counting. I only did all that because Jerome told me it was so important all the bloody time. While I intend on staying this size, I figure I deserve to relax a bit now we're not together. Anyway, I think most men don't actually mind buns that are a bit squidgier, so if mine are less steel and more sponge cake, I don't think it will matter all that much.'

'When you put it like that…' Emma dug her hand into the pack for another crisp.

'So what are you going to ditch now that you're not with Dougie?'

'Men.'

Tia raised her eyebrows.

'You don't believe me?' Emma asked. 'I know you're ready to move on, but I have a track record. I don't know if it's me, but all the men I've been with turn out to be Dougies in the end. He lasted a bit longer than the others but he ended up being the worst. I have no faith in my ability to choose a man so I'm better off not doing it at all.'

'Maybe you should let someone else choose for you.'

'Well they couldn't do a worse job than me.'

'Let me do it.'

Emma narrowed her eyes. 'Oh no, I know where this is going. Absolutely not!'

'You don't know what I'm going to suggest.'

'You go after Blake and then you fix up some *serendipitous*' – she waggled her eyebrows to accentuate the word – 'scenario where I date his brother and we all live happily ever after. Let me put you straight now – never going to happen.'

'You don't think he's attractive?'

'I'd be mad to think otherwise but that's not the point. It's a disaster waiting to happen.'

'God, you're so pessimistic sometimes.'

'And if it ends badly and we end up needing to employ them at some point in the future to work on the hotel… well that would be horribly awkward, wouldn't it? Sorry, Tia, but forget it.'

Tia shrugged. 'Suit yourself, but I think you're missing out on a golden opportunity.'

'I'm here, aren't I?' Emma said. 'One golden opportunity at a time is more than enough for me to handle.'

Chapter Thirteen

It was Emma's turn to cook, but she was exhausted and sore and she wondered if she went to Honeymoon Café and asked very nicely, Darcie or Tariq might take pity on her and plate up something nice to take away for supper. Tia was in agreement, as she didn't fancy cooking either, though they also agreed that they wouldn't be able to do this too often because regular takeaways would cost money they couldn't really spare. But as it had been their first day on site and a heavy one at that, they both figured they deserved to take a night off from the kitchen. The café was closer than the pub, and at least they knew they'd have a warm welcome from its owners. Besides, it would be a good opportunity to take a stroll through the village. There wasn't much to see, but perhaps it would start to feel like home a lot quicker the better they knew it.

So Emma gathered what little energy she had left and took a walk out into the evening. It was cooling rapidly, and a fresh breeze rolled down the high street, rattling the swinging sign of the Randy Shepherd pub, rustling through the leaves of the old oak tree that stood proud in its own special enclosure at the centre of the village, and sending streams through the grass of the tiny village green. Emma took it all in. Pretty as it all was, and hard as she tried to manifest the feeling of home, it still felt very alien. She felt like a traveller passing through, as if Honeymoon were somewhere that would soon be a pleasant memory as she moved on to the next place. It was hard to shake the feeling of transience even though she wanted to; harder still to shake the notion that, somehow, she didn't deserve to live in such a beautiful place, that fate would soon realise its mistake and take it all away from her.

Darcie was pleased to see her and only too happy to oblige her request. She recommended a smoked-salmon quiche made at her cousin's bakery and Emma took it, knowing they had fries in the freezer that they could throw in the oven for a no-fuss meal. She also took a couple of slabs of Madeira cake (they too had been made at the bakery) and, after a brief chat with Darcie and Tariq, filling them in on her day and bemoaning the absence of the contractors they'd been expecting, she headed home with her goodies.

When she arrived at the cottage, Tia was just ending a phone call.

'That was Purcell's,' she said, following Emma into the kitchen.

'Oh?' Emma put the bags of food on the dining table and went to get a baking tray for their oven fries. 'What did they say? I hope you got a decent explanation out of them.'

'They'd run behind on a job they'd been doing last week and had to go and finish it today.'

'And they couldn't let us know? Thoughtful of them.'

'That's what I said. Purcell said he'd asked one of his guys to give us a call. He said he'd look into why it didn't happen.'

'That doesn't explain why he personally didn't return any of the calls we made to his phone. He must have seen them.'

'I said that too.' Tia began to unwrap her quiche while Emma put the fries in the oven; she'd switched it on before heading over to the café. 'He told me he'd been so busy he hadn't noticed any calls come through.'

'And he'd been that busy until…' Emma looked up at the clock. 'Seven p.m.? Well I suppose we ought to be thankful he called eventually. Is he planning on coming tomorrow?'

'He said so.'

'You don't think he will?' Emma turned to her. 'Surely they wouldn't let us down again?'

'I don't buy the story he gave about today. It's hardly the way to start a professional relationship.'

'Where could they have been then?'

Tia shrugged.

'I suppose you're right, but we don't have a lot of choice but to take it at face value and give them another chance.'

'We do, actually. So I told him he was fired and not to bother coming tomorrow.'

Emma stared at her. 'You did *what*?'

'Em… we're two women. We have to work harder to get respect from these people. If someone like that thinks they can play us for fools and get away with it things will go downhill from there pretty quickly and the piss-takes will get worse and worse. Every sunny day, every heavy night, every more lucrative last-minute job that comes in… there'll be excuse after excuse for them to turn up when it suits them and to leave us in the lurch when it doesn't. We have to start as we mean to go on – we take no bull and show that we mean business.'

'That may be but you should have consulted me before you did anything – we're supposed to be business partners.'

'We are, but, Em, I've been in business before and you haven't. You're too nice and too soft, which are lovely things to be in life but not in business. Trust me, you can't afford to be forgiving when it comes to people like Purcell.'

Emma turned back to the oven and peered through the glass door to check on the food. She didn't like what Tia was saying, but she couldn't deny the logic of it. She looked round again.

'So what are we going to do?' she asked, though she had a feeling she already knew the answer to that question.

'We'll get someone else. There must be people out there who want the work.'

Emma took a bottle of water from the fridge and placed it on the table. Something about this situation irked her. It felt somehow engineered by Tia, even though there was no way she could have been responsible for the no-show of their original contractors. She'd seized on the opportunity to fire them a little too eagerly, though – or at least that was how it looked to Emma.

She didn't want to believe Tia would do that, but she didn't know what else to think. From the moment she'd seen the Ronson brothers in Darcie's café, Tia had seemed determined to find a way to involve them in the hotel renovations, and this situation had provided an opportunity that seemed just a little too perfect. Now, as Emma waited for her obvious answer, Tia had suddenly become coy and was skirting around it. They wouldn't always see eye to eye on everything over the coming months and years they were business partners, but this sense of frustration with her friend so early in proceedings didn't bode well for the survival of their future relationship.

'Are we talking any people in particular?' Emma asked, trying to keep her voice neutral.

'Well we have reliable tradesmen on the doorstep. Everyone keeps telling us how good they are. They're local and we did say we wanted to spend our money in the village to win people over – it would make sense to ask them first.'

'We don't know for sure they're reliable or good. They might be able to fix a leaking tap for Nell well enough but that means nothing on a renovation like ours.'

'They've got to be more reliable than the ones we've just got rid of. We can ask them, and if it's too big for them I'm sure they'll say so.'

'You mean the ones *you've* just got rid of? We don't know anything about the quality of their work, and they might well say yes just to get some money in and then leave the job when it gets too tough. You hear about contractors ditching work all the time.'

'You're thinking of big firms with no ties to the area they're working in. The Ronsons live right next to the site – it wouldn't be so easy for them to leave us high and dry. And we've only heard really good things about them.'

'Do you really think their neighbours and friends are going to say bad things about them in a village this small?'

'If they were no good I do think people would say so. Or they'd at least say nothing at all.'

Emma shook her head as she checked on their fries again.

'Don't be angry, Em.'

'I'm not,' she said. 'I just wish you'd told me what you were planning to do before you did it. We're meant to be equal partners and already I feel like you're becoming more equal than me. I know I've never been in business before but I do have common sense enough to make a decision on a situation.'

'I'm sorry; I didn't mean it to come across that way. Purcell was on the phone, you weren't here and I did what I thought was best.'

Emma dropped onto a chair and poured a glass of water.

'I don't suppose I have a better plan, so we'll have to talk to the Ronsons tomorrow to see if they can fit us in. You're right; it makes sense to get someone local, if only to show we want to be a part of this community. If they're not free, then I suppose it's back to the online trade listings.'

'You still don't sound very happy about it,' Tia said. 'I'm not really forgiven, am I?'

'I'm tired, that's all. I was hoping for a quiet night and then we have all this.'

'We can have a quiet night now we've sorted it.'

Emma put her glass down. '*Have* we sorted it?'

'You worry too much,' Tia said with a smile far brighter than Emma could have managed. 'You needn't; something will turn up eventually.'

That mantra again. This morning Emma thought it was contagious. Right now, she just wished Tia would stop saying it.

'So that's settled,' Tia continued. 'I'll see if I can track them down tomorrow and we'll ask them.'

'Maybe we should tackle that groundwork first,' Emma said. 'Seeing as we now have nobody to work around, it might be a good idea to clear the area before we get them in.'

'OK...' Tia said, but she'd picked her phone up and was scrolling down a page, and Emma couldn't be sure she was actually listening to a word she was saying. Wearily, she went to take their fries from the oven. She was too tired and hungry now to care.

Had she stepped into a sitcom? Emma and Tia arrived at the station to start work at eight thirty the following day to find half a dozen pensioners (presumably locals) standing around with plaques that seemed to suggest they were less than impressed by the plans for Honeymoon Station. And the man who appeared to be the ringleader was Sid – at least, he was talking to them with a loudhailer in a way that asserted his leadership, when he could have quite easily addressed everyone present in a loud whisper and they still would have been able to hear him.

'This is the beginning of the end!' he shouted. 'The destruction of our peace and quiet, our way of life! It's only a little hotel, they say! Corporate annihilation starts with a little hotel and before you know it there are arcades and nightclubs and chavs from all over the country congregating here!'

There was a ripple of (unenthusiastic, Emma thought) agreement and a few signs shaken in the air to reinforce it. Emma's gaze ran over them. They said things like: DOWN WITH HONEYMOON HOTEL and THE HONEYMOON IS OVER and SAVE OUR VILLAGE and GO AWAY CHAVS!

Sid had his back to Emma and Tia as they inched closer to the station entrance, where the crowd had congregated, and at this point some of the protestors began to realise the owners of the station had arrived. Some of them looked rather embarrassed, and they began to whisper amongst themselves.

'What's going on?'

Sid whipped round at the sound of Tia's voice, his clipped razor of a moustache quivering on his indignant top lip.

'It's our constitutional right to voice our opposition to your plans!' he said through the loudhailer.

'Well yes,' Tia said mildly, 'but that's usually more productive before the planning permission is granted. As the station building was sold with planning permission already granted, that horse kind of bolted long ago. I'm afraid you're slightly wasting your time.'

'We can still stop you from getting on,' he said.

Tia reached to lower the loudhailer from his mouth. 'Yes, you could do that too,' she agreed. 'But how long do you think you can keep it up for?'

'As long as we need!'

'Really? Are you sure about that? I mean, we've got literally nothing else to do but be here, and I'm sure you all have other things you need to get on with at some point.' Tia glanced at Emma and then back at Sid before she continued. 'We don't have to start work now. We can go away, get a cup of tea and come back when you've all had enough and gone home.'

He put the loudhailer to his mouth again. 'Then we won't go home!' he boomed.

'Look,' Emma said, 'can't we please be friends? We're not trying to destroy your village – we love it. We want it to stay exactly as it is because we think our guests will love it too.'

'Ah!' Sid yelped. 'But that's just it! That's just why you can't be here! All those guests will overrun Honeymoon and ruin it. And once word gets out there's money to be made, more business will come to cash in and our village will be gone forever!'

'We won't have enough rooms to overrun anywhere,' Emma said. 'We're not trying to turn Honeymoon into Las Vegas; we just want to run a little guest house where people can come to enjoy a quiet, pretty rural location. To expand from that would kind of defeat the point of why we're here.'

'I don't believe you! You're trying to gain our trust so we'll let you get on with it!'

Tia screwed up her face. 'It really is difficult to concentrate on what you're saying when you're shouting at us through that megaphone. Could you put it down for a second so we can talk like civilised people?'

'No!' Sid yelled through it.

Tia turned to the crowd of pensioners, who seemed quite enthralled by the performance. 'Why don't you see for yourselves what we plan to do? I'd be happy to meet with you all to go through it – maybe at the café or the pub? I can show you our plans and documents, and if you still hate them you can come and protest as much as you like. But quite frankly I think you'll realise all this fuss is a bit of a storm in a teacup.'

'We want nothing more than to be a part of the community and to be friends with you all,' Emma said. 'We'd even like to think our business will bring a bit of prosperity. I mean, some people in the village are already on board.'

There was a tentative but encouraging murmur of what sounded like approval from the protestors, but Sid was far from convinced.

'Oh, get everyone drunk so they'll agree to this… how very nefarious!'

Tia folded her arms. 'Work will be starting either way,' she said.

'But we'd rather have everyone onside,' Emma added. 'We're all going to have to live together after all.'

'We're hardly going to welcome you into our midst when you're hell-bent on destroying our way of life!' Sid scoffed.

But when he looked to his crowd for support, they didn't seem quite as resolute. Emma was beginning to see that one or two had most definitely been coerced into coming along today when they probably hadn't been quite as enthusiastic about the cause as Sid. Most of them looked a lot older than him and likely to fall over if they were expected to stand out there for much longer.

'I'd go to the café,' one lady said quietly. 'I'd like to see the plans.'

'Will there be trains running again?' another asked.

'Will there be pensioner discounts?'

'Will you be doing ballroom dancing nights?'

'What about Christmas parties?'

Sid turned his quivering moustache and disapproving glare on them and they immediately fell silent.

'Are you all soft in the head?' he demanded. 'First that café and now this! Slippery slope – that's what this is! Next you'll be inviting Richard Branson to turn us into a theme park!'

'Seriously, Sid?'

Everyone looked now to see Blake and Aidan Ronson standing behind Emma and Tia. Blake was grinning lazily, but though he appeared relaxed and unconcerned, there was a steel in his eyes that suggested otherwise. 'We're seriously doing this?'

Aidan folded his arms and fixed his stare on Sid now too. 'Wasn't it bad enough that you made Darcie and Tariq feel about as welcome as shingles? Now you're doing the same to these ladies. That's not the kind of place Honeymoon is and we're not about to start. Or have you forgotten our granddad? If he'd arrived in Honeymoon today, would you have led a protest to hound him out too?'

'No, but—'

'Then clear off,' Blake said.

'But they don't just want to live here,' Sid began to argue, and now the loudhailer was down at his side. He waved his hand at Tia and Emma. 'They want to—'

'They want to make a decent living,' Aidan said. 'Isn't that what we're all trying to do in one way or another? Everyone has a right to make a better life for themselves wherever they choose to settle.'

'Not here,' Sid said, but he sounded sulky now, as if he already knew he'd lost the battle.

'If Honeymoon is anything,' Aidan said, 'it's a place that welcomes anyone who needs a new start.'

Emma wondered vaguely if there was something about her and Tia that screamed 'women who needed a new start', but she was impressed by Aidan's eloquence nonetheless. It seemed his reminder of Honeymoon's values was persuading the other villagers too. As one, they lowered their banners and began to mutter amongst themselves.

'Well,' Sid said haughtily as he eyed the brothers, 'don't say I didn't warn you.'

Blake folded his arms across his broad chest and gave a wry smile. 'We won't.'

Sid's accomplices started to shuffle off. Some of them asked after the brothers' health or parents. One or two even mumbled apologies to Emma and Tia, like well-behaved children who'd been led astray by a naughty boy but who were now regretting it, which was a bewildering turn of events but very cute. Sid himself was less generous, and Emma had the feeling they hadn't seen the end of him or his disapproval. But he left with the last of his crew, admonishing them as they went.

Aidan turned to Emma and Tia. 'Are you alright? I'm sorry about that – it's not the sort of welcome you'd usually get in Honeymoon.'

'Well I suppose we're not your usual sort of visitors,' Tia said.

'We do understand their fears,' Emma added. 'We just don't know what we can do to settle them.'

'Time,' Aidan said.

Blake nodded. 'It's mostly Sid. He's a bit weird about newcomers and he likes to stir up trouble.'

'I think he just needs a decent hobby to keep him out of mischief,' Aidan said. 'He's got far too much time on his hands.'

'You mentioned Darcie and Tariq,' Emma began. 'Weren't they treated kindly when they moved here?'

'Oh, that was mostly Sid too,' Aidan said. 'Most everyone else either liked them or had no opinion either way. I think Darcie is a bit of a nervous type…'

'I got that feeling too,' Tia said.

'Yes,' Aidan continued. 'So I think she was spooked and I can understand why – even one voice shouting for you to leave feels unkind when you're in a new place trying to fit in, and especially when you're as unsure of yourself as Darcie is.'

'Most people were just glad to see the café stay open,' Blake said. 'Personally I think they're both decent people and you won't find a better fry-up than Darcie's in this county.'

'But you don't seem like other people round here,' Tia said.

Blake raised an eyebrow. 'You mean our knuckles don't drag on the floor when we walk? Don't worry – you can say it. Honeymoon must seem quaint and backwards to you.'

'God no!' Emma exclaimed. 'We weren't going to say anything like that at all, were we, Tia?'

'Believe me,' Tia agreed warmly, 'you hit the nail on the head when you said we were looking for a new start, and this place looks like a pretty good new start to me. We both intend to stay and we intend to make the most of it.'

'New start, eh?' Blake regarded Tia with hungry interest now. Emma saw it clearly – he fancied her as much as she fancied him.

It seemed that Aidan noticed it too – the knowing look he shared with Emma said it all. And if she wasn't mistaken, it seemed a little weary. As Nell at the shop had said, everyone knew Blake had an eye for a pretty girl and it looked as though Tia was next in his sights. *As long as it doesn't end in a car crash*, Emma thought. The idea that she had enough to stress about without throwing a disastrous fling into the mix wasn't a new one, but she was beginning to wish she didn't have quite such strong cause to keep worrying about it.

Emma took a moment to appreciate that while Blake was obviously the player, Aidan was handsome too, certainly better-looking than she'd originally given him credit for. He was less muscle-bound than his brother, but there was no mistaking the seductive qualities of his brown eyes and thick hair and more-than-capable physique. There was a softness and intelligence that was very appealing, something his brother didn't show so obviously. While Blake would waste no time in ripping your clothes off, Emma thought that perhaps Aidan might take the time to really know you first, and she couldn't deny that was quite attractive too. If life had been different for her right now – if she'd been minus the hurtful break-up, crippling debt and stress of a building project that was already beginning to cause her to question her sanity in taking it on – she might have been very interested. But she wasn't like Tia and she couldn't juggle it all. She didn't think Tia could, for that matter, but her friend was clearly very willing to give it a go.

'So,' Blake said, tearing his lustful gaze from Tia for a moment. 'You want to show us your plans?'

'Plans?' Emma asked, glancing at Tia.

'What you want out of us?' Blake continued. 'We can't give you an answer about taking on the work if we don't know what it is.'

'Right…' Emma said slowly, trying to communicate silently with Tia without anyone else being able to decipher it. They'd discussed employing the brothers the previous evening, but goodness only knew when Tia had organised it because Emma certainly hadn't seen her make the call and they'd been together pretty much since. She must have done it quickly too – it was the only way to explain them being here this morning. The suspicious side of Emma had to wonder if her friend had engineered all this even before she'd sacked their previous contractors, which meant she'd intended to fire them as soon as she'd learned there was a more attractive option in Honeymoon. Emma didn't want to believe that, and she had a feeling Tia would deny it if asked, but it was hard not to see it as a red flag.

'I can show you round,' Tia said, already edging closer to Blake.

'Both of us ought to do it,' Emma said deliberately. 'It is our joint venture after all.'

Tia gave a careless shrug. 'I just thought you might want to get started on other things while I filled Blake and Aidan in.'

'There's not a lot I can do in the meantime – we did a lot of clearing yesterday and it's probably better to work from now on bearing in mind what Blake and Aidan need to get their work done…?' Emma looked to them both for support and Aidan nodded agreement.

'That makes a lot of sense. No point in you ripping out a load of old flooring or something to find we needed to do something else first.' He paused. 'I take it you both plan to labour on site alongside us? Or are you wanting to leave it all to us?'

'We don't mind either way,' Blake put in. 'Though, of course, it keeps the costs down for you if you pitch in.'

'That's the plan,' Tia said.

Aidan turned to the station building and folded his arms, a thoughtful look on his face. 'It's not my property but even I'm excited to see it brought back to life. I've always thought it was a shame to see it neglected and falling down.'

'I can't see what Sid and his cronies were moaning about,' Blake agreed.

'I thought that,' Tia said. 'But I didn't like to say it. Surely anyone would want to save a beautiful old building like this.'

'I think it's us and what we plan to do with it rather than the building that's the issue,' Emma said. Blake and Aidan stayed silent, but Emma could tell by their faces that she'd hit the nail on the head.

Aidan shrugged. 'Some people adjust to change quicker than others.'

'And some people don't like it at all,' Emma replied.

He smiled warmly at her. 'I like change. Some I like very much.'

Emma flushed. She could feel the heat travel from her feet to the roots of her hair and was instantly irritated by the fact that she couldn't control it. Was he talking about her arrival? With Tia already panting over one half of the building team, this absolutely could not happen. What even was this? He'd smiled at her and now she was all giddy? Had she learned nothing from her time with Dougie? Charming men couldn't be trusted, no matter how they tried to sell it.

She tore her gaze away and very deliberately cleared her throat. 'Right! Shall we get started?'

Chapter Fourteen

It hadn't taken Tia long to swing into action. They'd shown Blake and Aidan around, who had then agreed they'd start work the following day after they'd tied up a few loose ends on existing jobs. Tia and Emma had gone on to do a little more clearing on site, according to their advice, packing up at around six.

Emma was exhausted again. So far she was finding the days long and stressful, but Tia assured her she'd get used to the physical work, and that the stress would get easier to shrug off. Emma couldn't deny it was a shock to the system for someone who had spent her working life desk-bound, and with very few real decisions to make where the running of the office was concerned. It had been a case of Margot telling her what to do (everything) and Emma doing it.

She'd expected them to settle in for a quiet supper and then off to bed for another early start, but Tia showered and announced she was going out.

'Out?' Emma repeated. 'Where?'

'If we're going to make our home here we ought to get to know the residents,' Tia said, pulling on a black dress. 'So I'm going to the pub to do a bit of mingling with our new neighbours.'

'Do you think I should come then?'

'Um… you're tired – you said so. Stay in; I've got it.'

'But I ought to—'

'It's fine, honestly, Em. Have a long bath and enjoy having the cottage to yourself.'

Emma frowned slightly, cogs whirring in her sluggish brain.

'Are you going out with Blake?' she asked.

'Well,' Tia began, and to her credit she looked a little sheepish, 'he did say he'd be in there about eight.'

'Without his brother?'

'Um... I think so,' she replied evasively.

'So this mingling is more like a date?'

'Maybe a little bit... sort of, yes.' Tia turned from the dresser mirror to face Emma, who was standing in the doorway to her bedroom. 'It's just a bit of fun – what harm is it doing anyone?'

Emma sighed. 'Please just be careful. Don't jeopardise this; we've already come too far and stand to lose too much.'

'What do you think is going to happen?'

'I don't know. I just...'

Tia didn't wait to hear the rest, which was just as well, because even Emma didn't know what the rest ought to be. All she had was a vague, unnamed misgiving that Tia wasn't taking their venture quite as seriously as she was and that some disaster waited to trip them up. She'd thought it before but felt it more forcefully this time – they had to focus. If they were going to make this work, nothing could distract them from their purpose, and distractions didn't come much bigger than men like Blake, especially when he and Tia would have to work together after the romance had ended.

'I'd better go or I'll be late,' Tia said, hurrying out of the room past Emma.

'It's seven forty-five and the pub's, like, two doors away – what's the rush?' Emma called after her.

The only reply was the sound of the front door opening and then shutting again.

Had Tia not made it so obvious that her company wasn't required at the pub, Emma might have been tempted to follow her there – if only to see for herself what it was like. Yes, she was tired, and yes, she might have appreciated the peace, but she'd also been looking forward to Tia's company. They had a lot to talk about and it was useful to take stock at the end of the day, not to mention that Emma enjoyed being with Tia, even if she was sometimes a little exhausting.

So what did you do on a weeknight in a tiny village where the only public entertainment venue was off limits, you didn't have a date and you didn't have any friends there yet?

She phoned her dad for a chat, but that lasted all of five minutes because a programme he wanted to watch was starting and apparently getting it later on catch-up would be far too inconvenient. Patricia and Dominic were out with friends and couldn't really talk, and Elise was in a minibus on her way to the Blue Lagoon to do some geothermal bathing and possibly quite a lot of geothermal drinking too, so she couldn't really talk either, though she promised to call her back the following evening to tell her all about it. So Emma made a quick meal out of a bowl of pasta and simple sauce, slurped it down and headed out for a walk.

Though it had been only a few days, Honeymoon was becoming completely familiar to her. Yesterday, when she'd gone to the café to buy their supper, she'd felt like a traveller passing through, but today she felt as if she might be starting to settle. The grey stones of the houses, the little roundabout at the end of the high street with the pink and peach flowers, and the standing stone that told everyone the way to London were becoming old friends now. That old oak tree in its own circle of land, gathering the village into its shadow, was a real sight to behold now that she looked at it properly, and though she didn't know much about these things, she thought it must be hundreds of years old. Perhaps that was why it had a fence to protect it.

There was a church – more of a chapel really – with a rose-adorned wooden gate, moss cushioning the base of the old walls, yew trees shading the centuries-old gravestones and a memorial to remember Honeymoon's sacrifices to two world wars. Emma pushed open the gate and had a wander around the graves in the evening sun, stopping at the very worn ones to try and make out the dates. But that didn't take long.

From there she could see the pub, the Randy Shepherd – out of bounds, of course – and at the other end of the street was Nell's all-sorts shop, which occupied a tiny old worker's cottage. She'd pulled in the coloured awnings for the night and, while it looked small enough during the day, shuttered up it looked miniscule. Emma wondered how all that stock she knew to be in there managed to fit in at all.

A few steps further on was the little cul-de-sac that was home to Honeymoon Café. Road traffic on the high street was rare, and it was even rarer that any of it stopped in the village. Emma supposed that if she and Tia were successful that would change, and she could see why that prospect might scare some of the older residents like Sid.

Honeymoon Café had closed for the day. Emma looked up at the locked door and wondered whether to knock to say hello to Darcie and Tariq and maybe chat for a while – after all, it felt as if they had a lot in common, and if anyone understood how it felt to be a newcomer here it was them. But she quickly decided against it. They'd probably be busy cleaning down and getting ready for the next day's trade, or else grabbing a few precious moments together, and they wouldn't want Emma hanging around them like a friendless teenager.

It was as she was walking away that the air was filled with manly laughter. She turned to see the door had opened and Tariq was on the step, seeing Aidan out.

'Mate, I don't know where you get these jokes from but you need to stop,' Tariq said. 'They're awful.'

'Yeah, but you're still laughing.'

'If I didn't I'd cry at the tragedy of them.'

Aidan chuckled. 'Bit harsh, mate.'

'See you tomorrow,' Tariq said. It was then he saw Emma. 'Hey… how's it going?'

'Good thanks.' Emma smiled. 'All good with you and Darcie? Oh, the quiche was amazing, by the way.'

'Ah, good. We'll be sure to tell her cousin you liked it. We thought we might see you at the café today but Aidan tells me you've been busy at the station.'

'Best labourer I've ever seen,' Aidan said warmly. 'Not a word of complaint, will tackle anything.'

'You were only there for ten minutes,' Emma said with a light laugh. 'Wait until you're there all day tomorrow; I'll be moaning my head off.'

Aidan and Tariq both grinned. For a moment she wondered if Tariq might invite her in or perhaps call Darcie to the door, and she was really rather hoping he would, but he did neither.

'Maybe we'll see you for breakfast tomorrow?' he asked her.

'Probably not breakfast but we'll be sure to pop in for some takeaways in the afternoon.'

'Great.' He looked at Aidan. 'See you later, mate… and thanks for sorting out that tap.'

Aidan nodded and, with a last acknowledgement of Emma, Tariq went inside and locked the café door.

'I'll see you tomorrow,' Emma said, turning to go, but Aidan called her back.

'The pub's that way…' He pointed in the direction she'd just come from.

'I know. I'm not going to the pub.'

'Oh. Where are you going? If it's not too rude a question, that is. I only ask because if you're looking for a nightclub you're going to be disappointed. It's pub or church, and that's about it.'

'God, no!' Emma laughed. 'I'm too boring for nightclubs – always have been.'

'Me too,' he said with a smile. 'Blake loves them – always trying to get me to drive out to one with him. They're alright once in a while, but once you've seen one you've seen them all.'

'So you're the quiet brother?'

'Someone's got to be the quiet brother, right?'

'I know what you mean. I'm not just the quiet sister, I'm the boring sister too.'

'You don't seem boring to me.'

'You'd think so if you met my sister. I'm wandering here like a lost puppy, and she's currently partying at the Blue Lagoon in Iceland.'

'Wow.'

'See what I mean?'

'Well now you put it that way…'

'Hey! You're not supposed to agree with me!'

He laughed. He had a nice laugh; it was kind and strong and confident.

'We don't have a blue lagoon here,' he said. 'But we do have Mary's Stream. I could take you to see it. If you aren't too busy?'

'Like now?'

'You're here, I'm here... I've got nowhere to be... I mean, if you'd rather not... But it might be nice to see a bit of the area – after all, you'll have to know it if you're going to be selling it to tourists.'

'True.' Emma smiled. 'And I guess it's quite obvious that I'm not doing much else right now.'

'I wouldn't say that – you look like a woman on a mission, but I know all the missions round here close at eleven.'

She giggled. 'OK. You got me. Mary's Stream... why not? Like you say, might as well get to know the area.'

'I was hoping you'd say that.'

It was roughly a fifteen-minute walk from the centre of the village. Along the way they'd seen clouds of starlings swooping and diving across the sky while rooks flapped noisily over a distant field as they gathered for the evening. Aidan had pointed out places of interest as they'd walked and named them for her: Two Acre Lane that led to a dairy farm, Halfpenny Track that led nowhere in particular and wasn't worth bothering with, Strumpet's Lane – Aidan told her she could probably guess what used to happen there – and so many other names and places that there was no way Emma was going to remember them.

The sun was low now, slanting through the trees as they headed through a small copse, burnishing the foliage gold. The stream was hidden by thick vegetation but Aidan knew the path well and didn't hesitate for a moment as he led her to it. They chatted easily as they walked, about Honeymoon Station and the work that needed to be done, but, when they reached the crystal water racing over mossy stones and lush fronds of aquatic plants, the conversation changed into something that felt more personal. At least, it felt to Emma that, as he talked, he revealed more and more of his soul, and it was hard to deny that she liked what she was hearing. He talked of his childhood in Honeymoon, of his brother and how close they were, of his parents who ran an import and export business from their house on the outskirts of the village, of two grandfathers he admired greatly and grandmothers who had spoilt him rotten, of his hopes for the business he shared with Blake.

There was no mention of a romantic partner, which led Emma to believe there wasn't one.

'It's pretty,' she said as they stood at the water's edge where it churned momentarily, frothing in a little whirlpool before continuing down a gentle incline and away out of sight, hidden by long grass.

'Not very impressive I know,' Aidan said, 'but clean. We used to drink it all the time when we played here as kids.'

'Really?' Emma couldn't hide her scepticism and he laughed.

'Honestly, it's fine; you can drink it. Have some…'

He bent down and cupped his hands, bringing some to his mouth to take a slurp.

'I'll take your word for it,' she said.

He looked up. 'I'll bet you've never drunk from a stream.'

'If you'd grown up where I grew up you wouldn't either. They don't taste so good when there's a shopping trolley in them. Why is it called Mary's Stream?'

'Oh, it's an old name,' he said, getting up and wiping his hands down his trousers. 'Nobody's really sure if the stories are true or not.'

'Stories?'

He nodded. 'This stream, many years ago, marked the boundary between two estates.'

'Estates? Like manors?'

'That's it, like landowners' land. Apparently these two lords were big rivals, didn't get on at all, so they stayed off each other's land and didn't mix and nobody who lived on their land was allowed to mix either. But the guy on this side' – he hopped to the left of the water – 'had a daughter, Mary. She was supposed to marry someone her dad had fixed up for her, some boring old toff from another county who was probably twice her age and had already got through ten wives. But the day before the wedding she met a boy walking on this side…' He hopped back across to the right side of the stream. 'Turns out he was a servant to her dad's mortal enemy. She fell in love with him instantly because he was really hot…'

Emma giggled and he grinned before he carried on.

'And so did he, because not only was she hot but she was also loaded. She went straight home to tell her dad she didn't want to marry the boring old toff. As you can imagine, he lost it, and when he found out the reason she didn't want to marry this guy was because she'd fallen for a servant at the neighbouring estate he marched straight up there to have it out with the master. The servant was fired on the spot and banished from the land. Mary was told she'd have to marry the old toff whether she liked it or not. She didn't like it one bit, and in the dead of night she came and stood in the stream, delirious with grief, waiting for her lost love to come to her.'

At this point Emma took a breath, realising only then she'd actually been holding it. 'What happened?'

'She stayed here all night but he didn't come. In the morning they found her here, frozen to death.'

Emma stared at him. 'That's awful! I thought there might have been a happier ending than that! Now I definitely don't want to drink the water!'

'It's only a story,' Aidan said. 'I quite like it.'

'Do you?'

'It's got a kind of romance to it, don't you think?'

'You've got a funny idea of romance.'

He laughed. 'It's probably why I'm still single. So this guy you left at home…'

Emma blinked at the sudden conversational swerve. 'How do you know I left a guy?'

'You must have mentioned something…'

'Did I? Are you sure?' Emma tried to recall if she'd mentioned Dougie. It didn't seem likely, but if she had that was bad news – it meant he was on her mind and his name came out of her mouth more than she'd like.'

'I think so. Or perhaps I imagined it. Either way it's obvious there's a guy in your life because there's no way a woman like you would be single.'

Emma tried not to blush – or to read too much into his statement.

'I didn't just leave him at home like I'm one day going to fetch him. It's over. I *left him* left him.'

'Ah, right. I was just asking because…' He shrugged.

She began to walk the line of the stream. 'My energy and attention are totally reserved for the hotel until it's up and running. Tia might find it easy to split her time, but I don't.'

'Yeah. I get that. Want to go and see a really tragic cliff?'

'Oh God, did the servant throw himself off it when they found Mary frozen?'

'No.'

'Good. So what's tragic about it?'

'A farmer fell off it and died, and his dog wouldn't leave the spot for the next twelve years until he died too.'

Emma raised her eyebrows. 'You sure know how to show a girl a good time.'

'Don't I?'

The funny thing was, despite the sarcasm in her tone, she *was* having a good time. That was what worried her.

Chapter Fifteen

Tia stumbled into the kitchen just as Emma was finishing her breakfast.

'Here she is,' Emma said with a wry tone, 'the dirty stop-out.'

'Sorry,' Tia said sheepishly. 'It got a bit lively in the pub. It might be a tiny village but they know how to party.'

'Really?'

'Honestly.' Tia took a seat at the table and felt the teapot before pouring out some lukewarm and slightly stewed tea. 'I know the average age in this place is about ninety but I'm not even joking.'

'I'm glad to see you going above and beyond and doing such valuable work to ingratiate yourself with the locals.'

'Oh absolutely. I mean, someone's got to do it.'

'Well' – Emma got up to take her cup to the sink – 'if anyone has a natural talent in that regard then it's you.'

Tia grinned.

'I should ask about your date,' Emma added, turning back to her.

'It wasn't really a date…'

'Of course it wasn't,' Emma said. 'Whatever it was then.'

Tia's cup halted halfway to her lips, a faraway look in her eyes that would have been comical had it not been so earnest.

'He's a great kisser,' she said.

Despite her doubts, Emma couldn't help but laugh. It was hard to stay mad at Tia for long, and she definitely had a knack for bringing the lightness out in any situation.

'Well I hope you can control yourself on the job today because we don't have time for kissing.'

'We'll keep it strictly to lunch breaks.'

'Ugh,' Emma cried, her laughter getting louder, 'too much already!'

As she left to get her shoes from the bedroom, she heard Tia call after her, 'Let's call at the café on the way to the site – I need a bacon sandwich!'

'I'll bet you do,' Emma called back with a grin.

Darcie greeted them with a warm smile and was only too happy to furnish Tia with two slices of doorstep bread filled with thickly cut bacon.

'Just a coffee for me,' Emma said. She looked slyly at her friend. 'I'm not the one trying to cure a hangover.'

'I won't have a hangover once I eat this,' Tia said. 'Never takes me long to get back on my feet so you don't need to worry on that score.'

'Oh, I wasn't worried,' Emma said. She was about to make some quip about how she'd crack the whip no matter how delicate Tia's state was when a van came to a halt outside and Darcie nodded at it.

'Your boys are here. They probably want bacon sandwiches too; I'd better put some more on.'

Blake walked in first and winked at Tia, who grinned and almost drooled the coffee she'd just sipped at right out again. Aidan came in a few seconds later.

'Morning!' Blake said cheerily. He was addressing them both but Emma felt distinctly invisible all of a sudden. Neither he nor Tia alluded to their evening together; they simply grinned at each other like naughty kids sharing a secret. Emma resisted the urge to roll her eyes. She smiled at Aidan.

'Alright this morning?' he asked her. 'Not too tired after your ramble?'

'Raring to go.'

Tia threw her a questioning look. 'What ramble?'

Emma laughed. 'While you were getting to know the local people, I was getting to know the local area. So I wasn't being completely idle while you were hobnobbing in the pub.'

Tia looked between her and Aidan and, as something apparently clicked into place, she looked suddenly smug. 'You sly fox,' she said.

Emma opened her mouth to set things straight when Blake spoke.

'We've got the van outside – we could give you two a lift down to the site.'

'It's not that far for us to walk,' Emma said.

Tia stepped over. 'I'll have a lift!'

Aidan looked at his brother. 'A bit cosy in the van with all four of us. It's a nice day; if Emma wants to walk I'll walk with her – you take Tia in the van.'

'I'd be so lucky,' Blake said with a cheeky wink at Tia, who began to giggle like a schoolgirl. Emma shot a look of barely disguised despair at Aidan, who threw one of warning to his brother.

'I've got the bacon on,' Darcie said as she came back through from the kitchen behind the counter.

'You know us so well,' Blake said. 'I'll have a double this morning; got to keep my strength up.'

'One for you?' Darcie asked Aidan.

'Why not?' he said amiably. 'It's going to be a busy day – might as well kick it off right.'

Once they'd got their packages of food, Blake and Tia climbed into the van and were gone, leaving Emma and Aidan to walk the mile or so to the old station house.

'I'll have a word with Blake,' he said.

'About Tia? Don't, I'm sure it will blow over in no time.'

'That's what I'm worried about. He's a good lad, you know. This track record with women that you might have heard about… it's a reaction.'

'To what?'

'He was hurt badly a few years back. Cut him up, and since then it's been about having fun, but deep down he's just trying to fix himself.'

'In that case he and Tia are well matched. Tia's divorce was tougher than she makes out. I think she's probably just looking for fun too right now. My only worry is if it interferes with our plans for the station. I have a lot riding on it – we both do, only Tia doesn't seem quite so aware of that.'

'You put a lot of money in, I suppose.'

'Worse than that – I put a lot of my dad's money in.'

'Hmm. I can see now why you might get a bit nervous. I'll talk to Blake and tell him to cool it, but you don't need to worry about us on site; he'll be professional when we're working.'

'Thank you.'

Aidan bit into his sandwich and chewed solemnly for a moment. The sun was throwing a gentle warmth over the morning, while rooks in a distant field were cackling and causing a ruckus, probably the same ones they'd seen when walking to Mary's Stream.

'See that tree over there,' Aidan said suddenly.

'Where?'

'Well more of a stump really…' He pointed to something that looked like it might once have been a tree but now resembled the leftovers of a fire. It was at the roadside, almost buried by the long grasses and delicate yarrow that grew in the shadow of the hedgerow, and if Aidan hadn't brought it to her attention Emma might never have noticed it. She certainly wouldn't have given it a second thought.

'Oh, right. What about it?'

'The hanging tree. It's where they used to hang criminals in the days before it was done properly.'

'Like any hanging is proper,' Emma said with a shudder. Then she gave him a sideways look. 'Don't you have any nice stories about this place?'

He grinned. 'Well that's sort of where I'm going next. The story goes that this guy was wrongfully accused of killing his wife – at least, most people thought she'd been having an affair and the lover had actually done it. On the day of his execution there was a rainstorm. Just as they kicked the stool away and the rope straightened, a bolt of lightning struck it, cut him free and set fire to the tree. He ran away into the storm and was never seen again.'

Emma gave him another wry look as he bit into his sandwich. 'Is that actually true?'

He shrugged. 'I have no idea, but it's what I was told.'

'If we ever need a local tour guide, I think I might have found our man.'

'I think you might.' Aidan turned to her with a grin. 'Not to toot my own horn but I think I'd be pretty good at it.'

'We could call it the misery tour.'

'How about the Tour of Terrible Tragedies? More of a ring to it.'

'So have you got more stories for this tour?'

'Loads. But if I tell them all to you at once I'll have nothing left when I want to impress you.'

'So I have to be rationed? Hardly seems fair.'

'It just means you'll have to spend more time with me if you want to hear them.'

'Or I could go and buy some local history books.'

'True,' he said, 'but they wouldn't tell it with such panache.'

'And I think we'll be spending a lot of time together anyway – you are building a hotel for me after all. You won't be finding excuses for more – you'll be trying to get away.'

'You know, I think it's great that you're taking that place on. It's special.'

'I think so too. So you have a tragic story for it?'

'Loads. I could keep you entertained for hours.'

'Well,' Emma said as the roof of Honeymoon Station came into view, 'there's something to look forward to.'

'Are you being sarcastic?'

'Me?' She grinned. 'As if!'

When Emma and Aidan arrived at the station, Tia and Blake were standing close, heads bowed over Blake's phone. Emma couldn't help but reflect that they looked very comfortable together already, though how long that would last with the baggage of two damaged pasts was anyone's guess. It did make Emma wonder if she'd been too quick to judge and perhaps it was about more than a roll in the hay. On closer inspection, she could see that they were studying web pages, though it was hard to make out what the photos were.

'Anything interesting?' Aidan asked as they looked up.

'I was just showing Tia some of Hank's jobs.'

'Who's Hank?' Emma asked.

'We've got this contact in Winchester for specialist stuff,' Aidan said. He looked at Blake. 'I'm guessing you're thinking of him for the timbers?'

Blake nodded. 'I mean,' he added, looking at Emma now, 'as I was just explaining to Tia, we could bodge the timber sections of the walls well enough and they wouldn't look too bad from a distance, but if you're having guests and trading on the fact you're a renovated station you probably want them looking their best. Hank's pricey, there's no getting around that, but he will do you a cracking job. His work is beautiful.'

'He's certainly a craftsman,' Aidan agreed.

Blake came over with his phone to show Emma the photos. There was a white house on stilts sitting in mudflats by the sea, a section of windmill, a house set into a hillside, another renovated railway station and a line of seafront properties, all rendered in beautiful lacquered and painted wood.

'Might be worth spending the extra,' he said as Emma pored over them.

After a moment she looked up at Tia. 'Maybe we can talk it over later?'

'OK,' Tia said.

Emma handed Blake his phone. 'When do we need to tell you what we decide?'

'I'd book him as quick as you can; he's in demand and you might have to wait months.'

'Oh, just get him in that case,' Tia said.

Emma stared at her. 'We don't know how much he costs yet,' she said, trying to keep her voice level. 'Or if we have the extra to spare in the budget. We *really* need to look at it properly before we decide.'

'But what's the point of scrimping? Blake said it – if we want it to look top class we have to hire the best.'

'I'm not scrimping, I'm being realistic. It's pointless having beautiful wood panelling and then not being able to afford a roof!'

Blake and Aidan exchanged an awkward look. Emma was aware it wasn't her finest moment and she probably sounded like a tyrant, but one of them had to be practical about this.

'Fine,' Tia huffed. 'If it makes you happy we'll hang fire.'

Once they'd discussed who needed to do what and prioritised jobs, work began. Despite her hangover, Tia threw herself into every task. Blake was like a machine, clearing away rotten bits of the structure, preparing what surfaces they could save and rebuilding parts they couldn't. Emma fetched and carried like any good builders' mate, and after Aidan had shown her how to mix the cement, she kept them topped up. Aidan tended to the things that took a more delicate hand while overseeing the works more generally so that everything ran at maximum efficiency. It very quickly became apparent to Emma what the dynamic between the brothers was. Aidan was the brains and Blake the brawn. Aidan, she'd discovered, was also the oldest by two years. He was sensitive and thoughtful where Blake was enthusiastic and gregarious. That wasn't to say Aidan was without charm and lively wit, but it was of a more subtle tone than his brother's raucous joking.

By the time lunch arrived, even Emma was flagging and she couldn't imagine how Tia was coping. Self-inflicted, she thought, but it still must have been tough.

'I fancy something from the café,' Blake announced.

Aidan looked at him. 'We have sandwiches in the van.'

'They're not as good as one of Darcie's pies.'

'Which means you'll have to eat at least two?'

Blake patted his six-pack. 'I think I've earned them.'

Aidan grinned. 'Don't be long then. You might as well pick one up for me too.' He looked at Emma, who was pouring tea from a Thermos flask. 'Want Blake to pick something up from Darcie's for you?'

She shook her head. 'We've got lunch, thanks.'

'I'll go with Blake,' Tia said. 'I fancy something.'

'But we've got lunch here,' Emma said.

'Yes, I know, but then Blake mentioned pies and I really fancy one.'

Emma shrugged. At this rate it would take less than a week for Tia to undo years in the gym, but she'd said before she didn't care about that, and who was Emma to stop her? Obviously, when Tia had said she was fed up with watching her diet, she'd really meant it.

'Besides,' Tia added, 'it's a good thing to spend money in the village supporting all the local businesses. In the end it benefits us.'

'It's alright,' Emma said, 'you don't need to convince me. Get your pie with my blessing.'

'Don't you want anything at all from there?' Tia asked her.

'Thanks, but I'll make do with what we have.'

'OK... we won't be long!'

Tia skipped to follow Blake to the van. A moment later the calm of the moment was shattered by the sound of his engine starting up and they left. Emma handed Aidan a mug of tea from her flask.

'Lovely,' he said with a grateful smile.

'Want to share this lunch now that Tia's not eating it?'

'What is it?'

'Tuna wraps.' She pointed to a cool bag. He wrinkled his nose.

'Sorry but not really a tuna kind of guy.'

'Seriously?'

He nodded.

'Well,' Emma said, 'now the wedding's off.'

He chuckled. 'All the more tuna for you.'

'I'm not going to lie; I could quite easily polish both lots off.'

'Go for it...' He sat on a tree stump and sipped at his tea. 'Labouring does work up a fair appetite.'

'You must have to eat mountains of food, the amount you do then.'

'I do. If I ever stopped doing this job I'd be like a whale.'

'Better not stop then.'

Emma took a seat close by on a pile of bricks. Even a couple of weeks ago she'd have been horrified at the thought of sitting amongst the dirt and rubble, but already that felt like a very different Emma. Her aunt Patricia would have been shocked to see her now; Emma had always been such a fastidious child, and it had been something of a family joke over the years. She half thought about taking a selfie to send to Patricia and Elise, but she would have felt silly doing it in front of Aidan.

Still, she had to muse that she might quite like this new Emma, who had muddy jeans, calloused hands and sweat stains on her T-shirt but didn't care. The mess was, in a strange way, symbolic. All her life she'd tried so hard to maintain order and keep things neat. She'd been so busy making sure life for everyone around her ran like clockwork in the absence of her mother that she'd forgotten how good a little chaos could feel. Here in Honeymoon she was finally beginning to realise that sometimes mess was the start of something beautiful. And if she could steady the project and keep Tia on track, their hotel could be that beautiful something.

Aidan let his gaze wander to the station building and Emma's followed it. The place looked almost worse than when they'd started, but so much of the structure had needed removing before they could begin to rebuild that it was hardly surprising. But the bones were there, more visible than ever.

'What do you think?' Emma said into the comfortable silence that had fallen between them. He turned to her. 'Think we're nuts yet?'

'Oh I thought that when you first arrived and announced your plans,' he said with a chuckle.

'Think it's doable though?'

'Yes,' he said after a pause. 'It's doable. At first glance the building's surprisingly sound considering how long it's been battling the elements out here. As long as we don't find anything nasty lurking we'll be OK.'

'Think we can get it done by the autumn?'

'That's harder to say in all honesty. Some companies would bull you but I won't. If you do manage, it'll be by the skin of your teeth.'

Emma nodded slowly. 'I appreciate the no-bull approach.'

'I thought you might.'

'Want some more tea?'

'I wouldn't mind.'

'You and Blake have lived in Honeymoon all your lives,' she said as she topped him up.

'Yep.'

'It's unusual, if you don't mind me saying. I mean, Nell was saying that the younger generation all leave to find work, but you didn't.'

'I think Blake might still move out given half the chance, but he doesn't because it would break Mum's heart.'

'So that's why you stayed too? For your mum?'

'Partly. But I love it here. Yes, it's quiet and there's not much to do and there's a big world out there to see. Maybe one day I will go and take a look, but right now I'm happy where I am.'

'Is that why you're so knowledgeable about the history of Honeymoon?'

Aidan lifted the cup to his lips with a smile. 'It's just stories; mostly my granddad's. Blake was never interested but I liked listening. It made me feel closer to my granddad, I suppose. When he died they became like heirlooms, these little treasures he'd left me.'

'I never thought of a story that way,' Emma said. 'Are they actually true or just stories?'

'I think there's a nugget of truth in most of them – no idea quite how big the nugget is though.'

'Maybe they're more fun that way.'

'Maybe.' He looked across the clearing. 'How much of this land belongs to you?'

'Up to that line of shrubs that way' – Emma pointed north – 'and out to that ridge that way' – she pointed south – 'to the track there and the old car park that way.'

'What are you going to do with it?'

'Don't know yet. Gardens, probably. Maybe even a pool… Who knows?'

'You'll have to fence that apple tree off.'

Emma blinked and scanned the grounds. 'Apple tree?'

'Granted, it's hard to spot because there are no apples on it now but there will be in a few months. Blake and me used to come and pick them all the time.'

'Nice memories… I can see why you'd want it to stay.'

He nodded. 'That, and it's a very important tree.'

'Is it?' she asked doubtfully. 'Oh… is this where you tell me someone died there? Did a freakishly large apple fall on their head and kill them?'

He laughed. 'No. It's King Edward's tree.'

'King Edward's tree?' she repeated slowly. 'Surely you're not going to tell me he lived here?'

'Nope. But one day he came through on a train, finished the apple he was eating and threw the core out of the window. It grew into that tree right where it landed. So that makes it King Edward's tree.'

Emma burst out laughing. 'Is that one of your granddad's stories?'

'Nah, that one's Nell's at the shop.'

'If there's a nugget of truth there it must be microscopic!'

'Yeah, but you like the idea, right? Your guests will too.'

Emma was thoughtful for a moment, the smile still fixed to her lips.

'You know what?' she said finally. 'You might just be onto something there.'

Chapter Sixteen

Emma's lunch had been demolished, and Tia's had too. They allowed a few minutes more for Tia and Blake to return, but when there was no sign of them Aidan was forced to phone his brother. There was no reply. Emma tried Tia and got no reply there either. Neither Emma nor Aidan were unduly worried, and while she didn't say it, Emma imagined them pulled up in a remote spot doing goodness only knew what. Though she wanted to credit Tia with a little more maturity than that – they were supposed to be working today after all.

When they'd waited as long as seemed reasonable, they picked up their tools again, having decided it was pointless to waste any more of the day, and were digging out a rotten floor together when Tia and Blake finally returned. They were completely oblivious to Emma's annoyed frown.

'What happened?' she demanded. 'We were beginning to worry.'

'We ran into some trouble at the shop,' Tia said.

'I thought you were going to the café?'

Tia stared at her. 'Alright, calm down. We went to the shop as well to get some gum.'

'I got you some too.' Blake threw a packet of gum to Aidan, who caught it neatly and shoved it into his trouser pocket.

'So what happened?' he asked.

Tia rolled her eyes. 'Sid!'

'He decided to give Tia a piece of his mind,' Blake said.

'Oh God! He's still upset about the hotel?' Emma asked, dreading the obvious reply. If they couldn't get the village onside, their idyllic vision of life here might quickly crumble. Sid could cause a lot of damage if his objections got any purchase.

Tia nodded shortly. 'You could say that. Anyway, Nell told him off. She threatened to bar him from the shop. Then things got heated between them and when he finally went—'

'With a bit of persuasion,' Blake cut in darkly.

'Yes,' Tia continued, 'Nell was so upset she had a funny turn.'

'Angina,' Blake said. 'We had to find her tablets and sit with her until she was alright again.'

'I served in the shop while she had a rest,' Tia said brightly. 'I can do shop work now!'

Emma gave a tight smile.

'She's alright now?' Aidan asked.

'I think so,' Blake said. 'Darcie and Tariq said they'd look in on her through the afternoon to make sure she doesn't have another turn. We can call in on the way home tonight and check on her as well.'

Aidan nodded agreement.

'What about Sid?' Emma looked from one to the other. While it was comforting to see that they didn't seem too concerned about what had happened, the notion of him out there causing mischief still troubled her.

Blake rolled up his shirt sleeves. 'Probably went home.'

'He's going to be a problem, isn't he?'

'Nah...' Blake grinned. 'He's all bark and no bite. Nobody listens to him anyway; he's complained so often about so much that it's all just noise when he opens his mouth now.'

Emma tried to let that reassure her but was still finding it hard to settle. She did, however, feel guilty for thinking the worst of her friend. There was so much riding on this project personally that it was hard to remember sometimes that this was Tia's dream too. It meant as much to her as it did to Emma; she just had a different attitude to the life she lived around it.

'OK,' Tia said, 'now we've sorted all that, someone pass me a pick and I'll get stuck into that floor with you.'

Blake laughed. 'Oh God, when you talk like that it does things to me.'

She winked. 'That's the idea!'

Aidan looked across and grinned at Emma. Tia and Blake's incessant flirting was something they were just going to have to get used to.

The rest of the afternoon passed without incident and everyone worked harder to make up for the time they'd missed. As they packed up, Emma felt much happier to see that they'd made progress and the floor they'd been trying to remove was almost ready for new concrete to be poured in. These were the sorts of necessary jobs that would be invisible once the hotel was finished and yet would probably take up most of their time and money. Making it pretty at the end, Aidan had said, would be a snap in comparison.

Tia and Blake had spent the afternoon throwing innuendos around and so it came as no surprise to hear that they'd arranged to go to the pub together again that night. Emma smiled and assured Tia that it was OK. She was hardly going to say otherwise, but she couldn't help being a little disappointed that she was being abandoned again when she'd been hoping for a night in with her friend. She felt they had a lot to discuss, as always, and even if they hadn't she would have enjoyed the company.

Tia and Blake met up the next night too, and the one after that. By the end of the week they'd been out together every night, mostly in the pub. Emma honestly didn't know how Tia found the energy after a day on site because she was always exhausted. Aidan had hinted to Emma that they should go too, but it felt worryingly like a date and so she'd politely declined. She'd fretted that she might have offended him, but he hadn't seemed bothered at all, and, of course, as soon as she realised that, she'd wished he would be bothered and that she'd said yes.

Instead, she'd taken walks out to explore, or visited Nell in the shop, or Darcie and Tariq, always getting back in time for a decent night's sleep.

Apart from the previous night. She hadn't had a decent sleep that night at all, having been woken at midnight by the sounds of enthusiastic sex. Tia and Blake had clearly taken things to the next level, and all Emma could do was hold a pillow over her ears and hope they wouldn't take too long.

Tonight, Emma had managed to catch Elise on the phone, who also seemed to be busier than ever and was increasingly difficult to get hold of.

'It sounds as if she's embracing her new freedom,' Elise said.

'Oh she's doing that alright.' Emma tucked her legs beneath her as she curled up on the sofa, phone to her ear.

'Maybe you should just fight fire with fire. Get your own man and be louder than them.'

'Jeez!' Emma said, unable to prevent her laughter. 'Any louder and you'd be able to hear from there.'

Elise giggled. 'It does sound like a flatmate I had in the first year at uni. She was a total nightmare.'

'You never mentioned her before.'

'I was too embarrassed to tell you. It embarrassed me just to hear her. She sounded like a wounded cat.'

Emma snorted with new laughter. 'Sounds delightful. So I'm getting the full student experience now?'

'You are,' Elise said. 'Enjoy.'

'Great.' Emma smiled. But then she was serious. 'Do you think I'm overreacting?'

'To the sex or the actual relationship?'

'I don't begrudge her the sex one bit… not even the relationship. I just wish she'd take this huge leap we've made a bit more seriously.'

'It sounds like she is. Sounds like she's jumped right into her new life to me. Are you sure this is not more about feeling abandoned? You've just got there and already she's doing her own thing so you're left alone to work out what you're supposed to do?'

'Maybe,' Emma said slowly. 'I hadn't really thought about it like that.'

'Couldn't you go to the pub with her?'

'Of course I could, but I'd feel like a bit of a gooseberry. I mean, they'd be smooching and I'd be sitting there trying not to watch.'

'I'm sure they'd tone it down for you.'

'You haven't seen them together – they can barely tone it down when they're working.'

'Didn't you say his brother had offered to go with you? Couldn't you go with him? And there would be other people at the pub –

couldn't you just talk to them? And you're really telling me they're so loved-up that they couldn't keep their hands off each other long enough to share at least one drink with you?'

'They might, but I'd know that they were thinking about having their hands on each other and wishing I'd bog off.'

'I'm sure they'd have more self-control than that.'

'I'd still feel as if they didn't want me there. The pub just feels like her space now, not mine. Like the place she goes to that I don't belong in.'

'Well maybe that's on you and not her.'

'Probably. Listen, could you just stop making so much sense for a minute? I'm the older sister and I'm feeling a lot like a silly kid right now.'

'I don't think you're silly. Perhaps you're feeling a bit overwhelmed and oversensitive right now and it's totally normal. Everything is still very new there and you're bound to feel unsettled by things that wouldn't usually bother you.'

'Is that how you've been in Iceland?'

'It's not the same, Em. I've got a whole team here to lean on. I've got so much support it's like I can't even sneeze without someone racing over with a hanky.'

Emma moved to get comfortable as one of her legs started to go to sleep. 'I'm glad to hear that – it's one less thing for me to worry about.'

'You wouldn't have needed to worry anyway. You've done your years of worrying about me – time to think of yourself now.'

'Easier said than done.' She stretched her legs out and wriggled her bare toes.

There was a knock at the door and she got up to look through the window. Tariq was outside.

'Can I call you back?' she asked Elise.

'I'm heading into town for a drink shortly so maybe I can phone you tomorrow.'

'OK. Have fun.'

'Love you, Em.'

'Love you too. Bye.'

Emma ended the call and rushed to open the door.

'I'm not disturbing you, am I?' Tariq asked.

'No, not at all. Would you like to come in?'

'I won't stay if that's alright… accounts to do. I just came to give you this…'

He held out a plate covered in tinfoil. 'Some leftover cake,' he said. 'We'd normally throw it away but Darcie remembered how much you'd liked the coffee and walnut and wondered if you might like what's left of this.'

'That's so kind.' Emma took the plate. 'I'll have no trouble finishing this off at all. Do you want some payment—'

'Oh no. We'd only be throwing it away so it's good that it hasn't gone to waste.'

'How is Darcie?'

'Tired,' he said. 'She'd have come herself but I was on my way out anyway.'

'You do long days at the café.'

'Yes, but we wouldn't swap it for the world. You'll know all about that once you get the hotel open.'

'I suppose we will, if we ever get there.'

'With Blake and Aidan on the job? They won't let you down; they're good guys. Did a lot to help us when we first moved here.'

'Yes, they're great,' Emma said neutrally.

Tariq paused. 'Are Tia and Blake...?'

'An item?' Emma raised her eyebrows. 'I think that's pretty obvious to anyone.'

'Hmm. We did wonder but didn't like to ask.' He smiled. 'It doesn't take him long.'

'Do you think it will last?'

'No idea.'

'You talk to them a lot?'

'Aidan mostly. He calls every now and again for a chat. Blake's always in a rush to get to the pub.'

'Don't you fancy going to the pub with him?'

'I don't drink so there doesn't seem much point. What about you? Aidan told me he'd asked you but you didn't fancy it.'

'I'm always so tired after a day on the site,' she said. 'I'd be terrible company and asleep in my beer by nine.'

'Perhaps you could go at the weekend then.'

'I expect I'll be on site at the weekend too. Whatever it takes.'

'Oh yes, we know all about that. Seven-day working weeks were a regular thing when we started out too.'

'You're still open seven days,' Emma said with a smile.

'True, but we manage to give each other bits of time off now we've got into our stride. Darcie's even talked about getting help when the hotel is open... We're sort of counting on your business bringing us a bit more business too.'

Emma laughed. 'Wow, I needed that extra pressure.'

Tariq grinned. 'Sorry. I'll let you get on with your evening. Enjoy the cake.'

'I will – thank you!'

He gave a casual wave as he made his way back along the high street. Emma closed the front door then peeled the foil back from the plate to see that Darcie had sent what looked like all the cake they'd had left, not just the coffee and walnut. There was Victoria sponge, lemon drizzle, chocolate, coconut… she'd never eat it all before it went stale. Even if Tia had been home to help they wouldn't have finished it.

A sudden idea occurred to her, and before she'd had time to decide if it was a good one or not, she'd fetched her phone and dialled the number.

'Hey… sorry to call you now and this is going to sound weird but I just wondered… are you planning to go out tonight?'

'Emma?' Aidan sounded bemused. 'Not really. Is everything alright?'

'Oh yes, it's nothing important. It's just… do you fancy some cake?'

Chapter Seventeen

'You know this cottage used to belong to the stationmaster of Honeymoon Station?'

'Did it? I thought it belonged to June's mother.'

'June's mum was married to Nell's granddad, who was the stationmaster. Second marriage – June's mum's first husband died of tuberculosis.'

'That's…' Emma shook her head. 'Too complicated for me to work out.'

'Most family trees around here are connected somehow. It's a wonder we haven't all got six fingers.'

Emma didn't know whether she was supposed to laugh or not, but then Aidan did and she relaxed.

'Did you also know he was one of the first people to climb Mount Everest?'

'I thought that was that famous guy… what's his name…?'

'I said he was *one* of the first, not the first.'

Emma narrowed her eyes.

He held his hands up. 'Honest, ask June!'

Emma laughed. 'Do you look at anything and not have a story to tell about it?'

He made a point of examining the kitchen carefully until his gaze settled on the plate sitting on the table between them. 'This cake.'

'Ah, well I can tell you the story of this cake. Darcie's leftovers – end of story.'

'There's another thing I don't have a story for.'

'What's that?'

'Actually, a person. You.'

Emma flushed, her gaze going to the depths of her teacup. 'That's because there is no story worth hearing. I mean, look how boring I am. Tia is out at the pub and I've got you here eating leftover cake and drinking tea like an old lady.'

'Well I came here willingly for tea and cake. I guess that makes me boring too.'

'No way. You're not a bit boring. Tell me your story; it'll be more interesting than mine.'

'You're not getting out of it that easily. I asked you for yours. You can hear mine from anyone in the village – everyone knows everything about me here.'

'Say I didn't want to ask anyone in the village. Say I felt rude asking other people about you?'

'I'd say you'd get far more entertainment asking Blake for his life story.'

Emma rolled her eyes. 'Oh, I know all about Blake. No offence, but I'm sick of hearing about Blake – Tia doesn't talk about anything else.'

'That can't be true.'

'Trust me, it's not far off the truth. She's got it bad.'

'I have to admit,' Aidan said, thoughtful now, 'she's making quite an impression on him. For a while it looked like he'd never get over Stacey…'

'Is that the girl who was supposed to have broken his heart?'

He nodded.

Emma nibbled on a chunk of walnut. 'But you think he might be serious about Tia?'

'She's older than the girls he's been dating since his break-up with Stacey. More assertive and wiser too. Maybe that's what he's needed all along. I haven't seen him like this over a woman in a long time.'

'What about you?' Emma twisted another walnut from the cake in front of her and popped it into her mouth.

'What about me?'

'You must have had loads of girlfriends.'

'A few, but none worth mentioning. How about the guy you left at home? He's definitely history?'

'I thought you didn't know my story.'

'I know that bit. Am I not allowed to know anything else? Is there a rule because I'm working for you?'

'It sounds so weird when you put it like that… to have someone working for me. I'm used to being the employee and not the employer.'

Aidan leaned across the table and looked straight at her. 'That's not answering my question.'

She shook her head. 'I'm having a good time; don't ruin our perfectly nice tea party by making me talk about him.'

'Is that what this is?'

'God, now it really does sound boring, doesn't it? Maybe we should go to the pub after all.'

'We could… I don't know about you but, as much as I love Blake, I don't want to sit at a table and watch him slobber over your friend.'

Emma laughed. 'Me neither. So that's a no to the pub?'

He smiled slowly. 'I've got a better idea. Give me ten minutes to run home and get some stuff. And while I'm gone maybe you want to find some good boots and a warm coat.'

He'd arrived back shortly afterwards with blankets, wine and two flashlights.

'What on earth do we need all that for?' Emma had asked.

'I'm going to take you to the best spot in Honeymoon. Actually, it's a bit outside Honeymoon and it's a bit of a climb. It'll be worth it, though, I promise.'

His promise had held good. The climb had left her breathless, but the view from the top of the hill as the sun set, huge and blazing across the woods and fields and rivers of the countryside, had left her dizzy.

'Wow.'

'I told you it would be good,' he said with a grin. 'Should I put it on my tour?'

'Why?' Emma watched as he spread blankets on the ground for them to sit. 'Is it tragic? Don't tell me something horrible happened up here.'

'Don't worry; it's just a hill. Pretty good view, though, don't you think? On a clear day you can see right over to the coast. My granddad said it was the closest you could get to heaven without going there.'

'I think he might be right.' Emma sat on the blanket and took a wine glass from him. 'It even smells amazing.'

'No pollution, see. Just clean air as God intended. And the best sunsets you'll ever see.'

Emma eyed him with a wry smile. 'Do you bring all newcomers to the village up here?'

'No, just you. But then, we don't get that many newcomers.'

'But you must bring your girlfriends up here? I mean, all those amazing sunsets…'

'One girl,' Aidan said, but then suddenly went quiet. 'She didn't get it,' he went on after a minute. 'The closest I ever got to *the one*, I suppose. The fact she didn't get it should have told me it wouldn't last. Still… all in the past now.'

'Well,' Emma said, trying to find the brightness of a conversation that had taken a sudden melancholy turn, 'I definitely get it. There's nowhere like this where I come from; it's beautiful.'

'Wait until the stars come out.' He poured some wine into her glass. 'They don't call it Shooting Star Hill for nothing. I guarantee you'll never see as many anywhere else as you do up here. You can make as many wishes as you like.'

Emma took a sip of her wine. It was a bit warm, but she didn't mind. 'I can't wait; it's a definite must for your tour then.'

'Is this tour becoming an actual thing?' Aidan asked as he poured his own wine.

'I think it might be. Interested?'

'I might be. I'm expensive though.'

'I'm sure you'll be worth it.'

She looked across, and his skin looked gold in the setting sun. He looked good… handsome… exactly her type… The girl he'd brought up here before must have been a fool to let him go…

She tried not to think about it as she tore her gaze away.

'So,' Aidan continued, looking appreciatively at the wine as he tasted it. 'What will you wish for if you see a shooting star?'

'I suppose I'll wish for the hotel to be a success. It's very sensible and boring but it's all I have going on right now.'

'What if you could stop being sensible for a minute and wish for something crazy?'

'I don't know…' she said, gathering her knees to her chest, her gaze on the horizon. 'I'd have to think about it.'

He placed his glass down and lay back on the blanket with his hands behind his head, staring into the sky with eyes that seemed to see the whole of the universe beyond. Emma looked at him and found her gaze dragged to those deep, dark eyes.

She hadn't been telling the whole truth. She did have another wish. It had been the first one actually. She was very afraid she was falling for Aidan, but it was too quick and too soon after Dougie, and there was too much else going on, and she wished she could do something to stop it. But as she watched Aidan now, smiling into the sky with a head full of stories and a heart as kind as any, she wondered if there would ever be enough shooting stars in the sky to make that one come true.

Chapter Eighteen

'Nothing happened. We had a few drinks, watched the sunset, talked about cement mixing and planning laws and then I came home.'

Tia's expression was more than a little sceptical as she ate her porridge.

'Scoff all you want,' Emma said, 'but it's the truth.'

'You must like him though. Blake's pretty sure he likes you.'

'I'm sure Blake must be wrong.'

'Why would he be wrong? Surely he knows his own brother well enough.'

'Don't go getting any ideas!' Emma warned.

'I'm not, I'm just asking. It's an innocent enough question.'

'No question is innocent when it comes from you.'

Tia grinned and then scooped the last of her oats into her mouth. 'Any of that toast left? I'm still starving.'

'I'm not surprised. You must be famished after another workout last night.'

Tia stared at her, and then turned a deep crimson.

'Oh, Em… I'm so sorry! I didn't realise you'd…'

'I hate to break it to you but the walls are pretty thin. You might want to bear that in mind next time you bring Blake back.'

'Oh God, how mortifying.'

Emma took her bowl to the sink. 'Forget about it. Let's chalk it up to experience and move on.'

'Did I keep you awake?'

'Not for long to be honest. There's nothing like a late-night climb to send you off to sleep.'

'I should get Blake to take me up there one day.'

'You should – it's lovely.'

'Romantic, eh?' Tia waggled her eyebrows.

'If you're up there with a partner, yes I'm sure it is,' Emma said, ignoring the jibe.

'What about a prospective partner?'

Emma looked up from the sink with a frown and Tia laughed.

'OK, OK… I've dropped it already. I won't mention it again.'

'I'm too busy for romance, even if I wanted it.'

'See, that makes me sad. No one should be too busy for romance.'

Emma smiled thinly. 'There's no need to be sad – you can have enough romance for the both of us.'

Tia was silent for a moment. She looked up from the toast she'd been buttering. 'Em… do you think it's too soon for me?'

'What do you mean?'

'For me to be seeing Blake?'

'I don't know. I thought it was just a bit of fun.'

'So did I.'

'Something's changed? Is that why you're asking me the question?'

Tia nodded. 'I really like him. And I think he might like me. And before you remind me of his reputation as a Casanova, I know all that. I'm not sixteen and I can see for myself when someone's a bit naughty, and if I didn't think he could change I'd run a mile. But I think he can change, and I think he might for me. Is that arrogant? Misguided?'

'The one thing that's always struck me about you is the way you read people,' Emma said. 'You're really good at it. You get the measure of someone straight away. I think you can trust your instincts because I think you might be right.'

Tia's doubtful frown turned into a smile. 'Did Aidan say something about it? He did, didn't he? He's told you what Blake's been saying about me, hasn't he? Tell me, please!'

'I only know what Aidan thinks, not what he knows for certain. I wouldn't want to feed you false information.'

'Oooh!' Tia squeaked, leaping up to hug Emma. 'I knew it! I knew I was right!'

Emma smiled. 'You must really like him,' she said gently.

'I do. I've been so fed up and I felt like no one would ever look at me again.'

'Why? You're gorgeous!'

'But I didn't feel gorgeous. I felt bruised and broken on the inside and I felt like it showed on the outside. And even if it doesn't last with Blake, I feel as if I'm starting to mend and it's thanks to him.'

'That's down to you, not him.'

'It's down to you too,' Tia said. 'Now we have to do the same for you.'

'Me? I'm fine; I'm not broken.'

'Maybe not, but we all have room for a little more love in our lives, even you!'

'Please don't think me ungrateful when I say this. I love that you want to look out for me but please… please don't get any ideas about trying to fix my love life. I don't need it fixing, and I don't want it.'

'But—'

'Tia, please. If you have any respect for me as a friend and business partner you'll leave it alone.'

'OK…' Tia let out an impatient sigh. 'Fine. But I think you're missing the obvious.'

'Which is what?'

Tia sat back down and bit into her toast. 'If I have to tell you then you really are more gormless than I thought.'

'Thank you!' Emma said.

'You know what I mean. There's a reason you spend so much time with Aidan.'

'Yes, it's because you're always missing.'

'And…'

'And because we're friends. We enjoy each other's company. He's showing me the local area so that we can tell our guests about it. There are a million reasons why I spend time with him and none of them are anything to do with sex.'

Tia gave her an impish look. 'Who said anything about sex?'

Emma snatched the plate from in front of her and dumped it into the sink to wash. 'Never mind that; we're running late.'

Chapter Nineteen

Three weeks had passed since they'd started work on Honeymoon Station and things were going as well as could be expected. At least, that's what Aidan and Blake had told them. Sid was doing his best to make his feelings known at every opportunity, but at least nobody seemed to be listening, and he hadn't dared turn up at the building site again. He simply glared at Tia and Emma whenever he saw them in the village, his moustache quivering indignantly. They were falling behind schedule with the renovations, a little more every day, but the boys had told them not to worry, that all builds ran into setbacks and that they'd do their very best to pull the time back. Despite this, every day Emma could see a little progress: a few more bricks here, a rendered wall there, a drainage ditch, some pipework. It wasn't exactly The Ritz, and there was nothing pretty about it yet, but that old station was slowly and surely becoming new again.

Tia and Blake spent almost every evening together now, and although Emma was getting used to it, she still craved Tia's company when they'd finished work and gone home for the day. By now she knew she wouldn't get it and had to be content with calling Patricia or her dad or Elise, or wandering around Honeymoon to see who was free for a chat, or taking a walk out into the countryside around her new home, sometimes with Aidan and sometimes without.

On site, every time Emma happened to look up from her work either Tia was watching Blake or Blake was watching Tia. And whenever they caught each other's eye there was a shared grin, or a wink or a blown kiss.

'It must be love,' Aidan said one morning in a low voice as he came to fetch a newly mixed batch of cement from Emma.

'You've noticed too?'

'It's kind of hard to miss.'

'You can say that again. By the way, I never said thanks for showing me that cave last night.'

'Oh, it was nothing that spectacular.'

'I mean, I'm not convinced that pirates used to hide rum in there but I still thought it was cool. Our guests will too.'

He laughed. 'Scout's honour. It was fun anyway, so it was no bother. Where do you want to go tonight? There's a field full of ghost cows. We think they're ghost cows because people can hear mooing when there's nothing there. It could be coming from the dairy farm up the road, of course. And there's the Honeymoon stone circle. It's not exactly Stonehenge, more of a garden centre ornamental rockery, but it's cute, and legend has it that at midsummer it's where the fairies go to dance to celebrate the longest day. Or…' Aidan paused, 'I don't know… maybe I could take you somewhere civilised. Like out to dinner…'

'Aidan…' Emma gave him a pained look. 'I'm not like Tia.'

'What do you mean?'

'I'm not where she is' – she tapped her head – 'in here. I'm just looking for friendship right now, nothing else.'

He frowned, and then he looked horribly embarrassed and awkward, and Emma suddenly realised she'd assumed too much and insulted him into the bargain.

'I mean…' she began to backtrack, 'it's not that I don't—'

'Please,' he said, 'forget that I suggested anything. I'm sorry if it came across as anything other than friendship. I was only thinking you must be sick of eating at Darcie's café or cooking your own food and you might fancy a change. I overstepped the mark.'

'No, no you didn't! I'm sorry, I didn't mean—'

'Aid!' Blake called from where he was installing a damp-proof course. 'Can I borrow you, bro? Need you to look at this.'

Without another word to Emma, Aidan went to join his brother. She watched him go. If she could have punched herself in the face she would have done. Of course he was just trying to be her friend. Why did she have to be so suspicious of everyone's motives? Maybe the real problem was that she wanted there to be more in it than friendship but couldn't bring herself to open up to that. Not every man was out to use her like Dougie and others before him had done. She was a different woman now too: stronger, more independent – the sort of woman who forged her own path. If she'd met Dougie today she wouldn't let him walk all over her like before. And Aidan wasn't even like that. He was kind, respectful, good company, fun to be around, so why couldn't she allow herself to like him as more than a friend? After the way she'd just blown him off, even that was in jeopardy now. Why did she have to be so stupid?

Another thing that had become a regular occurrence in the weeks they'd been in Honeymoon were lunch breaks during which Blake and Tia disappeared. Today was no exception – as the clock struck one, Blake announced his intention to go and pick something up from the café and Tia announced hers to go with him and off they went, leaving Emma and Aidan alone.

Aidan sat on a pile of bricks munching solemnly on a cheese sandwich. Things still felt a little awkward between them since their mortifying conversation of earlier that day, but Emma was determined to fix it.

'You want some tea from our flask?' she asked.

He gave a vague smile. 'That'd be good, thanks.'

Emma poured some and handed it over.

'If the offer's still there…' she began, doing her best to keep her tone light, 'I'm actually pretty desperate to see a field of phantom cows. And garden centre rockeries full of dancing fairies are really my favourite things.'

He gave her a small smile. 'Emma, it's really OK – you don't have to—'

'No, I know. I really want to. I love you showing me around and, let's face it, if I'm going to sell holidays here then I really need that local knowledge.'

His smile grew a little. 'I mean, the cows are cool.'

'I think they'd go down a storm on TripAdvisor.'

He sipped his tea, and Emma was relieved to see he looked a little more like his normal self.

'You know what? I'm an idiot,' she said after a silent moment. 'I have some trust issues right now, but that's not your fault and I was wrong to make you a victim of them.'

'I hardly feel like a victim.'

'You offered me friendship – and God knows we need friends in Honeymoon right now – and I threw it back in your face. I'm sorry… Forgive me?'

'Of course – there's nothing to forgive. And you're really not that unpopular in Honeymoon.'

'There's Sid and his friends. They're not exactly our biggest fans.'

'Ah, I really wouldn't worry about what they say; nobody else does. Everyone else likes you.'

'That's probably down to Tia.'

'To be fair, she's very popular in the pub.'

Emma laughed. 'I bet! So this field full of ghostly cows… when did you say you could take me to see it?'

Aidan downed the last of his tea and handed her the empty cup. 'Maybe I can do better than an empty field. How does a genuine Iron Age settlement sound?'

Emma smiled, so glad the air had been cleared. 'That sounds amazing.'

'Tonight?'

'Tonight is perfect!'

'What did you say was supposed to be here?'

Emma looked across the expanse of meadow. There wasn't a lot here apart from the usual things you'd expect to find in a meadow: grass, flowers, rabbit droppings…

'Are you sure this isn't your empty field?' she asked.

'What, the phantom cows? Honest, I have brought you to the right place – there was a settlement here. I mean, I know there's not much of it left.'

'There's none of it left. I think we can safely strike this from your tour itinerary.'

'You say that but don't be too quick to judge. You know it's my tragic tour? Well this is kind of tragic, right?'

'As in it's tragic there's nothing to see?'

'Now I'm offended!'

'OK.' Emma smiled. 'I'm sold. Impress me.'

Aidan began to walk. 'See here? The bit that's raised all along here… would have been the walls of a house. And here… there's another.'

'It just looks as if the field needs a good steamroller to me.'

'You need to use your imagination.'

'Well that's where you're going wrong because I don't have one.'

'I don't believe that for a minute. Anyone who looked at Honeymoon Station and saw a hotel must have an imagination.'

'That was Tia, I'm afraid.'

'But you came on board; you must have seen something. I don't think you give yourself enough credit.'

'I suppose…' Emma began to wander the field, looking at the ground. 'Well how do I know what's just lumps and what used to be a building?'

'Most of the raised sections would have been the site of something.'

'What did they look like?'

'Stone, I guess. Maybe mud. Maybe some straw roofs.'

Emma narrowed her eyes. 'You're making this up as you go along, aren't you?'

He grinned. 'Maybe the details. But there was definitely a settlement of some sort here; I know that for sure.'

She smiled at him. The sun was low in the sky now, playing hide and seek with fast-moving cloud that kept changing the light, so that sometimes it was soft, and sometimes it was dark and epic. When Aidan was this animated he was twenty times more attractive, and she knew she'd be thinking about this moment later when they'd parted ways, trying hard not to but failing miserably. She'd never been interested in Iron Age mounds of earth, but when he talked about them she wanted to hear more – even if it *was* largely made up.

'I suppose you're going to tell me something awful happened to the village here,' she said.

'I don't know about that,' Aidan said cheerfully, 'but they do say it's haunted.'

'By who?'

'The chief of the tribe who was overthrown by a naughty nephew. He's still trying to reclaim his land, even after all these years. Won't stop haunting until someone gives it back.'

'So why doesn't someone just come here and tell him it's his? Case closed.'

'You know, I don't think anyone's ever thought of that.'

'That's ridiculous. It's the most obvious thing in the world.'

'To someone with half a brain cell, perhaps.'

'To anyone with an ounce of practicality.' Emma gave a wry smile. 'I guess that would be me – no imagination but practical to the last. Kind of sad, right?'

'No, I don't think so. You do it.'

'Do what?'

'Tell the chief he can have his land back.'

'Don't be daft.'

'Don't you want to exorcise the land? What if your guests don't like being haunted by an ancient chieftain as they walk around here?'

'Now you're just being silly.'

'Come on, just say it.'

'Now?'

'Why not?'

'I don't want to do it. I've just been insulting his mounds; he might not take very kindly to me.'

He laughed. 'Maybe not then.'

Emma gave him a coquettish look. 'You do it.'

'Chief!' he called out. 'It's all yours! Now bugger off!'

Emma giggled, and then a strange silence fell over the meadow. It was hard not to get caught up in the idea that something supernatural had just happened. On the horizon the tiny clump of rooftops that represented Honeymoon flickered in the light and shade of an ever-changing sky, and a flock of distant birds streamed across the heavy banks of cloud.

After a moment Aidan broke the quiet. 'How about I show you something you can't fail to see? It's a bit of a drive out; we'd have to go back to Honeymoon and get the van.'

'Depends what it is.'

'The Cerne Abbas Giant. Know it?'

'Not really. Is it a real giant or just a field where a giant used to live? Because if it's that, you could be showing me fields all day and I'd have no clue whether you were making any of it up.'

'It's a real giant alright. Carved into the hillside with his great big willy hanging out.'

Emma laughed. 'Seriously? This I've got to see!'

'So how are you feeling about the hotel?' Aidan asked as they began to walk back to the village. Twilight had turned the sky pink and the hedgerows had that intense evening scent, and Emma wondered how they were going to get to Cerne Abbas before it went dark. But he seemed so keen that she didn't want to burst his bubble so said nothing. 'Happy with how it's going?'

'I suppose so,' she said. 'Are you? You're the expert.'

'I don't think it's been too bad so far – I've certainly been on worse builds.'

'I'm not sure that fills me with confidence but I'll take it. It's exhausting, I know that much.'

'I think it's coming along nicely. There – does that make you feel better?'

'I wish it did. All I see when I look at it is work that will never end. We're there every day and we never stop, and when we go home it looks exactly the same. It's disheartening sometimes.'

'It'll come together all at once – at least it will look that way. One day, in the not-too-distant future you'll get the exciting stuff in. Right now it's all invisible but necessary work – foundations and walls and stuff. But when we start seeing changes at the end of every day, that will be encouraging for you, I promise. You'll forget this depressing phase soon enough.'

She nodded. 'I suppose you're right. Do all your clients complain as much as this?'

'God no! You're an absolute pain.'

She gave a broad smile, her gaze on the ground as they kept pace beside each other. 'I know it'll be better soon and I know these things take time. I suppose I'm just nervous. I've never taken a risk like this before; it's so out of my comfort zone I still can't quite believe I made the decision to come to Honeymoon at all.'

'Well I'm glad you did.'

She looked up to see him gazing warmly at her. His hand brushed against hers as they walked and for the briefest second she was seized by the maddest impulse to reach for it and grab hold.

But as they reached the first lamp post on the road into Honeymoon, the thought was pushed out of her mind as a poster pinned to it caught her eye.

'Seems not everyone is glad I'm here,' she said slowly, going over to take a closer look.

Cars!
Pollution!
Litter!
Noise!
Queues in shops!
Swearing louts!
Fights in the pub!
Rising crime!
If you don't want these things in our village, take action!
Say no to Honeymoon Station Hotel!

Aidan ripped it down. 'Sid… It's got to be; it has his outraged fingerprints all over it.'

Emma said nothing, but the conviction that if Sid felt like this then lots of others must do too grew in her. She'd feared it since they'd arrived but had been soothed by Tia and Aidan and Blake, and seeing little outright evidence apart from Sid's grumbling, she'd persuaded herself that she was being paranoid. But this poster was no paranoia and, as far as she could logically tell, his couldn't be the only voice of dissent. Even Darcie had told her how difficult life had been for her and Tariq when they'd first taken on the café, and that was the kind of business that would hardly change the nature of life in the village at all. There was no denying it, the hotel would change Honeymoon, for good or bad, and she could see why some people might not like that.

'I'm going to see him,' Aidan continued, rolling the poster into a tight tube as they began to walk again.

'Don't. We don't know it's him for sure and I don't want to make things worse even if it is. It's just one poster.'

'Make that two,' Aidan said, striding over to another lamp post and tearing a second poster from it. 'Littering,' he said, crushing this one, 'I'll show him littering! I'm going to shove these up his—'

'He's just trying to protect his home,' Emma cut in.

'It's not for him to say who does or doesn't live here or how they earn a crust. Don't be swayed by this, Emma – there are plenty in the village who welcome the hotel. There'll be jobs for a start – everyone's got to make a living. And Sid's attitude proves we need new blood in the village. He'd be more at home in that Iron Age dwelling we've just come from than here in the village with his stupid phobias of out-of-towners.'

'It doesn't matter. He's still entitled to his opinion. Maybe I should try to talk to him properly. I could ask him to meet me for lunch and explain exactly what we're planning and try to put his mind at ease. When he sees it's really quite a tiny hotel, he might—' She spotted another poster and went to take it down. She could try, but it looked as if he was going to take some convincing.

'He must have his own bloody printing press.' Aidan frowned at the poster she'd just removed. 'Where the hell did he get all these copies done? Certainly not in the village. Unless… the only person I know with a photocopy service is Nell, but she wouldn't let him make these.'

'Unless she didn't know what they were for?'

'I'd say it's pretty bloody obvious what they're for.'

'But Nell wouldn't…' Emma's dread deepened. Had they really gauged the mood so very badly? Could it be that even the people they considered allies weren't as keen to have them in the village as they'd imagined? If Sid had recruited Nell to his cause – Nell who'd shown such pride in her family connections to the station and seemed so enthusiastic to see it beautiful again – then this was a battle Emma and Tia were sure to lose. If Nell had turned against them, they had no hope with anyone.

It took less than five silent minutes to get to the shop, five minutes too long for Emma, whose thoughts were maudlin and pessimistic and not at all constructive.

Despite the lateness of the hour, the door was open and Nell was behind the counter. She greeted them with a bright enough smile.

'Where are you two off to tonight?' she asked.

'Nowhere,' Aidan said tightly. 'Not until we sort this out.'

He slapped the poster Emma had taken down onto the counter. Nell's smile faded as she read it.

'Oh… that's not good.'

'They're all over the village,' Aidan said.

'I expect it's something to do with Sid.'

Aidan gave a brusque nod. 'That's what we thought. But where did he get all the copies done?'

Nell's complexion suddenly lost half a dozen shades.

'Oh, Aidan, I never… He came in wanting to use the copier but I didn't stay with him. I never saw what it was… I'm ever so sorry – you know I would never—'

'We know,' Emma said gently, relief flooding through her. How could she have thought for one second that Nell would betray them like that? She'd been nothing but kind since they'd arrived in Honeymoon, and any fool could see she was a generous, tolerant person. Emma's heart went out to the owner of Honeymoon's everything shop – she seemed ready to burst into tears.

'Emma, my love.' Nell looked at her with watery eyes. 'I'm mortified. I should have known that snake was up to something when he wanted to do his copies all by himself! I should have looked what he was up to!'

'Don't be,' Emma said. 'You mustn't blame yourself. At least we know now who's responsible. I'm going to talk to him.'

'Give him a piece of your mind,' Nell said.

'I think I might get a better result trying to reassure him,' Emma said.

'There's no knocking any sense into a head that thick,' Nell said, drying her eyes.

'I'll be happy to try,' Aidan said grimly.

'He's an old man,' Emma said. 'You can't go around scaring him.'

'Can't I? That's exactly what he's trying to do to you.'

'Tia and I will talk to him – I think it will be better coming from us; at least, we can try. After all, we're the people he has an issue with and we need to convince him to trust us. I'll go round and see him tomorrow. Nell…' She turned to the shopkeeper. 'Do you know which cottage is his?'

'Hawthorne,' she said. 'Can't miss it; has a big side garden where the others don't.'

'You won't need to find his house,' Aidan said, nodding at the entrance. 'He's here now.'

Sid walked in, and as soon as he saw Emma his lip curled. She had to be impressed by his spirit – for such an old man his apparent loathing of her must have been taking quite a bit of energy.

'Oh, it's you,' he said directly to her, not even acknowledging that there was anyone else in the shop.

'Yes,' Emma said as calmly as she could. She held up a poster. 'Are these yours?'

'I don't have to explain myself to you,' he said coldly.

Aidan stepped forward. 'Well maybe you can explain yourself to me.'

'I'm a British citizen – I have a right to object when I don't like something,' Sid replied. 'It's called freedom of speech.'

'In that case,' Aidan said, 'Emma has a right to settle where she likes and to make a living there as she sees fit. You're so fond of reminding everyone of your rights as a British citizen – aren't they the most important of all?'

'Now, lads—' Nell began, but Sid cut across her.

'Respect for traditions, respect for your elders, decency, honour… those are British values that nobody around here seems to care about anymore.' He jabbed a finger at Aidan. 'Especially you and your brother, up and down the village chasing any bit of new skirt that arrives, helping them destroy the place I love! If this village is not to your liking the way it is, why don't you get out!'

Sid looked so furious Emma wondered if the effort might finally finish him off.

'Sidney Charteris!' Nell shouted. 'If you're going to insult my customers then you're barred from my shop – and I really mean it this time!'

'I'm one of your customers!' he yelled back.

'Not anymore you're not! Out!'

He looked as if he might try to have the last word. But then he stepped back towards the door. 'I'm going! I wouldn't shop here if it was the last place on earth! Everything's overpriced and out of date anyway!'

He slammed the door as he left.

'Out of date and overpriced,' Nell huffed after his retreating figure. 'Let's see how you like having to go miles out to the supermarket!'

Emma turned to her, vaguely alarmed at what she'd just seen – partly because she was worried that Nell might have another angina attack, and partly because it might have just made everything twenty times worse with Sid. 'You're not really going to bar him, are you? Not on my account?'

'Of course not,' Nell said gruffly. 'He'd starve if I did because he'd never set foot in the supermarket. But I'll let him stew for a day so he gets the message that he needs to behave when he's in here. And I'm sorry about the posters… That's the last time I let him use the copier.'

'I'm sorry you had to have all this in your shop. I feel as if we've caused so much trouble since we arrived, I wouldn't be surprised if people started to feel fed up with having us here.'

'Nonsense!' Nell said. 'It's certain people causing the trouble, not you. Personally I think Honeymoon needs your hotel – there's no work hereabouts and the hotel will at least be something to help with that. Sid thinks driving you away will protect the village but he's doing the opposite. If everyone keeps moving away to find jobs there'll be no village left.'

'Put that to him when you meet up with him,' Aidan said.

'Meet up with him?' Emma said, looking faintly alarmed now. 'I don't think he'll come to meet up with us now, not after what's just happened.'

'Give him a couple of days,' Nell said. 'I'll talk to him when I see him again, if that helps.'

'Thanks.' Emma gave Nell a grateful smile. Then she looked at Aidan. Their buoyant mood had disappeared and maybe it was time to call it a night; she could see in his face that he felt it too.

'Do you mind if we give the giant willy man a miss tonight?' she asked. 'I ought to go and find the rest of these posters before I turn in, and we've got an early start in the morning again.'

'I'll help you—' he began, but she stopped him.

'I've already dragged you in and pitted you against your neighbour.'

'What – Sid? He's had a bee in his bonnet about one thing or another for as long as I can remember; I wouldn't worry about him.'

'Even so… I can manage. I'll see you tomorrow?'

'Of course you will,' he said. 'Now that I know Sid really hates me working on the hotel I'll enjoy it twice as much.'

Emma tried to smile at his joke, but it was hard to find the energy. The evening had started full of promise but had ended like a deflated balloon. And Sid was just one obstacle. Even if they won him round there was a mountain of other worries, and she was beginning to wonder if they'd ever conquer it.

Chapter Twenty

The following morning the skies were low and grey, and rain poured steadily in heavy sheets, but Emma didn't take much notice, and there was no change in the plans to start work on the hotel as usual. Tia had woken late and so they'd decided Emma would go ahead to meet Aidan and Blake on site. While she grabbed a quick breakfast and filled Tia in on her encounter with Sid, she tried not to show her impatience. She was annoyed that she'd had to deal with it on her own (or at least without the one other person it affected as greatly as her), and she was equally vexed by the fact that if Tia had got home from the pub at a decent hour she wouldn't have been running late now. At least Tia had taken on board Emma's plea for less noise; if she'd brought Blake home after the pub, Emma hadn't heard anything.

When she got to the station, Aidan and Blake were already there, deep in conversation. Aidan turned to her with a worried look as she bid them good morning.

'I think we had a fair bit of rain overnight,' he said.

Emma immediately saw what he meant. Everywhere they'd worked, digging to shore up foundations or lay pipes or terraces, was now waterlogged, swirling with mud and pools of filthy water.

'Normally the vegetation would catch most of it,' Blake said. 'But of course we've pulled a lot up and this soil must be a lot less porous than we thought, so the water is just sitting on the surface and not going anywhere.'

'It's going to make it difficult to do a lot today. Equipment is going to get soaked or start sinking into the mud.'

Emma stared at him. 'But we can't waste a whole day! And what if it's still not dry tomorrow?'

'We could perhaps do a few jobs inside the building,' Aidan said doubtfully, 'but with the roof still incomplete even that's going to be difficult. Whatever we do might end up wet and that means we'd just have to do it all over again at some point.'

'I'd say take a day off,' Blake put in. 'We could always do an extra few hours at the weekend to make up the time.'

'Take a day off?' Emma said. 'For rain? We've worked in rain before.'

'Not this heavy,' Blake said.

Emma shook her head. 'I can't just stand around.'

'You could use the time to go and see Sid,' Aidan said.

'I'll bet this is his doing,' she said darkly. 'Bloody rain spell or something.'

'I don't think he's that clever,' Blake said.

Emma turned to Aidan. 'After yesterday's run-in I don't think it's wise to see him today. I think it needs a bit of breathing space.'

He shrugged. 'It was just a thought.'

'A sensible one but I'd rather stay here and see what I can get done, rain or not. Every day is too precious to waste. We're already running behind – every day we add to that is way more stress than I need.'

'There were always going to be days when the elements were against us,' Blake said. 'That's the thing about working outside.'

Emma looked at the swirling vortex of mud that currently occupied the space where their terrace would eventually be. 'It's an absolute mess.'

'It looks worse than it is – it'll dry out soon enough. A good day of sun and it will be gone. We'll work to put something back in the ground as soon as we can so it doesn't happen again. Even a bit of grass and a few shrubs will help. We were probably a bit too efficient at clearing it in the first place.'

'You mean I was,' Emma said miserably. 'You can say it – I was responsible for most of the ripping out.'

'I'm just as much to blame,' Aidan said. 'If I'd foreseen problems I would have stopped you.'

Blake glanced up at the leaden sky. 'I don't think you're getting any sun today.'

'The forecast isn't too bad for the rest of the week though,' Aidan said. He gave Emma a reassuring smile, though she was finding it very hard to be reassured. 'I vote we head to the café for now. We might not be able to do much here but we could put our heads together over a coffee and try to come up with a workaround that would enable us to do at least something with the rest of the day.'

'What sort of workaround?' Emma asked.

He shrugged. 'There must be something. And even if we don't come up with something, it might be a good opportunity to discuss concerns, things you want to change, things you want to implement later on in the build that we might need to know about now. At least it won't feel like a total waste of the day either way.'

'You mean like the wood panelling?' Emma asked, coming round to the idea now. Aidan's suggestion didn't exactly make her happy but she didn't have anything better. 'We were going to discuss hiring that specialist. I suppose we might be close enough now to that stage to figure out whether we're going to – we could do that at the café. Tia could meet us there as soon as she's ready.'

Blake frowned slightly. 'You mean Hank?'

'Yes,' Emma said. 'That's his name, isn't it?'

'But Hank's already booked… I did it last week.'

'What?'

'Tia told me to get him. She said it was all sorted.'

'But we never… Ugh!'

Emma spun round and began to march back through the clearing in the direction of the village.

'What's wrong?' Blake called after her.

'What do you think?'

A moment later Aidan was walking alongside her. 'I'm guessing you didn't agree on Hank.'

'No,' Emma said through gritted teeth, 'we didn't.'

'And Tia took it upon herself to get him anyway?'

'It looks that way.'

'That's not good. Want me to put him on hold until you sort it?'

'I want…' Emma fumed, 'I want for my business partner to start treating me like one!' She drew a sharp breath. 'Look, I'm sorry, I shouldn't be taking this out on you. It's not your fault, and I realise it makes things awkward for you and Blake.'

'I doubt she's doing it on purpose.'

'I know. I know Tia and I'm sure she's not. She probably thinks she's being super efficient and saving me the stress. She'll be used to making that sort of decision too, from when she ran the gym. She won't realise it's different for me – scarier. I can't just snap my fingers and say yes or no.'

She sighed, all the anger draining from her to be replaced by a sense of defeated frustration. 'I'm beginning to wonder if I've made a huge mistake. I've been feeling like that for a while but I kept going… But Sid doesn't want us here – probably others too who are too scared to say. Tia's missing half the time, and when she's around she's making decisions on my behalf, and even this rain today… I don't know, call me melodramatic but it feels like the universe is trying to tell me to go home.'

'Melodramatic.'

She glanced across to see Aidan smiling slightly. Not to mock, but to encourage.

'It's just rain,' he said. 'It's really as simple as that. As for Sid, he'll come round. Tia just needs to understand your point of view and get used to being part of a team. The bit about going home… well, I thought this was home for you now.'

'I did too,' she said. 'Maybe I was mistaken.'

He pulled out his phone and tapped a brief message.

'Come on,' he said, putting it away again, 'let's go to the café. I've asked Blake to go and get Tia. If you feel we've achieved nothing there when we're done then you don't have to pay us for today. How's that sound?'

She couldn't help but smile, though she felt far from certain about anything he'd said.

'Alright then,' she said. 'I don't suppose I can argue with that.'

'I wasn't expecting you at this time of the day,' Darcie said as they walked in. 'Not that I mind one bit. What can I do for you? Fancied a takeaway coffee, did you?'

'Actually we're hoping to make you our office today,' Aidan said. 'We promise to order lots of tea and sandwiches.'

'Of course!' Darcie beamed at him. 'It'll make us look full – nothing wrong with a bit of positive publicity! I hate it when the place is empty; it stresses me out. I get scared we'll never have another customer again. Tariq says I'm daft but I can't help it.'

'Right now I can totally understand where you're coming from,' Emma said. 'I'm stressed we'll never even have a finished hotel to be empty at all.'

'Oh dear,' Darcie said as they made their way to a table. 'That bad?'

'It's just the weather messing us around,' Aidan said. He pulled out a chair for Emma to sit. 'As soon as everything dries out we can crack on again.'

'At least we never had that to contend with,' Darcie said. 'Oh, Emma, I do feel for you.'

'Don't,' Aidan said. 'She's being melodramatic—' He shushed her objection. 'You said I could call you that – remember?'

'Hmm.' Emma took a menu from Darcie. 'I said you could call me that but it's a one-time only deal.'

He laughed. 'OK. I'll owe you one in return then.' He shook his head at the menu Darcie offered him. 'I know exactly what I'm having.' He threw an impish look at Emma. 'We're here and not in any particular rush until it stops raining… we might as well treat ourselves to a full English.'

Emma narrowed her eyes. 'I think you're enjoying this.'

'Of course I'm not!' he said with mock offence. 'I'm just making the best of a bad job. And you can't complain because if we don't get any work done today you won't pay us. That's not going to happen though. We're going to get loads done and it'll be a nice break from being on site for you.'

'I suppose in that case I could have breakfast,' she replied, being persuaded against her better judgement. 'I expect Tia will want one when she gets here too; soak up last night's booze.'

'Probably.' Aidan looked up at Darcie and she nodded.

'Don't worry – I got it. And you want teas too?'

'Thanks, Darcie.'

Emma watched her go to the kitchen and then turned back to Aidan. 'At least one of us has slotted right into village life without a fuss.'

'Darcie?'

'No, Tia. I'll bet she spends more time in your local than your locals do.'

He was thoughtful for a moment. 'You know, in her own way I think she's struggling to adapt and fit in just like you are. The difference is she goes to the pub to try and find that connection.'

'Maybe I should start going to the pub then.'

'Maybe you should. Come tonight with me. And before you turn me down, I'm asking you as a friend, just to meet a few more of the villagers.'

At that moment the café door burst open.

'Guess who I found on our doorstep!' Tia cried. 'They say they're your aunt and uncle but I have no clue!'

Emma frowned. 'Tia, are you still drunk?' But then she leapt up from her chair with a squeal as Patricia and Dominic followed Tia into the café. She rushed to embrace them both. 'What are you doing here?'

'It's a long story,' Patricia said. 'But the gist is we decided it was high time we had a holiday, and where better to go than Dorset where our favourite niece is.'

'It's lucky they caught me,' Tia said. 'I was just on my way out. A minute later and I'd have left.'

'We would have phoned ahead,' Patricia said to Emma, 'but we wanted to surprise you. And before you start fussing about where we're going to stay, we're passing through on our way to Bournemouth so you don't have to worry about looking after us. We just thought we'd take a quick detour to see how you're doing, but we'll be on our way in an hour or so and you can get on with your work.'

Emma smiled. 'Well you picked a good bad day. The ground at the site is pretty waterlogged so I don't think we'll be doing much there anyway.'

'That's a shame,' Dominic said. 'Must be frustrating.'

Emma shrugged. 'These things happen – it's just rain.'

Aidan shot her a knowing look and she smiled at him. Then he got up.

'Listen, I'll clear off for a bit and let you talk to your family.'

'Oh no,' Patricia said, 'you don't have to go on our account—'

'I'm sure you'd like to catch up.' Aidan looked at Emma. 'I'll be back later – say about twelve? We'll see what the weather's doing then and decide if it's worth trying to get anything done on site or if we'll have to leave it for today.'

'What about breakfast? Darcie will have started it…'

'I'll go and ask her to put it in a takeout box.' He grinned. 'And if you don't want yours now I can absolutely eat two.'

Emma laughed. 'Take them both – give one to Blake or something. I was only having it because you were and it's really very bad for me so you're doing me a favour.'

'That's exactly what I'm doing,' he said, his grin spreading.

'I can take that off your hands,' Tia said. She looked at Aidan. 'You and Blake can come back to the cottage for a while and we'll eat there.'

They disappeared into the back to find Darcie, and Emma barely had time to smile at her aunt and uncle and ask them about their drive down when they emerged again with their food.

'She'd nearly finished cooking it,' Aidan said in reply to Emma's silent query.

'Ah,' Emma said. 'Well enjoy.'

'We will,' Tia said. She shifted her attention to Patricia and Dominic. 'It was lovely to meet you.'

'You too,' Patricia said. 'Thank you for bringing us here, and we look forward to staying in your hotel one day.'

'We look forward to having you,' Tia replied. She turned to Aidan. 'Let's go and find your brother.'

He nodded before bidding farewell to Patricia and Dominic. 'Nice to meet you, Emma's aunt and uncle.' He glanced at Emma. 'See you later?'

'You will; I'll call you.'

They watched Aidan and Tia leave.

'They both seem very nice,' Patricia said. 'Who's the man?'

'Aidan… one of our contractors.'

'Oh?' Patricia asked with interest. 'Is that the one she's dating?'

'No, Tia's going out with his brother.'

'He's very friendly... You have quite an informal working relationship then?'

'It's kind of how things are round here,' Emma said.

Darcie came through from the kitchen, drying her hands.

'Hello,' she said, sounding suddenly shy. Emma had noticed she was always like that when confronted with an unfamiliar face, and often wondered what had possessed her to take on an occupation that required a far more outgoing personality. If they did get the increase in custom from hotel guests they were hoping for, Darcie would be in a permanent state of stress from dealing with all the new faces. 'Aidan said...'

'This is my aunt and uncle,' Emma said. 'Patricia, Dominic... this is Darcie, who makes the best coffee and walnut cake in Dorset.'

Darcie blushed. 'Actually my cousin makes it but thank you. Can I get you anything?'

'I wouldn't mind a slice of that famed cake,' Dominic said cheerfully.

'Me too,' Patricia said. 'A pot of tea wouldn't go amiss either.'

'Make that three teas and three cakes,' Emma said. 'Not exactly a full breakfast but just as nice.'

'Coming up,' Darcie said before going to the counter to get their order.

'Now then,' Patricia said to Emma, 'I know you'll be fretting about everyone at home so let's get that out of the way. They're all fine, including me and your uncle. Your dad says you call him almost every day and you're to stop because he's not totally useless and he can fend for himself. Of course, I wasn't supposed to tell you that. That said, I do check on him most days myself anyway and I can confirm he's quite useless – but we'll let that slide because he's managing to survive quite nicely in his own rubbish way.'

Emma gave a broad smile. 'It's so good to see you – such a lovely surprise.'

'We couldn't be in this corner of the world and not come to see you. Although, you took a bit of finding this morning. We went to your cottage first but there was no reply. Then we went to the post office to see if we could find out where the station is, thinking you might be there, but it hadn't opened yet. So then we were going to text you – which would have ruined the surprise, of course – but we saw your friend coming out of your house. She said she must have been in the shower when we knocked, and she brought us here. She is so lovely, by the way. Not a bit spoilt like we expected her to be.'

'She's very sweet, although she's more of a handful than I remember her being at school.'

'I can imagine,' Patricia said. 'I very much get that impression from talking to her today. Very excitable.'

'But it's going well?' Dominic asked. 'You're happy?'

'Of course,' Emma said, trying not to think about how wretched she'd felt that morning and how she'd been thinking more and more about home in Wrenwick and how she felt like this project was bigger than she could cope with and she was convinced she was going to fail and lose all her dad's money. 'It's going great,' she said. 'If you want I'll take you to have a look.'

'We'd love that,' Dominic said. 'But it won't hold you up?'

'There's not much going to happen today,' Emma said, and she couldn't mask the tone of defeat she'd been trying so hard to hold back. Her aunt and uncle exchanged a worried look that she didn't miss. 'I'm

OK,' she added. 'It's just taking so much longer than we'd planned. Honestly. I don't think we'll be ready this year, let alone this summer.'

'These things always take longer than you think they will,' Dominic said sagely.

Darcie came back with their drinks and cake.

'Now this is what I call breakfast!' Dominic accepted his slice from Darcie with a smile.

'I'd say we're closer to elevenses now,' Patricia said.

Emma glanced at the clock with a vague agreement, though it only reminded her of how much of the day they'd already wasted. It was lovely to see her aunt and uncle, of course, but it was hard to relax and enjoy their company knowing how much work she had to do, that every lost hour let the schedule slip further and further out of reach. Later, she was going to have to talk to Tia about putting in some evenings and weekends on the site, and she knew Tia wasn't going to like that one bit if it stopped her from seeing Blake.

'Your friend could have stayed a while,' Patricia said. 'It would have been nice to get to know her.'

Emma gave Darcie a grateful smile and watched for a moment as she returned to the counter to give them some privacy. 'I expect she's keen to get some work done. It's very frustrating having the ground flooded and all this stupid rain.'

'I expect it'll dry out soon enough,' Dominic said.

'That's what Aidan told me this morning.'

'These men…' Patricia poured some tea from the pot. 'They're reliable? You had trouble with your first ones, didn't you?'

'Oh, Blake and Aidan aren't like that at all – they're really good,' Emma said. 'They're local too, so they're always close at hand and know the area well.'

'Hmm, sounds like they're quite a find.'

Emma nodded. 'They are.'

'I suppose they've got family here then?' Patricia asked.

'Yes,' Emma said. 'Honeymoon born and bred. I haven't met their parents… I suppose it might be a bit weird if I asked. They just work for us after all.'

'Perhaps,' Patricia agreed. 'No children?'

'No, they're both single… though, of course, Blake isn't technically single now.'

'It does make things easier when there are no ties – they can concentrate on the job and give you more time if you need it,' Dominic said.

'I suppose so…' Emma stirred some milk into her tea.

'So you haven't met anyone since you've been here?' her aunt asked.

Emma frowned slightly. 'You know I would have told you – I tell you everything.'

'I know, I know…' Patricia smiled slightly. 'But still, I don't expect you to and I was just asking… So no burly Dorset farmer has taken your fancy?'

Emma laughed. 'No.'

'Well you'll be pleased to know that Dougie is out of your hair for good now.'

Emma looked up sharply, fork dug in her cake.

Patricia nodded. 'He's moved in with an older lady… I think she's a good ten years older actually. Two kiddies tagging along, so I don't imagine he'll be spending his days at the fishing lake for much longer. He'll have to get a job now too, I expect.'

'We all have to grow up eventually,' Dominic said. 'Even your Peter Pan.'

If they'd been trying to make Emma feel better about Dougie they'd failed in a spectacular fashion. Far from better, she felt worse. She'd been doing well, trying to keep Dougie from her thoughts and succeeding most of the time, but now he consumed them once more.

It hadn't taken him long to move on, and already it sounded like he was willing to give more to this new woman than he ever had to her. Had that been her fault? Was there something about her that said: *Please use me – please take advantage of me because I don't matter*? What had this new woman got over Emma? Dougie had told Emma he'd loved her – had he ever even meant it once? They'd been engaged – had that meant nothing to him either? If she couldn't even trust the truth of that, how could she trust anything?

'That's good,' was all she could say. 'I'm glad he's sorting himself out.'

'You're better off without him,' Dominic said, patting her hand. 'He's someone else's worry now.'

Patricia regarded her steadily for a moment. 'Perhaps I shouldn't have told you about that…?'

Emma forced a smile. 'It's fine. It doesn't bother me what he's doing – why would it? I left him; why would I care what he does now? I can be a grown-up about it and wish him well… I'm glad he's settling down with this woman. She might be a better influence than I ever was.'

'But you were very fond of him,' Patricia said gently.

Fond. Emma supposed she had been fond of him. But you were fond of a dog that constantly seemed to find mud to roll in whenever you took it out, or a naughty little cousin who always got crumbs on your sofa, or a forgetful great-aunt who embarrassed you in front of your friends. You shouldn't be fond of the man you're supposed to be marrying; it ought to be so much bigger than that.

Looking back, she and Dougie had never been suited. They'd had nothing in common, no shared goals or dreams, and should never even have been together, let alone engaged. She'd been lonely and lacking in self-esteem; he'd been lazy, homing in on a handy opportunity, and somehow, for a while, that had been enough for them both. She had to wonder now what had possessed her to think it could work, and thanked her stars that they'd never got as far as marriage after all.

'This cake is good,' Dominic said. 'I could move to Dorset just for this cake.'

'Darcie's are the best,' Emma said, shaking herself from her destructive musings. They were serving no purpose and were ruining her time with her aunt and uncle and she wasn't going to let them. Dougie was welcome to his woman and her kids, and good riddance.

'That's the young girl?' Dominic asked.

'Actually, I think she's about twenty-six, but she looks as if she could still be at school, doesn't she?' Emma sipped at her tea.

'I thought she was the Saturday girl when she came to serve us,' Dominic said.

'It's not Saturday,' Patricia said, and Emma laughed.

Dominic pushed his plate away and patted his belly. 'Lovely – just the ticket after a long drive.'

'You must have started out early,' Emma said.

Patricia rolled her eyes. 'Don't we always? It's your uncle's obsession with being on the road before anyone else wakes up.'

Emma laughed. 'Oh yes. I remember those day trips well – getting up almost before we'd gone to bed.'

'It's lucky for you,' Dominic replied, looking faintly wounded at Emma's remark. 'It means we're here nice and early so we don't hold you up.'

'True,' Emma said. 'Thanks for thinking of me.'

'I wouldn't mind if he thought of *me* once in a while,' Patricia said. 'I don't want to be dragged out of bed with the lark.'

Dominic drank the last of his tea and looked expectantly at his wife. 'I'm done. Ready to move on when everyone else is.'

'Give me a minute to finish,' Patricia huffed.

'Don't rush on my account,' Emma said. 'I'm happy to wait. I'll warn you, though, the building site is very muddy… If you have a pair of waders in your luggage, now might be the time to get them out.'

Emma managed to lay some spare plywood down, and although the ground was boggy, there was at least a path through to the entrance of the station house. The rain had eased off too, and she was hopeful it might mean they could resume work once Patricia and Dominic had gone. For now, she was excited to show them around, the sour mood she'd started the day with chased away by their arrival and the chance to make them proud. She'd always been the disappointing niece, the non-achiever, while Elise had flown high. Just for once, maybe Emma could be the achiever, and her aunt and uncle might leave today approving of what she was doing here.

'It's smaller than I thought,' Patricia said. 'It looks bigger in the photographs.'

'It's only a rural station,' Dominic said. 'It was never going to be big.'

'We're going to get some train carriages as extra rooms,' Emma said. 'They'll be parked up alongside the main building where the track used to run. Tia's been trying to source some.'

'They'll be popular,' Dominic said. 'People love those; you see them on travel shows all the time.'

'I hope so,' Emma said. 'Want to go inside?'

'If we can,' he said.

'Of course you can.'

Emma smiled and led them across the little plywood bridge she'd laid. It wobbled, and mud bubbled up around the edges, but it held firm. The front door had been taken off to protect it while they did structural work. It was in the corner of the room standing against a wall, and when they were able to put it back up it would be stripped and repainted. Emma frowned slightly as she walked in and she noticed water running down it from a gap in the roof, but there was little she could do about it right now. That wasn't the only gap in the roof or the only leak. She tried not to think about what damage the water might be doing.

'What do you think?' she asked as she ushered Patricia and Dominic in through the yawning entrance.

Patricia scanned the room. 'There's not much in here.'

'Well no,' Emma admitted. 'We had to take the furniture and a lot of the old fittings out for now. It's in storage until we can sort what's good to keep. We've got gorgeous rosewood counters and tables – we're just hoping we'll be able to clean them up and make them good as new again so we can put originals back in. It'll be cheaper to do that too.'

'I know you said you were a bit behind,' Patricia said, 'but I thought you'd be further along than this… When did you say you wanted to open?'

Emma hesitated. 'Maybe autumn… with a fair wind and a good sail,' she added, repeating a phrase Aidan had used.

'It's not far off autumn now,' Dominic said, wandering over to gaze up at the rafters where a pigeon was huddled.

'You don't think we're going to be anywhere near ready?' Emma asked.

'I didn't mean that,' he replied.

'But you were thinking it?'

'Of course not…'

'I think what Dominic is trying to say,' Patricia cut in, 'is that it just looks very far off to us. But then, what do we know? We're not builders. I expect it's only because it's empty. It's hard to imagine it finished when there's just a shell here. Will there be much trade when you open? Won't you have missed peak season?'

'Well yes…' Emma said. 'But we're going to try for some Christmas bookings to see us through. We thought we might put on special events and Christmas dinner and things like that. It means I won't be able to come home for Christmas of course, but…'

'I'm sure your dad will understand, and he can come to us for Christmas lunch,' Patricia said. 'Who's going to cook it for your guests? Surely not you?'

'Thank you for that endorsement of my cooking,' Emma said with a wry smile. 'We'll have to find a chef, I expect.'

'Do you have many chefs round here?'

'I've no idea,' Emma said, realising that it hadn't even occurred to her to check how she might go about employing a chef for their hotel at all.

'I expect there will be someone willing to travel,' Patricia said soothingly.

'And then you'll be empty after Christmas?' Dominic asked. 'Until the summer?'

'I suppose we might not be very full in low season,' Emma said.

Dominic was thoughtful for a moment. Emma watched him walk the space. 'If you needed to loan some money to keep going we might be able to spare a little,' he said, glancing at his wife, who nodded her agreement.

There was a peculiar, crashing feeling in Emma's stomach as the realisation of what he was saying hit her. If he'd hoped to reassure her with his offer, it'd had the opposite effect. They both clearly thought things were so bad she'd need bailing out. They didn't think the hotel would be ready on time. They didn't think she knew what she was doing. Now that they'd seen it with their own eyes they thought it was a mistake – they thought this enterprise was doomed to failure.

What if they were right? What if she did fail? What if she lost all her dad's money? What kind of madness had made her believe she could do this?

Panic bubbled up in her. Patricia exchanged another loaded glance with Dominic.

'We didn't mean to infer you couldn't manage,' she said. 'We only meant just in case… If things were worse than expected…'

'Yes, I know,' Emma said quietly. She drew a breath. 'It's kind of you, thanks, but… Anyway… do you want to see where we're going to put the kitchens?'

'Yes, that would be lovely,' Patricia said, and Emma began to walk them to the area where the café had once been filled with travellers bidding farewells to their loved ones over tea served in Wedgwood china. Once, the idea of that would have made Emma proud and excited. When they'd first arrived, that enthusiasm for the station's romantic past had had her waxing lyrical to anyone who'd listen. But now, her heart just wasn't in it, and she didn't even mention the travellers or the Wedgwood china. She looked at the bare brick walls and the concrete floors stripped of their beautiful tiles and a roof that still showed patches of sky and she realised that her aunt and uncle were right. They were never going to be open on time at this rate. And if it dragged out much longer, they were going to run out of money and Honeymoon Station Hotel might never open at all.

Chapter Twenty-One

By the time Emma had seen her aunt and uncle on their way, having spent the morning looking as bright and optimistic as she could manage for their benefit, she was emotionally spent. She'd arranged to meet up with Aidan, Blake and Tia back at the café, feeling as despondent and heartsick as at any time since her split with Dougie. She'd loved seeing Patricia and Dominic, of course, and was happy they'd made the effort, but almost everything they'd said had made the bad mood she'd already been in worse, even if they hadn't meant to.

'Hello!' Tia said as she walked in. 'I thought you might have brought your aunt and uncle back to say hello.'

'Oh, they had to get on,' Emma said, although that wasn't strictly true. They'd been too polite to ask if she had more time to spare, wondering aloud if they were holding her up, and she'd been so dejected that she hadn't corrected them. So they'd gone off to their holiday chalet with a kiss and a promise to see her on the way back if she had time. She'd felt rude and inconsiderate afterwards, regretting that she hadn't made more of an effort, but they were on their way and the damage had been done now, and she just hoped they wouldn't be too hurt.

'That's such a shame,' Tia said. 'Well I expect they'll come to stay lots at the hotel when it's open.'

'You mean in 2090?' Emma asked.

Tia exchanged a puzzled look with Aidan and Blake.

'Is everything alright?' Aidan asked. 'You're still upset about the flooding on the site?'

'No.' Emma sat down at their table. 'I mean, that's not helping but I've accepted that there's nothing we can do about it.'

'Emma… about Hank…' Tia began, and for the first time since they'd come to Honeymoon together, she sounded nervous.

Emma glanced between the three of them. Aidan and Blake had obviously filled Tia in on her reaction to the news they'd booked their timber specialist without her agreement.

'Forget it,' she said. 'It's done. We can't very well cancel him now because if we decide we do need him further down the line he'd probably turn us down for messing him around in the first place.'

'But I'm sorry,' Tia said. 'I should have—'

'It's fine,' Emma said. 'Can we move on? We've got other things to talk about, haven't we? I'm going to get a coffee.' She got up. 'Darcie?' she called at the unmanned counter, assuming that the café owner was in the kitchen out back. 'I don't suppose you could make me a drink?'

'She's on the phone to her cousin,' Aidan said from behind her. Emma turned to him. 'Tariq's at the wholesalers. I told her I'd keep an eye out for customers. I know where everything is – I'll make you a coffee.'

'Thanks.'

'What did your aunt and uncle have to say?' he asked as he busied himself behind Darcie's counter. 'It was good to see them, I expect?'

'Yes,' Emma said in a dull voice.

'Hmm… I'd have thought you'd sound happier than—'

'I am happy,' she cut in, in a tone that suggested she'd never been happy in her life and didn't even know what the word meant.

'OK…' Aidan said slowly. 'I'm glad we got that cleared up. You know, if you're getting stressed about the build you can talk to us. Blake and I would do our best to put your mind at ease without bulling you. We've always been transparent and honest with you, haven't we?'

'Yes, of course.'

'So do you want to tell me what's eating you?'

'It's just… hard to boil down into a worry I can express.'

'Sounds strange, but go on – try.'

'It feels like a big cloud of worry, like a spaghetti plate of worry where I can't separate the strands, and even if I could some of the spaghetti has stuck together in big clumps.'

'It's getting stranger, I'm afraid.'

Emma let out a sigh, her eyes filling with tears that made her feel stupid and childish but that she couldn't hold back.

'Hey…' he said gently. 'It will come good in the end. I've seen a million jobs like this and they always look like a mess before they start to look amazing. It's going to be fine.'

'I know,' she said.

He placed a cup down on the counter for her. 'Do you?' he asked, leaning close to hold her gaze.

She paused, looking into his eyes, an alternate universe where everything was good and right and safe. How she longed for that place to be her real universe, instead of this confusing mess she had now. She had no idea how long they'd been silent, heads close and eyes locked, when he spoke again.

She blinked herself free, and he gave a smile that made her heart ache. 'I still owe you a trip out. Do you think a giant chalk man with a giant chalk willy might make you feel better?'

Emma returned his smile, sniffing back tears. 'Maybe,' she said. 'But if you don't mind, maybe not tonight?'

'Not tonight.' Aidan nodded. 'No problem. Whenever you're ready, you just say the word. I'll wait for as long as you need.'

The afternoon had brightened but it had been too wet underfoot to do much at the station. Emma had cleaned up inside where the roof had let in rain, while Tia had taken some measurements so they could decide where new internal walls should go, discussing the space with Blake but being very careful to repeat every suggestion to Emma as they went. It was obvious she was mindful of what had happened earlier that day, and it should have made Emma happy, but it didn't. Now she felt like the delicate cup that nobody dared take down from the shelf to use. This over-consideration was almost as bad as not being considered at all. The only thing she'd ever wanted was to be an equal and respected partner, and now she felt like Tia thought her a basket case.

It didn't help that Aidan kept asking if she was alright in soft, solicitous tones, and every so often when he did, she'd glance across the space to see Tia watching, who'd then pretend she hadn't been watching at all and declare to Blake in a loud voice how busy she was just to prove it.

Later that evening, back at the cottage, Tia told Emma she was staying home for a change, which cheered Emma up a little, and they even made plans to cook their own pizza from scratch and watch a film together. But Tia's phone pinged so often with messages that were so obviously from Blake that Emma felt guilty for making her stay home and told her to go and meet him after all. When she refused, it made Emma feel even worse, but without turning it into another awkward thing between them she couldn't do anything but relent and let Tia stay with her, phone pinging all the way through their movie.

'How are you feeling?' Tia asked her the following morning.

'Good, actually. Much better than I did yesterday.'

The sun spilling mellow light into the kitchen and a decent night's sleep had made the world of difference to Emma's mood. As she'd woken, Aidan's words of encouragement at the café the day before had come back to her. It would be alright, and one day when the hotel was full of happy guests and their lives were the amazing dream they'd hoped for, she'd look back and wonder why she'd ever feared otherwise. She had to have faith, she had to be strong and she had to keep going. Didn't they say that fortune favoured the brave? The way she looked at it, she and Tia had been pretty brave, hadn't they? They were definitely owed that favour by fortune.

Tia looked pleased as she poured tea from a pot she'd just made. 'I'm glad to hear it. You know, for a horrible moment yesterday I thought I'd lost you.'

'For a moment so did I,' Emma said. 'I'm sorry for being such a drama queen; it's just that everything gets on top of me sometimes.'

'I understand that; it gets on top of me too.'

'You never show it…' Emma accepted a cup from her. 'You always seem so cool and collected.'

'Just because I'm not showing it doesn't mean I'm not feeling it. Spending time with Blake has helped too – he's so steady and so good for me.'

'He must be special. You spend all day with him and then want to see him again at night – not many couples who could say that.'

'He is. They're both good company, aren't they? I mean, you spend a lot of time with Aidan away from the site.'

'Not as much as you do with Blake. It's different anyway – he's showing me places of interest, mostly, for when we start to get guests so we can make recommendations to them.'

Tia regarded her over the rim of her cup. 'Why do you have to pretend you don't like him all the time?'

'I do like him.'

'You know what I mean. I know you're going to be annoyed with me for saying it, but I think you're a little bit in love with him.'

Emma choked on a mouthful of tea. 'What? Where did that come from?' she cried, grabbing a tea cloth to mop up.

'I've seen you together,' Tia said. 'You can deny it, but you can't hide it.'

'That's ridiculous. It would never work anyway.'

'Why not?'

'It just wouldn't. You're with Blake for a start.'

'So?'

'Tia – we're not ABBA! It's a recipe for disaster – them business partners and us business partners and them working for us… it's far too complicated.'

'You're scared.'

'I'm being practical.'

'But you didn't deny being scared.'

'I'm not scared, I'm sensible.'

'You mean boring.'

'Thank you.'

'Anyway, they won't be working for us forever – then they'll just be two guys in the village.'

'Two *brothers* in the village.'

'What does that matter? You're finding excuses that don't exist.'

Emma took the tea cloth to the sink. 'OK, suppose I did like him a little bit… even then, nothing is going to happen.'

'Why?'

'I've told you before, I'm not like you. I need some time on my own. I'm not ready for a relationship and I'm too busy even if I was.'

'That's just silly. You're not too busy to go out with him looking at God knows what but you're too busy to see him romantically? What's the difference? Do you fall into a time warp when you start kissing someone?'

'You might as well because it takes over your life.'

'Prove it.'

'What?'

'Prove to me it takes more of your life to be with someone in a relationship than the time you're spending with Aidan now.'

Emma sat down and reached for a slice of toast from a pile Tia had made. It had gone a bit cold but she buttered it anyway. 'This is stupid. This is all because you have some weird little fantasy where it's like *Little House on the Prairie* and the whole of Honeymoon is together like one big family.'

Tia folded her arms. 'That's just insulting. And you sound stupid saying it.'

'Me and Aidan – that's stupid.'

'No, *you're* stupid!'

Emma put her knife down. 'I know,' she said quietly, looking up at Tia now. 'Don't you think I know that? Don't you think I wish I could change this weird brain of mine? I can't; it's just how I am, and how I feel about Aidan right now is that we can't be together.'

'So what? You're going to make him wait until you're ready? You're going to risk losing him for good? Because he's a catch, and some lucky woman will snap him up if you don't. He likes you but he won't wait forever.'

'How do you know he likes me?'

'Because he told Blake so.'

'Did he?'

'Yes.'

Emma frowned. 'He's never said anything to me.'

'Well, duh! Of course he hasn't because you're giving off such ice-queen vibes. He's not going to put his neck on the block if he thinks you're going to chop his head off! Didn't it ever occur to you that there's a reason he keeps asking you to go to all these places?'

'Well I suppose so, but…'

Tia threw her hands into the air. Emma winced, because she couldn't deny that her friend had a point. Why was she pushing Aidan away? Was it just down to fear, or being busy, or any of those other reasons she kept coming up with? Or was it about stubbornly trying to prove something – that she didn't need anyone? She'd been trying to prove that since forever. She'd been projecting this mirage of strength and reliability and independence for so long maybe she'd forgotten how to stop. It had always been her, being the one who did everything for everyone, never allowing herself to accept or even admit she needed help or support or for someone to just carry her from time to time.

'Maybe I should talk to him, clear the air,' she said slowly.

'Good,' Tia said. 'That's exactly what you should do… for a start anyway. You can talk to him tonight.'

'He might not be free tonight. I'll have to ask him when we see them—'

'He's free,' Tia blurted out. 'For you he is. He'll be at the pub… waiting.'

She sat back looking supremely pleased with herself. Emma stared at her. 'What?'

'I was banking on you admitting you have feelings for him because I absolutely knew it. And Blake knew he liked you too, so we fixed up a date for you.'

'You did what?'

'Oh, don't look so pissed off – you'll have a great time!'

'I didn't ask you to fix a date for us! If we want to go out on a date we can fix it up ourselves! I can't believe Aidan's gone along with this too!'

'I'm sure he will, because he's not stubborn like you.'

'What do you mean, *you're sure he will*? You don't know? I thought you'd arranged it?'

'Blake's going to tell him about the plan this morning, just like I'm telling you. Well he's not exactly going to tell him the plan… he's going to make sure he goes to the pub later. That's what I was supposed to do… but then you forced my hand and I had to tell you.'

'Tia! You were going to send me there and you didn't even know he'd come? It's bad enough going behind my back but that would have just been humiliating!'

'But I knew he'd be there.'

'You knew nothing! You think you know everything but you don't! You don't know me; I'm not you! I don't want what you want and I don't think like you think. Just because a thing suits you doesn't mean it will suit me.' Emma stared at Tia. 'You were always so bloody spoilt and entitled at school but I thought you'd changed and matured. I should have known a leopard couldn't change its spots. Shame on me for being fooled – and now I only have myself to blame for being stuck with you in this godforsaken village on the building project from hell!'

She pushed away from the table so violently her chair fell back and hit the floor with a clatter. Stepping around it, she marched from the kitchen.

'Where are you going?' Tia called. 'You haven't eaten your toast!'

'To the station, so I can start work and get this thing finished as soon as possible. Then we can sell it and I can get back to a normal life away from this place!'

Chapter Twenty-Two

It was raining in sheets again as Emma marched down to the station house.

How dare Tia interfere! It was one thing to offer opinions she hadn't asked for, to book specialists she hadn't approved and make decisions she hadn't consulted on, but quite another to manipulate a match with a man when she had no idea of Emma's wants or needs or emotional state. It was more than annoying; it was downright presumptuous and totally out of order.

She was in too deep here. *Get the station house finished, keep your head down, don't get involved with the villagers, then you can sell up and ship out.* There was no future with someone like Tia who thought she knew more than everyone else and felt her God-given right to impose her rules on their lives. If this bust-up hadn't happened now it would have happened somewhere down the line, so perhaps today was a blessing in disguise. In the end, it would probably save wasted months and a more difficult disentanglement once Emma came to her senses and wanted out of the partnership. She'd spent her life pandering to others, being told what to do and what she ought to want; she'd let people like Dougie and Margot walk all over her. Not anymore. How she lived and who she loved was her choice, not Tia's and not anyone else's.

As she walked her blind rage calmed a little, though she was still angry and her resolve was unchanged. At least it was still early, so hardly a soul was up and about, meaning Emma didn't have to make polite conversation with anyone. She was in such a savage mood right now there was no telling what she'd say. And though Honeymoon and the road to the station were as quaint and charming as ever, all flowers and thatched roofs and cobbles, the rain and grey skies and her mood cast them in a new light, one that made her sad and full of regrets. Now that she'd tasted something different, sweeter, it would be harder than ever to leave this beautiful place and life behind and go back to her old existence. Maybe it would have been better if she'd never come at all.

When she reached the clearing, the shell of Honeymoon's old station building stood silent and dark in front of her. How she hated it right now – those mocking holes where roof tiles ought to have been, that gaping mouth of a door, the chasms of damp rooms beyond with no plaster and water running down the walls, where birds and rats came and went at will and used the building she'd spent her last pennies on like everyone else seemed to use her life: when she wasn't looking and without her permission. Was that how Tia saw her? A sap? A naive woman without a clue? No head for business but a willing source of income she could tap into to make her own dreams a reality, and to hell with anything Emma might want out of the deal? Did she see a stupid, pathetic, gullible doormat? Maybe she'd listened to Emma complain about Dougie and Margot and decided she could use a soft touch like that too?

Emma took a deep breath. She wasn't thinking straight at all. She didn't want to believe that of Tia. It might have been convenient at first, but they'd become good friends, hadn't they? And maybe she had only been trying to help when she and Blake had played Cupid. But Emma still had a right to be angry, didn't she? She had a right to expect her friend to respect some boundaries. She had a right to decide for herself what she wanted and who she wanted. No matter Tia's intentions, she'd crossed the line.

And Honeymoon Station hadn't finished with the business of making her miserable. Inside, she could see that all the places she'd spent so long cleaning the afternoon before so they could dry out were soaking wet again. She went over to inspect the biggest puddle, which might have been classified a pond in some quarters, and a large, cold drop fell from the ceiling, into her collar, running down her back.

'Well that made me feel a whole lot better,' she announced sourly to the pigeon that blinked at her from a bare rafter. It cocked its head to one side and cooed at her before flying away.

'Oh, that's it... bugger off. Thanks a lot for your support!'

Another drip landed on her head and ran down her scalp. Emma looked up at a jagged square of sky showing through the roof, and then back at the pool of water steadily growing at her feet. What was the point in cleaning it up again if it was just going to keep reappearing? They'd been waiting for a scaffolding delivery so they could tackle the whole roof, but waiting for scaffolding was making everything in the building waterlogged. Why wait when she could easily use some ladders, get on the roof herself and at least patch it up to keep the rain out? She studied it for a moment. Maybe there was even a way to do it from the inside, which would save her going on the roof and ought to be safe enough.

Trudging outside, she located a set of extendable ladders Blake had left lying under a tarpaulin at the side of the building and dragged them inside. They were a lot heavier than they looked and her arms were aching by the time she'd managed it. She cast around for somewhere safe to prop them, and then she had to get them extended, which was another heavy job, but finally she got them in position, only to realise she couldn't reach the hole from there. So she moved them along to lean on a joist that looked less than secure but took a chance anyway, the wood creaking and complaining but holding as she went.

Attaching a thick sheet of plastic with some nails stopped the rain getting in, and for a moment she was pleased with her work. But it soon started to fill with water and she'd barely begun her clean-up of the puddle when she looked up to see the sheet sagging. She'd have to remove it before it got so heavy it would bring half the roof down, and with a growing sense of frustration she decided the only way to solve the problem was to repair it properly.

Sweating now in her raincoat as she dragged the ladders outside again, she leaned them against a side wall. There were old roof tiles somewhere – she knew that, because they'd collected a load from the ground where they'd been shaken off by decades of storms and Blake had salvaged the ones that were still intact to use again. After ten minutes of searching she found them stacked in a corner of the old waiting room. There were around a dozen, but she guessed the hole needed maybe half of them. She picked one up – they were heavier than they looked too. Why was everything so much bloody heavier than it looked?

Deciding she could probably carry no more than three at a time and get them up the ladder, she tucked some under her arm and made her way outside. It was a pain, but she'd just have to get them up there in relays before she could do anything else.

It was at the top of the ladder, just as she was about to crawl onto the roof, that she heard someone shout her name.

'Emma! What are you doing?'

'What does it look like?' she shouted back, not daring to turn round in case she lost her balance.

'Get down!' Blake yelled.

'I'm fine! Why can't everyone stop babying me?'

'Emma, please…'

This time she recognised Aidan's voice. She twisted to look and lost her grip on the tiles. As they clattered back towards the ground, her first instinct was to grab for them, and in doing so she lost her balance, stifling a scream as the ladder fell backwards and threw her into the branches of the old apple tree.

'Em… are you alright?' Aidan called up, his voice now full of barely disguised panic. 'Hang on – we'll get you!'

She was balanced precariously in the boughs of the tree, like the cradle in the nursery rhyme that would fall with the slightest whisper of wind. There were only claws of branches holding her like a net and she needed to get control. If she could sit herself properly on a sturdy branch maybe she could shimmy along to the trunk and climb down. Feeling very stupid, and cursing her rotten luck that of all the moments Aidan and Blake could have arrived, it had to be now to see this, she started to wriggle cautiously to reposition herself more securely on the branch.

'Stay still!'

'I'm alright; don't fuss! I'll work my way—'

Her words were stolen by a loud snap, and suddenly she was falling.

Chapter Twenty-Three

The pain in her arm told her she'd badly injured it, pain that clouded her thoughts and threw her into confusion. It was all she could do not to scream out.

'Jesus, Emma, are you mental?' Blake shouted as he and Aidan ran to her.

'That's broken,' Aidan said shortly. He swept her into his arms. If she could have spoken she'd have told him she didn't need carrying, but she was concentrating too hard on not passing out to talk at the same time.

He hurried with her across the muddy grounds of the old station, Blake following. She closed her eyes, rain hitting her face as they went, thankful for its chill.

'Keys in my back pocket,' Aidan grunted as they reached the van. Blake got them out as Aidan put Emma in the front seat and fastened her in.

'Stay here and let Tia know what's going on,' Aidan said as Blake handed the keys over.

'Where are we going?' Emma asked in a small voice that spoke her pain. She was confused and dazed and felt sick.

'To put you back together,' he said.

'What, like Humpty Dumpty?' she asked with the sudden insane urge to giggle at her own joke.

There was no reply. The door slammed at the driver's side, the engine started with a throaty roar, and the van started to move. Emma laid her face against the cold of the passenger window and wished she could make all this pain go away.

Ten hours later Emma's arm was in plaster. She was doped up like a Glastonbury reject and lying on the sofa of the cottage while Tia fussed and kept repeating what Aidan had told her about their hospital visit.

'Your arm's totally smashed up,' she said. 'But if you hadn't landed on it how you did you'd have smashed a lot more. Having a messed-up arm is actually a good outcome in this scenario, which is ridiculous, when you think about it. Why were you up there? On your own, with no safety equipment and no scaffolding? You could have died!'

'I was fixing that hole – I told you. If I hadn't been distracted I'd have done it perfectly well without injuring myself.'

'If Aidan and Blake hadn't arrived when they did you'd have been lying in agony for hours. Nobody goes that way if they don't have a reason to.'

'You'd have been there soon enough.'

'You still would have had to wait. I got held up trying to… well, you know, I had something to sort out.'

'You mean that stupid date with Aidan?'

'Yes,' Tia said, looking sheepish and a little embarrassed. 'I managed to abort it just before Blake said anything to him, so you needn't worry now because he doesn't have a clue.'

It pained Emma now to see Tia upset about it, especially when she was making such an effort and was clearly stressed about the accident. 'Look,' she said, 'I'm sorry I flipped out about it. I know you meant well.'

'I'm sorry I interfered. Em—'

'Tia, sit down.'

'I will; I'm just going to get you some more pillows from upstairs.'

'Tia, please… just for a minute. I need to say this before we go any further.'

Tia sat on the armchair and folded her hands in her lap as she gave Emma her full attention.

'I want to go home,' Emma said.

'Oh,' Tia said. 'Well I expect it would be a good idea until your arm mends; maybe you should stay with your dad—'

'No – I want to go home for good.'

Tia stared at her. 'But what will I do?'

'You'll be fine. You've done more or less everything anyway. You're the one with the business head; I've just held you back while you've held my hand through everything. I don't know that you ever really needed me.'

'Of course I did!'

'I won't leave you in the lurch. I'll make sure to sell my interest to someone who wants to go ahead with the guest house just as we'd intended to.'

'But it won't be you!'

'No, but I expect it will be someone who knows what they're doing.'

'But I don't want someone who knows what they're doing; I want you!'

'You might not want them but you'll be better off with them in the long run. Being here is a mistake – like a rebound relationship after Dougie, only with a building instead of a man. It wouldn't have been a very good idea with a man either, but it would have been a darned sight cheaper.'

Tia shook her head. 'I refuse to believe that all this was about Dougie. I thought you believed in our venture. You hated your old life – you told me that all the time!'

'I did, and I probably will when I go back, but at least I can manage it. This feels too big and too complicated. Besides, I've proved how useless I am today.'

'That was an accident; you're not useless.'

'I had an accident because I couldn't keep my emotions in check. It's not just the hotel, Tia.'

'It's me?'

Emma hesitated. Better to get this out into the open, even though it might make her feel like a bitch. Tia had a right to know everything.

'Tia, you're fun and amazing and so good to be around but… I can't cope with you. Since we arrived… it's not just Honeymoon Station, it's Blake. You're with him and that's great and I'm really happy for you, but it's made you forget me. I feel so lost and lonely because you're never here. People in the village talk to me but it's not the same. I thought we'd be partners and friends but I don't have the friends bit anymore and I miss it. Before we came here I had this vision, this idea that life in Honeymoon would be pulling together and muddling through – you and me as a team – to this eventual triumph, but it's not like that at all. I see how close you and Blake have become and I see that you won't need me soon at all.'

'Of course I will, Emma! We *are* a team! Don't make this decision now – you're not of a mind to. You're high on painkillers and you're not thinking straight.'

'I'd already made it before today,' Emma said. 'I'd just been looking for a reason to think I was wrong before I told you about it.'

'And you didn't find anything?'

'No, I didn't. I'm sorry.'

'Em, please don't do this. I'm sorry if it looked as if I pushed you out or didn't need you. The truth is I need people – that's who I am. I need Blake; he makes me feel safe and wanted, otherwise I'd always be scared, but needing Blake doesn't make me need you any less. I've always needed you because you keep my feet on the ground and keep me on track and without you I get crazy. I'm a dreamer, no head for reality at all, and you're the driving force I need to keep me focused. When Jerome and I had the gym it was the same; it was always his common sense that kept everything straight. Without you, these dreams I have will always be just dreams. I can't make them real if you're not here.'

Emma closed her eyes. Her head was spinning; nothing made sense. Was she meant to be here or not? She'd felt so certain that Honeymoon Station was a mistake, but now she was scared that giving it up might be the real mistake. And giving it up meant giving Tia up. If what Tia had just said was true, then it was a hell of a burden to have on her conscience. Could she be the woman who left a friend in need like that? She'd spent her whole life looking out for people who hadn't asked her to, and now she was going to skip out on the one person who'd told her she needed her.

'I'm tired,' she said finally.

'Let's talk more in the morning then,' Tia said. 'Sleep on it. If you still feel the same then I won't stop you from leaving. But please, think what you're throwing away before you do.'

Almost every day since she'd arrived in Honeymoon had been so busy that Emma had slept well every night, but for the first time since her arrival, she'd had a terrible night's sleep. *Breaking your arm will do that,* she thought grumpily as she went down to breakfast feeling as if she hadn't had a single second of decent rest. But she was forced to recognise that there'd been more to it than her injury. The conversation with Tia the evening before, her plan to leave, the decision that had led to it… she didn't know what to think about any of it. This was the time when, usually, she'd call her aunt or Elise to talk it through, but this time she wasn't going to. She didn't want to worry them, and this felt like something big enough to have one or both of them heading straight to Honeymoon to sort her out, and that would disrupt their lives. It was bad enough that hers and Tia's would be thrown off course for a while without subjecting someone else to it.

'What are you doing up?' Tia asked. She was at the stove stirring a pan of oats.

'It's time to get up.'

'If you're working, yes.'

'I'm working. I'm not having a day off just for this…' Emma nodded at her plastered arm. 'I can't afford to.'

Tia turned down the heat on the stove then rested her hands on her hips. 'And what exactly do you think you'll be able to do?'

'I can carry things that only need one hand. And I can paint with one hand. I can get tea for you, go to the shop to get gum for the boys—'

'Emma, stop it. You need to rest and mend. Maybe in a couple of weeks you can pick up light duties, but until then…'

Emma slumped into a chair at the table while Tia went back to stirring her porridge.

'About what I said yesterday,' Emma began after a pause.

'Which bit?'

'The selling-up-and-going-home bit.'

'Right.'

'I was confused.'

Tia turned to her with a slow smile. 'So you're not going?'

'Honestly, I don't know. I just feel so… lost. I don't know what I'm supposed to do.'

'Do you still believe in the hotel?'

'I think so.'

'Then there's nothing else to worry about.'

'But we're so behind, and the money is running out, and now I'm laid up with this stupid arm which will make it ten times worse.'

'Something will turn up, Em. It always does. Things have a way of working themselves out.'

'You always say that.'

'And it's always true.'

There was a loud knock at the front door.

'Hold that thought,' Tia said. She turned the stove off and left the kitchen. Moments later Emma could hear the low hum of conversation and then Tia came back, followed by Aidan.

'How are you feeling?' he asked.

'A bit stiff. Tired mostly. You have no idea how hard it is to get a decent night's sleep with a broken arm.'

'Actually I do,' he said with a small smile. 'Broke mine playing rugby about ten years ago. Last time I tackle a guy who's taller and wider than my shed.'

Emma smiled. 'Ah, then I'll stop complaining.'

He held out a box of chocolates. 'Nell sent these. She says she hopes you get well soon. Sid sends his best too.'

Emma raised her eyebrows to their full height. 'Sid?'

'Nell's let him back in the shop. And he's a troublemaker but he's not a complete monster. He'll probably wait until your arm mends before he starts hating you again.'

'Hmm. Well it might have been worth breaking my arm just for the respite.'

'I'd say so.'

'Would you like a cup of tea?' Tia asked him.

'I've love one.' Aidan took a seat at the table.

'Toast?' Tia asked. 'Porridge? There's plenty to spare.'

'I've eaten, thanks.' He looked at Emma. 'I've called in a couple of favours to get the roof sorted.'

'But the budget—'

'Don't worry about the budget. These are favours which mean they will barely cost. I've factored it all in so it's absorbed; I just didn't want to give anyone any more reasons to get on the roof. One broken arm between us is enough.'

Tia placed a cup in front of him. 'Thank you,' she said. 'We really appreciate it.'

Emma gave an uncertain smile. 'I don't know what to say.'

'You're supposed to say *thank you*,' Tia put in.

'Yes, I mean thank you,' Emma said. 'It's more than we deserve.'

'Speak for yourself,' Tia said wryly as she spooned some porridge into a bowl and sat down. 'I deserve it.'

'Yes, but you're not an idiot,' Emma said.

'True.' Tia looked at Aidan. 'Help yourself to sugar.'

'He doesn't take it,' Emma said.

Tia bent her head to eat her porridge, but not before Emma caught a knowing smile.

As Tia ate, they chatted a little about the plans for the day's work and how they were going to manage without Emma. She continued to argue for being on site to assist in some capacity, while Aidan pointed out what a liability having an incapacitated person there would be, how many health and safety laws they'd be breaking and that she'd end up slowing work down rather than helping. She didn't like it, but in the end she had to agree to stay away, though only on the proviso that they reviewed the situation the following week. Her priority, for the time being, was admin, website-building for when they opened, stoking a social-media buzz and general public relations (by which they meant getting round Sid and his crusading pensioners).

'Right,' Tia said as she finished drying up the breakfast dishes. 'I'll pop back at lunch to see you're OK, Em.'

'I'll be fine.'

'I'd rather see for myself.'

'I'd rather you cracked on. I'm holding things up enough without you rushing back and forth to see if I'm OK.'

Tia hesitated and then nodded shortly. 'Ready, Aidan?'

'Give me a minute, would you?' he asked. 'I'll follow you down.'

Tia frowned slightly but then told Emma she'd see her at teatime and left them.

Emma waited for Aidan to speak. It felt like a telling-off was coming for her foolishness on the roof of Honeymoon Station, and if it was she'd already decided she deserved it and would sit quietly until he was done.

'Tia says you want to leave,' he said.

'Oh…' It wasn't what she'd been expecting and it threw her. 'I don't know… I'm just… well like I told you before, I'm sort of all at sea.'

'I know and, like I said to you then, the build will work out; have a little faith.'

'It's not just the build. It's me. Tia has slotted straight into the community here but I don't feel I have at all. I don't feel as if I belong and I don't feel wanted.'

'Who on earth has made you feel like that? Apart from Sid, who's treated Tia in exactly the same way. Everyone else has been friendly.'

'I know, I can't explain it. They've been friendly but I don't feel as if that really means anything.'

'I know it's hard being the newcomer. And village life is so different from what you had before, I expect. I can imagine if you haven't lived here forever it might not seem as if you belong in the way everyone else does. But people will accept you in time and you'll feel as if you've always been here.'

'That's not to say I couldn't get used to it, it's just… I had this dream of what it would be, like a postcard or an old cosy TV drama where it's always sunny and everyone is rosy-cheeked and welcoming and work on the station would be like a barn-raising or something with all your neighbours, done in a flash with a dance afterwards… Silly, I know. I mean, I didn't really think that was what it would be like but I had that dream… It's hard to explain.'

'Try. I'll do my best to understand.'

'Well I sort of had that image in my head of things being idyllic and people being pleased about our arrival, but the reality is some people are awkward and some situations are awkward, and we have to worry about every penny, and the work on the hotel is backbreaking and it feels like it will never end.' Emma drew a breath. 'I'm being melodramatic again, aren't I?'

'You don't think you could make Honeymoon your forever home at all?'

She shrugged.

'There's one story I haven't told you,' Aidan said. 'Want to hear it now?'

'I've got nothing else to do.'

'Right. Settle in, this one might take a while.'

Emma held back a frown, wondering now where this conversation was going.

'There was a boy,' he began. 'Many years ago he was chased across Europe with his family by a complete dickhead with a funny moustache—'

'It wasn't Sid, was it?'

Aidan chuckled softly. 'If only. This guy was a lot nastier than Sid. So the boy and his family kept running, from country to country, and along the way they lost their loved ones who got separated from them or captured or just got ill and died, until the only ones left were the boy and his mum. They found their way to a port and a kind fisherman took pity on them and let them stow away in the bottom of his boat so they could cross the sea to England, where they'd heard they could be free. They found their way to London and they managed to get a place to live. It wasn't great and life was tough, but they were thankful to be safe. But just as they started to settle the bombs started to fall and all the children had to leave. The boy said goodbye to his mum, not knowing when he'd see her again, and he got on a train with all the other kids to the countryside to stay with people he'd never met. The other kids on the train teased him – they told him the people in the village wouldn't want him because his accent was funny and his nose was big and his ears stuck out and he walked with a limp. He'd never been so scared, even when he was being hunted across Europe, because that was a different kind of fear. Nobody wants to be rejected, especially not a young boy.

'But when he got there a family came to meet him at the railway station and he saw in their faces right away that they wouldn't reject him. They took him to a tiny cottage where he had to share a bedroom with their own son, but they treated him kindly and it had been a long time since he'd felt so safe. Then, one day he was told he'd be going back to London with all the other kids because the bombs had stopped. He was sad to be leaving the people who'd cared for him, but he'd missed his mum so he was happy to go.

'But when he got there his house was gone and he discovered that his mum had been in it when the bomb fell. He didn't know what to do or where to go. Nobody in London wanted him. The only friends he had in the whole world were the family he'd lived with while the bombs had been falling on London and even they weren't really his… They were a borrowed family who'd simply done their bit for the war effort.

'The days went on and he kept thinking about that place in the countryside. Even if he had to sleep under hedgerows it had to be better than sleeping on bomb-shattered streets. So he scraped as much money together as he could. He wasn't proud to say it in the years to follow, but he stole and he begged and he sold the food the church had given him to survive and eventually he had a train fare.

'He arrived in that village and he didn't even know what would happen. The family would probably turn him away – he wasn't their problem anymore. He walked to their house anyway because he didn't have anywhere else to go and he told them everything…'

'And what happened?'

'The family who had once welcomed him as an evacuee now welcomed him back as a son. They took him in without a single question and they treated him just the same as they treated their own boy. He grew up in that village, and he married there and had sons of his own, and he spent the rest of his days there. You want to know who the boy was?'

'Who?'

'My granddad, Josef Aaronson. His mother had dropped the As from their name to make it sound more English, though he needn't have worried about that here in Honeymoon. Still, that's how we became Ronson. He came to Honeymoon full of doubt, full of fear, not knowing if he'd be accepted, but with hopes of a new life.' Aidan smiled slightly. 'Sound like anyone you know?'

'Wow…' Emma sat back in her chair. 'I didn't know… Your granddad must have been so brave.'

'What I'm trying to say is what my granddad always told me about Honeymoon: there's a kind of magic about it – it's special. If you let it, it will save you.'

'I'm not like Josef. I'm just a stupid woman who doesn't know what she wants.'

'No, you're not like Josef, but you're not stupid either. And I think you could use a little of that magic just the same.'

She twiddled with the handle of her cup, wondering what on earth she could say in reply to what he'd just told her that wouldn't sound trite or flippant, but she couldn't think of anything.

'Thank you,' she said finally.

He drank the last of his tea and stood to leave. 'You're welcome.'

'That one's not tragic enough for the tour,' she said with a faint smile as he started to leave. 'I mean, it's tragic, but it has a nice ending.'

'Good,' he said. 'That was kind of the point.'

Chapter Twenty-Four

Tia did her best to go through every little detail of what had happened at Honeymoon Station that day, careful to keep Emma completely in the loop. She'd been pleased to report that the scaffolding was up and the roof repairs were well underway, and that it was a big step towards making real progress on the renovations. It also meant no more reasons for Emma to get on the roof, an observation Emma had to acknowledge with a sheepish smile.

Tia had her head in the fridge, pondering what to cook for their supper when Emma stopped her.

'Let's eat at the pub tonight.'

Tia turned with a frown. 'But the money—'

'We need this. Why don't we put it down as an essential expense?'

'You're sure you're up to it? You must be tired.'

'I've done nothing all day; I'm pretty sure I can manage to stay awake for a couple of hours at the pub. Why don't you tell Blake to come and meet us there?'

'Really?'

'Sure. He's your boyfriend – maybe I ought to be making more of an effort.'

Tia beamed at her. 'I'll get showered and I'll be ready in five!'

*

A cheer went up when Emma and Tia walked into the Randy Shepherd. Blake seemed to be the ringleader and grinned broadly at them.

'I knew she'd come round to the delights of the Shepherd eventually!' he said, laughing.

Aidan stood at the bar with him. Had Tia told Blake to make certain he was there or had he just decided to come anyway? He gave Emma a knowing smile and she wondered if he'd told Blake about their conversation that morning and that she now knew the story of how their granddad had come to settle in Honeymoon.

'What are you having, Emma?' the barman asked as they made their way over. He stuck out a hand to her. 'I'm Walt, landlord. First one's on the house, my love.'

Emma shook his hand. 'Wow, thank you. I'll have a lager… Not sure what you've got but I'm not fussy.'

'I've got just the thing,' Walt said, taking a glass from the shelf. He turned to Tia. 'Your usual, my love?'

'Thanks, Walt,' Tia said.

A few people stepped forward to say hello to Emma as Walt got their drinks. June, who they already knew, of course, clinging to a sweet sherry in a tiny glass; Betty, who was June's friend; a slightly younger couple called Wendy and Jim who ran the post office; Barnaby, who tended the grounds of the church and kept the pots and flower beds around the village looking lush and weed-free; a lady named Tulip who said she did nothing in particular except live off her husband's generous pension and didn't care who knew she was a lady of leisure; and a pair of farmers called Stan and Ollie, which everyone still found hilarious after fifty years of them being in the village. They assured Emma that they weren't as accident-prone as their Hollywood namesakes, and – they added with a grin at her cast – certainly not as accident-prone as she was.

Everyone crowded round. They asked about her arm, about how she'd come to break it, where she'd lived before Honeymoon, how she knew Tia, what her family did and whether they'd join her to live in the village once the hotel was open, what their plans for the hotel were, and how it was that she hadn't punched Sid in the face yet. They were all interested in everything and Emma had never felt so fascinating before.

During a rare let-up, Aidan sidled over. 'I'm glad you came.'

Emma smiled up at him. 'Me too. I feel a bit of a miserable cow for not doing it before.'

He glanced across to where Blake was sitting at a table with Tia. Their heads were close as they talked, and it was obvious they had eyes for nobody but each other. 'I kind of get why you might have felt it wasn't really for you. But what you should have remembered is that they're not the only people in Honeymoon.'

'I know. I'll remember it from now on.'

'So you're staying?'

'Maybe for now.'

He raised his glass to his lips, but the look he gave her bordered on exasperated. 'Only for now?'

She gave a small smile. 'Maybe I could manage a bit longer than that.'

He set his glass down on the bar. 'You've got friends here, don't forget that. When you think things are getting on top of you, tell us – we want to help.'

'Ah, people have their own worries; they don't want to add mine to them.'

'Would you stop doing that! There's no shame in admitting you can't do everything on your own. Being able to ask doesn't make you weak; it makes you strong. It means you recognise your shortcomings and will do what it takes to put things right.'

'Got it,' she said.

Aidan regarded her carefully for a moment. 'I don't think you really have.'

'Maybe it's a work in progress then.'

'Well I suppose a work in progress is better than nothing.'

When Emma glanced up again, she saw that Tia was now alone at her table and Blake was making his way over. He seemed suddenly anxious.

'Got a minute, bro?' he asked Aidan, who looked at Emma.

'Don't mind me,' she said. 'I'll go and keep Tia company for a bit.'

Tia smiled up at her as she made her way over. 'How are you bearing up?'

Emma took a seat. She cast a quick glance around the room. It was furnished in warm woods, claret-and-gold carpets and curtains, and printed copies of oil paintings of the surrounding countryside. The decor looked old and traditional, but well cared for and very clean.

'Good,' she said. 'It's nice in here, isn't it?'

'I like it. I'm sure all my old friends from the gym back home would think it's horrible. Maybe I would have too back then, but I love it here now.'

Emma smiled at her. She had a feeling that had more to do with the people who came to the pub rather than the pub itself – one in particular. But she simply nodded.

'You want to eat soon?' Tia asked.

'You know what?' Emma said. 'I'm not too hungry now. All day I've been snacking out of boredom – I've probably eaten so many biscuits I won't be able to eat for another month.'

'I'm not that hungry either to be honest,' Tia said. 'And Walt looks quite busy on the bar so I feel a bit bad asking him to get the kitchen going.'

'He does look like he has his hands full. Doesn't he have anyone else helping?'

'Candace, but it's her night off.'

'And he doesn't have anyone else?'

Tia laughed. 'This is Honeymoon. Why would he need anyone else?'

Emma grinned. 'True. I suppose most of the time they don't have enough customers to keep Walt and Candace busy, let alone anyone else.'

'Exactly. If you want food here it can be a bit hit-and-miss if they're busy on the bar but you get used to it. There's a fish and chip shop in the next village – Blake's taken me there a few times. If we get hungry later we can always drive out to it.'

'I think we'll both be too drunk for that,' Emma said. 'Walt seems determined to make sure I'm legless for my first visit.'

'Well don't fall over on your other arm, for goodness' sake.'

'I'll try not to.'

There was a pause. Emma glanced over to the bar, where June and her friend Betty were now singing some unrecognisable old song while Tulip clapped along. Aidan and Blake seemed deep in conversation, and it looked quite intense.

'Em… do you think Blake's weird tonight?'

'In what way?'

'I don't know… like he's nervous.'

'He certainly didn't sound nervous when we came in, the way he was making fun of me.'

Tia smiled. 'True. His humour is one of the things I love about him.'

Emma hadn't noticed that Blake was especially funny, but each to their own. She supposed Tia saw him in a very different way than she did. Personally, she'd take Aidan's intelligent wit any day. Her gaze went across to the bar again to where he was talking to his brother. He was wearing a soft woollen sweater in a forest green that suited him well, and his hair was still a little damp after the shower he must have had before he'd set out, and she didn't think she'd ever seen him look so good.

She shook herself and noticed now that Tia was watching them too.

'They look very serious,' she said.

Emma craned to get another look, and as she whipped round in her seat her knee hit the table and knocked Tia's drink over.

'Oh shit! I'll go and get a cloth.'

'It's OK, I'll go—'

'Don't be daft,' Emma said. 'I made the mess. I'll go – it won't take a sec.'

She strode to the bar. Aidan and Blake were so deep in conversation they barely noticed her.

'Walt… I'm sorry, do you have a cloth? I've managed to knock Tia's drink over. And could you do a refill for her too?'

'No worries, my love,' Walt said cheerfully. 'Give me a tick.'

Emma waited. People in the bar had moved on to their own conversations now, which was fine by her as she'd found the attention earlier a little unnerving. Completely unconsciously, she found herself homing in on Aidan's voice.

'You don't think it's a bit soon?'

'No,' she heard Blake reply. 'It's not like it was with Stacey. She's the one – I know she is.'

'So you want to ask her tonight?'

'I don't see the point in waiting. If Emma goes, I don't want her to go too. This way, she'll stay no matter what happens.'

'That's if she says yes, of course.'

'She'll say yes.'

'You're sure about that?'

'Yeah, I think so.' Blake sounded suddenly anxious again. 'Do you think she might say no?'

'I think she's mad about you, but she's just got divorced.'

'That was months ago.'

'It will still be new to her.'

'I don't want to wait, bro. I can't wait – I need to know she'll stay in Honeymoon.'

'You're taking a risk.'

'That's what you think?'

'Yes.'

'What if I told you I'm doing it anyway?'

'Then I'd hope she says yes. I'd get to be your best man?'

'As if there was ever anyone else…'

Emma was pulled from the conversation by a tap on her shoulder.

'Your cloth, my love.'

'Oh…' she said, reeling from what she'd just heard. 'Thanks, Walt.'

'I'll bring your friend's drink over if you like. And one for yourself too?'

'Yeah… sure.'

Emma made her way back to the table. Was Blake planning to propose to Tia? It sounded like it. Should she warn her? What if she said no? It would be terribly awkward to work with him on the hotel then, and Aidan had a point – Tia had just got out of a painful marriage and there was every chance she wouldn't want to go there again for a long time.

Even more troubling was the prospect of Tia saying yes. Where would that leave Emma? She'd just decided to give Honeymoon another try, to make an effort to fit in and build a life here, and she was feeling optimistic about the hotel again, but Tia getting married would change everything. She wouldn't want to live with Emma at the hotel for a start, which had been the plan all along so they could be on site to run things. If she was married she'd want to live with Blake. He'd want that too, but she doubted he'd go as far as living at the hotel so they could be together.

Wordlessly, Emma began to mop at the drink on the table.

'Everything alright?' Tia asked.

'Yes, sorry, I…'

'Here's your drink!' Walt said cheerfully, putting it down. 'And one for you, Emma my love… Want me to take that cloth for you now?'

'Oh, thanks, Walt.'

Emma handed it over and he left them again. She'd just decided she was going to warn Tia about Blake's plans when Aidan came to the table.

'Moon's huge tonight, Em,' he said. 'Corn moon. Want to come and see it?'

Tia looked confused. Perhaps she was wondering why Aidan was asking Emma but not her, but Emma knew the answer to that. A second later, as Aidan was leading Emma out, Blake went to the table and sat down with Tia again. Emma flicked a last glance behind her as they left the interior of the pub, just in time to see Blake get up again and kneel in front of her.

*

Emma shivered as they stood outside. She could just make out the shadows of bats circling the eaves of the pub. She wondered if they were related to the bats that lived in the roof of their cottage.

'Are you cold?' Aidan asked.

'A bit, but it's alright.'

'If I was any kind of gent I'd offer you a jacket but I haven't brought one out.'

'That's alright,' Emma said. She perched on a wooden bench in the beer garden and looked up. The night was clear now, the sky peppered with stars, and the moon bore down as if about to fall to earth, amber and luminous and completely stunning. 'It's huge. I don't think I've ever seen it that big.'

'It's a beaut, isn't it?'

'So why's it called a corn moon?'

'To do with harvest time. Corn moon, barley moon, fruit moon… Last full moon of the summer.'

'I've never really noticed it before.'

'But you must have noticed sometimes the moon looks bigger than at others?'

'I must have done, but I never really thought about it.'

'There's no romance in your soul at all, is there?'

'I'm a city girl – what can I say?'

'Maybe we'll make a country girl of you yet.'

'Good luck with that.'

Aidan looked at her. 'You *are* cold, aren't you? Here…' He took off his sweater. 'You can't put it on obviously,' he said, draping it round her shoulders. 'Better?'

'Much. But now you'll be cold.'

'Nah, I'm used to being outside, aren't I?'

'Wandering round looking at all the places in your granddad's stories?'

He laughed. 'Working. But sometimes wandering round too.'

'You love those old stories, don't you?'

'I loved him, that's why. I loved his story and they came from that. He was so happy and grateful to find a home here he made an effort to know everything about it. He found out where everything was, all the interesting places, all the history. And when he heard a story or a myth – click… he filed it in his brain and he remembered it, and then he told them to us. Blake was never quite as keen to listen, but then he never could stay still for five minutes.'

'Is Blake going to ask Tia to marry him?' Emma blurted out. As Aidan turned to her with a shocked look, she blushed. 'I'm sorry, I overheard something at the bar.'

'I suppose we ought to have been quieter then. He wants to.'

'But you don't think he should?'

'I don't know… I don't want him to get hurt if she says no. What do you think? Will she say no?'

'I have no idea. I know she really likes him, and even if she says no it wouldn't be anything he'd done wrong – it would be because she's not ready yet.'

'That, to me, suggests you do think she'll turn him down.'

'I'm as much in the dark as you are.'

'Well,' Aidan said with a sigh as he looked back up at the moon, 'I suppose we'll find out soon enough.'

Chapter Twenty-Five

When Aidan and Emma went back into the pub, the table that Tia and Blake had been sitting at was empty and they were nowhere to be found.

'Did you see Blake leave?' Aidan asked Walt.

'No,' Walt said.

'I did,' June put in. 'About ten minutes ago. He left with Tia. I must say, they didn't look very happy.'

Aidan and Emma exchanged worried glances. That didn't sound good at all. It sounded very much as if Blake had asked the question and she'd turned him down, but they couldn't know that for sure. And it wouldn't explain why they'd gone off together, unless, perhaps, they'd gone somewhere quiet to talk it over.

Emma sent Tia a text, but after fifteen minutes with no reply, Aidan decided to phone his brother.

'Where are you?' he asked tersely. 'I don't need details, just want to know everything's alright.'

He nodded shortly as he listened to the reply, and then he ended the call and turned to Emma.

'They're at your place, talking things over – that's all I know.'

'She must have said no.'

'I'm guessing that too. I suppose they're figuring out where that leaves them. This will be kind of a big deal to Blake.'

'I suppose he'll feel foolish for asking?'

'More than that… That's why Stacey dumped him. He asked her and she told him she hadn't realised he felt that way about her. She'd just been having some fun and she didn't want anything that serious. He felt like an idiot for not seeing it. She gave him the elbow and that was that. Since then he's kept a distance, just having fun himself. I really thought Tia had changed that…'

'She has,' Emma said. 'She loves him as much as he loves her, but her circumstances aren't the same. He knows that, right? He knows it's only time that's in the way now? If she's said no now, I'm sure that won't be no forever, because I've seen the way she looks when she talks about him and I know that if she hadn't just been through that divorce, if this had been a year from now, she'd have said yes in a heartbeat.'

'As long as she tells him that.'

'I'm sure she will.'

'There's nothing we can do for a while anyway,' he said. He angled his head at the bar. 'Another drink?'

'As I can't go home, we might as well,' Emma agreed.

Last orders had been called and Emma and Aidan were pleasantly tipsy. Despite their worries about Blake and Tia, they'd managed to have fun. Aidan had told her more stories about Honeymoon, but these ones had been more down to earth. He'd told her about the time Nell had single-handedly fought off an out-of-town robber who thought he'd take a shot at the shop by hitting him with a broom, and the time Betty, June's friend, had been in the background on a TV news report and mooned the camera to win a bet. Emma couldn't believe some of the things she was hearing, and by the end of the evening she was looking at some of the drinkers in the Randy Shepherd in a whole new light.

'Well,' she said, downing the last of her drink and noticing that the pub was almost empty now, 'I suppose I'm going to have to go back, no matter what's going on at the cottage. I can't hang around here all night. I just hope they're not doing anything unmentionable on the kitchen table.'

'You could come back to mine… I mean… God, that sounded all wrong, didn't it? I meant, just to wait if you're worried about going back home.'

'Um…' Emma began, not wanting to make things worse but wondering if there had been any subtext in Aidan's offer and how she might feel about that. But she didn't get the chance to think of a reply because, as they left the pub, they saw Blake and Tia walking towards it.

'We thought we ought to come and get you,' Tia said.

'We wondered if you were hiding here until we were done,' Blake added.

'Kind of,' Aidan said.

'It's sorted now,' Blake replied. He looked at Tia. 'See you tomorrow?'

'Yeah, of course,' she said, and started walking back the way she'd come.

'I'll see you tomorrow too?' Aidan said to Emma.

'I'd like that,' she replied. 'Call in for a cup of tea on the way to the station tomorrow if you have time.'

'I will. Thanks for tonight – I enjoyed it.'

She smiled. 'Me too,'

They left her to go their own way and she strode to catch up with Tia.

'Well?' she asked.

Tia glanced at her. 'Well what?'

'What's happened?'

'Blake asked me to marry him.'

'Um… I kind of know about that. So am I to congratulate you?'

'I said no.'

'Oh.'

'I told him I wasn't ready.'

'I suppose that was kind of tough.'

'He was a bit upset. Offended, you know. It must have taken a lot of courage to ask in the first place.'

'So what happens now?'

'I told him I love him. Just because I turned him down it doesn't mean I don't love him – it just means the timing is off. I asked him to wait until we get Honeymoon Station Hotel up and running.'

'Why?'

'Because that's why we came here and that has to come first. We've come this far and we have to see it through now. I promised you at the start my relationship with Blake wouldn't get in the way and it won't.'

'But I never expected you to turn down a proposal!'

'I know.' Tia gave her a small smile. 'But I have. We'll finish this thing because it's about more than a business – it's about proving to ourselves that we can do it. We need this, Em, you and me. You stuck by me when it got tough, and now I'm going to stick by you. When we've done it, when those doors are open, then maybe I can think about something as big as marriage. Not before.'

'So what's going to happen with you and Blake? He hasn't… well, he hasn't ended things, has he?'

'It might be weird for a while but I told him I love him and I'm willing to carry on if he is. There's no reason I can see to break things off, and it's not like I'm never going to commit.'

'And what did he say?'

'He said he loves me too.'

'So you wait?'

'Yeah, we wait. And…' Tia turned to her with a wry smile. 'In a way, it does us a favour.'

'How's that?'

'The longer it takes to finish the work at the station the longer he has to wait to revisit the question…'

'So he'll work like a demon to get it finished?'

Tia's smile grew, and Emma couldn't help one in return, even though it felt a little inappropriate. 'Exactly!'

Chapter Twenty-Six

Winter had set in. The hedgerows were often frosted over, the trees bare and melancholy and the fields shrouded in mist until late in the morning. Walks with Aidan – when he and Emma had time for them, which was rarer these days – were always closer to home now, bundled up in coats and hats and sometimes with hot chocolate or coffee they'd bought at Honeymoon Café. June's little cottage had a wood burner that kept things cosy and Emma and Tia were snug enough in there, no matter how cold it was outside.

If only they could say the same for the days spent working in the bitterest winds. Despite their efforts and their determination to weather any storm to carry on, the hotel was still very much closed. Their hopes of offering Christmas breaks were a distant memory now, and every day felt like a battle with the elements just to keep work going. The shell was there, at least, watertight and secure, and it was beginning to look as majestic as the station had looked in its glory days. The interior was a different story. There was still plastering to be done, central heating and wiring, fixtures and fittings and finishing touches.

While Emma had been laid up with her broken arm she'd been busy creating social-media accounts and a website for the hotel. With no finished product to show, she'd started to document their progress in a blog and had gathered quite a few interested followers already, including railway enthusiasts who sent her endless photos of the station as it had once looked – monochrome snapshots of moments that would never be again with blurry figures in old-fashioned clothes – and accounts of its history. She'd shared them all with Aidan, who had listened with interest as she read them out and pored over the photos with her during his many visits to the cottage.

They'd been out to the café and the pub too, and Emma was always struck by how concerned everyone was for her welfare. There had been gifts of food and flowers and promises of help any time she needed it. Things were finally looking up – at least the village was beginning to feel like home. Even Sid had decided to be courteous whenever she saw him out and about – though hardly friendly – and there had been no more posters or protests. She suspected he probably fumed in private but didn't dare do much about it now that everyone liked Emma and Tia so much.

By the end of October her cast had come off and she'd been able to help out on the site again. The others had been careful to give her the lightest work, and often there wasn't enough of it to keep her going until the end of the day so she'd find herself wandering around asking people what she could do. She'd be set on tasks like filling planters with flowers (even though there was nowhere to put them yet) and restoring the old station signs, growing more and more frustrated by the day that she wasn't being given any proper work to do. The others were trying to protect her, but she didn't need it.

At night Emma and Tia would trawl through paperwork, filing receipts and guarantees for materials or pieces of equipment and keeping up to date with the social-media following they were so painstakingly building, applying for permits for this and that, checking eco requirements and health and safety rules, researching markets and room rates so they could figure out who their own target market was and what they should charge. Tia found it dull but Emma was happy to do these tasks because they felt like safe ground, like things she was well used to doing. A spreadsheet or a file – those were things she could understand and deal with. They were certain; they had an indisputable answer to any question; they told you exactly what you needed to know.

One rainy Monday evening they were doing just that. Emma was on her phone looking at a hotel in Sussex that offered rooms in old London buses, while Tia tackled the accounts. Tia always did the accounts, because Emma said she was better at figures and, as she'd run her own business before with her ex, she'd know what everything meant without having to look it up. Tia had argued that Emma was better at maths, but Emma had reminded her that maths at school was a very different animal to maths in the real world – knowing what *x* would be if you took *y* from it was hardly going to tell you how much you had to spend on shelving for your reception area.

With a cough, Tia took off her glasses and turned to Emma.

'You want the bad news or the bad news?'

Emma looked up from her phone. They'd decided on a working supper and the remains of their slow-cooker sausage casserole were still on the table.

'Bad news?' Emma asked uncertainly. 'I mean, what do you want me to say to that? Can't you give me a less scary-sounding option?'

Tia turned the laptop so that Emma could see the screen.

'Oh,' Emma said, taking a closer look at the spreadsheet. 'Oh shit.'

'My thoughts exactly,' Tia said.

'How did it get so low? I thought we had more than that to play with.'

'I've only just got this all up to date and all the receipts for everything on here. And of course, we're running way over… There's the rent on this place rolling on that we hadn't budgeted for, and we have to eat. The projections we started out with were based on us living at the hotel by now… Actually, they were based on us pretty much having been open for a couple of months by now.'

'Do you think we could move into the hotel as it stands? It would save some money, wouldn't it?'

'I suppose we could rough it – but that's not really the issue at this point. It won't recoup the money we're already short of – that horse has already bolted. I don't even know if there's enough here to finish… We'd have to do some more calculations and see what we could cut back on.'

'But we don't want to scrimp on the building.'

'I agree, but I don't know what else we can do.'

Emma blew out a long breath as she looked again at the screen. 'I could see about borrowing more from the bank.'

'With what collateral, Em? We have nothing – neither of us even owns a house now.'

'Yes, but we have the hotel.'

'We've already borrowed against that. I don't think we'd get any more.'

Emma ran a hand through her hair and gazed at Tia. 'There must be something. We've got to find it; we've come too far to fall at the last hurdle.'

'I guess we could try the bank,' Tia said, though she didn't sound hopeful. 'If they say no, I just don't know what we're going to do…'

*

Emma almost knocked Darcie over the following morning as she hurried to catch up with the others at the station. She'd spent the last hour on the phone to a very uncooperative and unsympathetic bank manager only to hear the one thing she'd been afraid of. It had been obvious from the start of the call that he wasn't going to give them any more money, but he'd gone through the motions with an imperious tone, and by the end, she'd felt utterly humiliated and dearly wished she hadn't bothered making the call.

Afterwards she'd spent some time scouring the web for some kind of alternative solution but didn't know if she could trust anything she saw. There were loan companies that promised quick cash with no strings attached, but when Emma took a closer look she'd decided that their honest company names ought to be something like 'We Love Kneecap Smashing' or 'No Pay, No Legs'. She'd have to talk to Tia later to get her take on the situation. She'd even thought about taking her aunt and uncle up on the offer they'd made a few months before of loaning her money if she needed it to get through the winter, but she'd already had a chunk from her dad and, not knowing when she'd be able to pay it back and even if what they could offer would be enough, she'd rejected that solution for the time being too. In the end she'd decided there was no point getting further behind on their build to mess around at home with this stuff and so had headed out, still turning it all over in her head as she walked. One thing she knew for certain – they'd come this far and through so much to get here, she wasn't about to lose it all for the sake of a few thousand quid.

Darcie was carrying a bucket of soapy water, having just cleaned the windowsills of Honeymoon Café.

'Oh God, I'm sorry!' Emma squeaked. 'In my own world, wasn't watching where I was going at all!'

'It's alright,' Darcie said cheerfully. 'You missed me, so no harm done. I was just thinking we haven't seen you for a few days.'

'And then I go and knock you over. You need to be careful what you wish for.'

'I know,' Darcie said. 'I just wondered if everything was alright? How's your arm?'

'Well on the mend now,' Emma said. 'We've just been busy, you know…'

She wasn't about to tell Darcie that they'd been keeping out of the café to save money. Knowing that Darcie and Tariq relied on the trade too, she and Tia had felt guilty about that, even though they'd both agreed that their daily takeaways ought to stop, for now at least.

Darcie gave her a sympathetic smile. 'I hope you don't mind me saying, but Blake told us about your cashflow problem. Will you… Do you think you'll be OK?'

Emma tried not to frown. Of course Tia would have told Blake – she told him everything – and Blake probably told Tariq, who would have told Darcie. Emma could have been annoyed about it but what was the point? Honeymoon was just that sort of place, and the sooner she got used to it, the easier it would be to deal with it.

'I don't honestly know,' she said. 'We're going to fight bloody hard to be OK, though. We've come this far…'

'I understand,' Darcie said. 'My cousin, Millie, had similar problems when she was renovating The Old Bakery. If it hadn't been for the villagers there and her husband Dylan – who wasn't even her husband back then – she'd have lost it for sure, but they pulled together and helped her get it over the line.'

'That must have been lovely,' Emma said.

While she could have done with a bit of fairy-godmother intervention, Emma wasn't sure she'd be able to cope with the sense of obligation that sort of help would bring. The idea of forever being in the debt of the entire village didn't appeal to her at all. Aidan kept telling her she could ask for help, and she was getting better at that, but nobody could expect miracles.

Darcie put her bucket down on the pavement for a moment, rolling clouds of steam rising from the hot water into the crisp air. 'Why don't I ask Dylan to come and help you?' she said. 'He'll help anyone in a jam – he's like that – and he has some knowledge of building as he worked on Millie's bakery.'

'Really, it's very kind but I'm sure he has enough on his plate running the bakery with your cousin. I couldn't possibly expect him to come and work on a hotel for a complete stranger.'

'He'd do it, though. Millie always says it's paying it forward. In her hour of need she got help, so it's only fair she repays her debt to the universe by helping someone else… I mean, that's what Millie says…' Darcie blushed. 'She's sort of witchy like that.'

'It's a lovely offer but, honestly, Darcie, we'll muddle through. Thank you.'

'Well…' Darcie looked unconvinced. 'If you change your mind you'll be sure to come and say so, won't you? I could phone Millie anyway, just to see if Dylan is busy in case you decide—'

'If it makes you happy. But please don't ask him to come just yet until we've exhausted all other avenues.'

Darcie nodded. 'OK. I hope you get it sorted one way or another.'

'So do I,' Emma said, and she hoped the universe had decided that she deserved a favour that might come from a little closer to home.

*

There had been a thick frost overnight and even now at midday it clung to cobwebs in the trees and iced the new slates of the roof of Honeymoon Station. The ground was hard and glittering, and in the shaded corners dew still clung to the grass in icy shells.

Aidan was teaching Emma how to plaster a wall. His hand pressed over hers, they moved the trowel across the surface together. Having him this close was so natural and comfortable now that she barely thought about it. They were together so often these days, either on the site, at the pub with the new friends that Emma had made there, in the café chatting to Darcie and Tariq, or wandering the shaded lanes and sweeping fields of Honeymoon and beyond, with a story for every sight or sometimes just a moment of silent admiration. Emma had ceased to find that remarkable too. They were like a pair of old slippers, Tia had joked, perfectly matched in boring, safe old shabbiness. Emma had been mildly offended by the quip but, when she really thought about it, she could hardly argue that it wasn't true.

'There,' Aidan said, leaning back to look at her with a broad smile. 'Looks pretty good.'

'That's because you did it,' Emma said, inspecting the new section of wall.

'No, you did it.'

'My hand was on the thingy but it was your hand telling it where to go.'

'Well you try the next bit without me.'

'Right… but don't blame me when it's a total mess.'

He chuckled softly as she scooped a blob of plaster onto her trowel as he'd shown her and slapped it on the wall. It simply fell with a wet plop, onto the floor.

'So that went as well as could be expected,' she said dryly.

'Here,' he said, loading up with some more. He applied it and gave her the trowel back. 'Now you can smooth it.'

As she worked, she could sense him watching.

'It's shit, isn't it? You're thinking it's shit but you daren't say. It's alright, I can take it.'

'Hmm, well I think there's room for improvement.'

Emma turned and flicked some plaster from the end of her trowel. It landed on his T-shirt.

'Oi!' he yelled. She giggled as he dunked his hand into a tub of water they were using for finishing and flicked her back.

'That's freezing, you pig!' she squealed.

They were both laughing so hard Emma thought she might stop breathing, until at last it died away and they simply faced one another, grinning like loons.

'Who knew we'd end up such good mates?' he said.

'And we almost had those other builders,' Emma replied.

'They wouldn't have been half as much fun as me and Blake.'

'Or as good-looking,' Emma said, 'which does help if I have to spend so much time looking at you every day… well, Blake is anyway.'

'Oh funny. I thought you said the other day you were sick of the sight of my bum sticking in the air? So if that's the case it doesn't matter what's going on at the face end.'

'That's true, but these days I can hardly tell which end is which anyway.'

'Oh! If I said something that cruel and heartless to you—'

'Can't,' Emma fired back. 'Because I'm the boss and I'd sack you.'

'You can't sack me – I'm my own boss; I decide if I want to work for you or not, so be nice or else.'

She grinned. 'You just keep believing that and I'll let you. Let's have another go at this plaster or we'll never finish this wall.'

Aidan loaded up the trowel and handed it to her.

'Corfe Castle,' he said into the pause.

'Huh?'

'Corfe Castle. I just thought… it's somewhere we haven't been yet.'

'Is it far?'

'Well maybe a little way out, but we could grab a couple of hours at the weekend…'

Emma frowned. He saw the change in her expression and his face fell.

'Aid… hasn't Blake told you about our finances?'

'Yes, he did mention something about it. Are you planning to lay us off? Is that what you're going to say?'

'We don't want to do that at all. I'm trying to figure out what we can do but I think the weekend jollies might have to go on hold for a bit… sorry.'

'It's alright – there'll be other times.'

'We need to be doing as much as we can here to get finished as quickly as possible now. We're so far over schedule – and we don't blame you at all for that – time is literally money to us right now. We have to work weekends. We're not expecting you and Blake to, of course. You do understand, don't you?'

'Of course. I'll come over at the weekend to help out then.'

'We can't pay you for extra hours.'

'I know,' Aidan said, giving the plaster in the bucket a stir.

'So why would you?'

He shrugged. 'To help a friend.'

He looked up from the bucket. There was a strange charged moment when nothing would come into her head to say. All she could do was lose herself in those eyes of his…

'Knock knock!'

They both turned with guilty expressions to see Nell at the door of the station house.

'What brings you here?' Emma asked, trying to calm her inexplicably racing pulse. 'Who's minding the shop?'

'Oh, the shop isn't going anywhere,' Nell said. 'Boring day, not much going on… I thought I'd come down here and see how you're getting on. It's looking lovely, isn't it?'

'I think so,' Aidan said.

Tia appeared at the door behind Nell, looking puzzled. 'Blake just said you wanted to talk to me, Nell.'

'Both of you,' Nell said, eyeing Emma and Tia in turn.

Aidan angled his head at the door. 'Should I…?'

'Just for a minute if you don't mind,' Nell said. 'I hope not to keep the girls for long.'

Aidan left and Nell turned to them.

'Don't be cross when I tell you this, but you must have realised by now that news travels around here like wildfire.'

'Sort of,' Emma said.

'So a little bird – I won't say which little bird because you could take your pick from dozens – tells me you're in a bit of a pinch with money.'

Emma and Tia exchanged a questioning glance before they both turned back to Nell.

'I'd like to help,' Nell said.

'But, Nell,' Tia began.

Nell held up a hand to stop her. 'Let me tell you my plan before you say I can't.'

'OK,' Emma said with a faint smile. 'What's your plan?' They'd hear her out, politely decline, and then they could all get on with their day.

'I'd like to buy a share in the hotel.'

Emma stared at her. There were many things she'd expected to hear from Nell, but that wasn't one of them. Tia looked as shellshocked by the offer as Emma.

'But why would you do that?' she asked.

'Would it help you?' Nell asked.

'We can't deny the money would,' Tia said. 'What would you want in return?'

'Nothing. Nothing more than a stake in the hotel anyway. And I wouldn't want to tell you how to run it… What's the phrase…? Oh, I know… I'd be a silent partner.'

'But why do you want that?' Emma asked, wondering if she was following the conversation correctly. Was Nell asking to buy part of the hotel? The one they hadn't even finished building and might yet end up bankrupting them?

'I think it would be nice,' Nell said. 'I've got some money saved for a rainy day… well, no day ever seems rainy enough for me to get it out so I've got quite a lot now. I thought you girls could use it and you'd never let anyone gift it to you – quite right too – but I can buy myself something far more useful and lasting than a pair of new boots or a holiday in Spain. Not that I ever get time for a holiday in Spain, because who would mind the shop…?'

'Well,' Tia said, sounding as dazed as Emma, 'how much would you want to buy?'

Nell thought for a moment. 'Depends how much you need me to buy.'

'This is all a bit unexpected,' Emma said.

'Of course,' Nell said. 'I'm in no rush.'

'Would you want to see plans… projections?' Tia asked. 'I feel you ought to see something up front before you decide if you really want to make an offer like this.'

'Perhaps you ought to talk to each other first to see if you're both happy with another person being involved,' Nell said. 'But if you decide the answer is yes then we can talk about how much.' Her gaze swept the space. 'I can still remember sitting on my grandfather's lap in this room. He had his uniform on… It always smelt of mothballs… and I was eating mints from the tin he always had in his pocket while he showed me how he waved his flags and explained what it meant when he blew the whistle. I remember how proud he was when the trains pulled in, smart and shiny. He loved his job and he loved this place more than anything. Broke his heart when it was closed down. He'd have been so happy to see you two bringing it back to life. If I can be a tiny part of that it would make me happier than I can say. I'd sit back and think of him looking down and know that I'd done him proud.'

Emma looked at Tia, whose eyes were swimming just as hers were. There was no need to discuss this, because she knew Tia's answer would be exactly the same as hers.

'When you put it like that,' Tia said, smiling, 'we can hardly say no.'

Chapter Twenty-Seven

By the time Nell's offer had been made good and work had begun in earnest to get the project finished, spring was on its way. The signs were everywhere – birds flitting from tree to tree with bits of grass or twigs in their beaks, daffodils and primula poking tiny faces from the hedgerows, and leaf buds on the bare branches of the oak that stood in the centre of Honeymoon. Close to a year since Tia had first seen photos of Honeymoon Station online – a sad, dilapidated wreck, forgotten and abandoned – it was almost ready to open its doors to travellers once more. Only these ones weren't on their way through to somewhere else – they were coming to marvel at the beauty of the building, to breathe in the nostalgia and enjoy their own little slice of heaven in the Dorset countryside.

Outside, the brickwork had been pointed, the roof made sound, the windows were new, the entrance door stripped, sanded and painted a rich royal blue, the platform canopy decorated with fresh timber finished in a pristine white, the old iron signs restored and re-enamelled, the platform refurbished with new flags and dotted with pots of flowers and a swinging seat. Inside, the old ticket office had become the reception, the rosewood counter they'd managed to salvage now gleaming as if new, and the station café was now the hotel restaurant. The offices where Nell's grandfather would have seen to his official business had been turned into bedrooms and the waiting room was a bar for hotel residents. Outside where the railway line would have run stood a row of fire-red carriages decked out with soft beds and sofas, showers, televisions and pretty net curtains.

Aidan, Blake, Tia and Emma stood together, surveying the fruits of their labours. They'd each said at least twenty times how incredible it looked, and they were simply delaying the inevitable. But then Aidan dared to say it. He gazed at Tia and Emma.

'This is where we leave you.' He extended a hand out to them both to shake. 'It's been an absolute honour to work on this. Thank you for asking us.'

'I won't know what to do with myself now,' Blake said. 'And every other job's going to seem boring.'

At this point Tia began to weep and Emma felt like she might too. There was utter joy and pride in what they'd achieved here, but it was more than that. A chapter in her life that had brought both happiness and heartache, optimism and uncertainty was closing. It had changed her profoundly as a person, and she was sad it was about to end. As for the hotel, she'd miss working on it now that it was done. No more listening to Blake's tuneless whistling, no more arguing with Tia about where this or that should go, no more having Aidan laugh at her attempts to master some new skill, and no more of those secret knowing looks they'd share whenever Blake and Tia were flirting and thought nobody had noticed. Emma wasn't going to see Aidan every day and she no longer had a reason to. As for their trips out, the hotel was going to keep her busy most weekends and evenings now, at least until they started to make enough money to take on more staff.

'Remember,' Aidan said, 'if you get a burst pipe—'

'Don't call us,' Blake interrupted, laughing. 'We're not plumbers.'

Emma smiled and Tia sniffed hard.

'When are your landscapers coming?' Aidan asked.

Emma's gaze went to the grounds of the station house. While the building itself was close to completion the garden still had some way to go. It looked almost as wild as when they'd first arrived, only barer where they'd removed undergrowth and rogue shrubs. New grass had started to poke through the mud, nature stating its intent to reclaim it if they let it, and crowds of dandelions, bluebells and daisies had gathered in the shade of the trees. Emma rather liked its wildness, but it wasn't the sort of look that visitors would want.

'Tomorrow,' she said.

Aidan's hands went into his pockets and he gave a solemn nod. 'Charli's good. Her lads will do you a good job.'

'If you recommended them then I'm sure they will.'

Blake picked up a toolbox from the ground beside him and took it to the van. As he came back, he reached to catch a tear from Tia's cheek.

'Take a walk with me, Ti?' he asked gently. 'There's something we need to talk about.'

Emma had a feeling she knew what they were going to talk about and Tia probably did too. The question of marriage had been put on hold for months now. Tia had told Blake she would consider it again once the hotel was open for business. It wasn't quite, but that day wasn't far off, and perhaps Blake considered it close enough. It was obvious to anyone he was still crazy about her and that she felt the same about him. The question of what Tia's marriage might mean for Emma still troubled her, but she couldn't very well let that influence Tia's decision.

'Looks like everything's about to change,' Aidan said quietly as they watched Tia and Blake walk into the woods beyond the grounds.

'Just what I was thinking.'

'Will she say yes this time?'

'I think she'd be mad not to. If I had a bloke who loved me that much and had waited that long I'd never let him go.'

There was no reply. As that fact slowly dawned on her, she turned to look at him. Without another word, he began to walk to the van and then locked the back doors.

'Aidan?' she called.

'Tell Blake I'll meet him at home!' he called back as he climbed in and started the engine. Emma watched him go, a deep frown creasing her forehead.

Emma and Tia had left the landscapers with a copy of the plans for the grounds and gone to meet Nell and Sid at Darcie's café. Nell, who knew Sid better than anyone, had come up with an ingenious proposal to keep him in line and out of mischief, and she was sure he'd accept.

The four of them sat around a table now with cups of tea and a large plate of assorted cakes between them.

'Well this is all very unexpected,' Sid huffed, doing his best not to look flattered. He wasn't fooling anyone. He was clearly incredibly flattered and feeling very important right now.

'Nobody knows Honeymoon like you do,' Tia said. 'If anyone should be the face of the hotel it's you.'

'You'd bring a sort of gravitas to the place,' Emma said.

Tia winked at her. 'Good word! Gravitas – exactly! You'd command respect, Sid.'

'You'd make the hotel look respectable,' Emma said. 'A respectable hotel for a respectable village.'

Sid seemed to grow a foot taller as he sat and soaked up their praise. 'And all I'd have to do is greet people?'

'In the stationmaster uniform,' Emma said.

'A recreation of the original,' Tia said. 'It's beautiful.'

'You might want to direct people to their rooms,' Emma said. 'If they're not sure where they're going.'

'Yes,' Tia chipped in. 'So welcome them, show them around if they need it, answer questions about the area, share a bit of the station's history…'

'I don't know,' Sid said, trying to shake off the seduction of their flattery like Mowgli trying to shake off the snake in *The Jungle Book*.

'Oh, come on, Sid!' Nell huffed. 'Nobody is fooled! We all know you're dying to get that uniform on if nothing else!'

He shot her a wary look. 'And would I get paid?'

'Naturally,' Emma said.

'I'd get to run things my way?' he asked.

'To a certain extent,' Tia replied carefully.

Emma nodded. 'You'd get to decide what duties the position entailed and how they're best performed, so if you decide you've had enough somewhere down the line your successor would be doing a job you'd essentially created.'

Sid ran his fingers over his moustache thoughtfully, but Emma could see he was already sold. 'Would I get to vet the guests?'

'Um, no, Sid,' Emma said, giving Nell and Tia a doubtful look. 'We couldn't go that far, I'm afraid. If someone books and pays, then they're staying.'

'Even if their shoes haven't been polished this month,' Nell said. 'So you'll have to be polite and respectful regardless, or you'll have me to answer to.'

'Why don't you think it over?' Emma said. 'When you've made up your mind come and see us.'

'I'll take it!' Sid said. 'Trial period. If I don't like what I see—'

'You'll be a good boy and go back to your miserable retirement and not bother anyone again,' Nell said sternly. 'Don't forget I'm a partner at the hotel now too. You tangle with these girls and you tangle with me – got it?'

He nodded sullenly. 'You won't be there, will you?' he asked her.

'No,' Nell said. 'I still have a shop to run, but don't worry, I'll know everything that goes on. And I mean, *everything*...'

'Well,' Emma said brightly. 'I'm glad we got that sorted. We're not quite sure when your start date will be, Sid, but we'll let you know.'

'Any other business before we wrap up?' Tia asked.

Nell beamed at her now. 'Just one thing. You know those little birds I hear so much from... One of them tells me you're soon to be Mrs Ronson...'

'Not too soon,' Tia said with a broad smile. 'But eventually.'

'Then I'd like to offer my congratulations,' Nell said warmly. 'I hope you'll both be very happy.'

Sid looked confused. 'Who are you marrying?'

'Blake Ronson,' Nell said proudly, 'and it couldn't have happened to two more deserving people.'

'Oh,' Sid said, eyeing Tia with a new dubiousness. Perhaps he was deciding that Tia really was someone he couldn't afford to get on the wrong side of from now on.

'I'm sorry to break things up,' Emma said, 'but I think at least one of us ought to be at the hotel to make sure everything's alright. I don't mind going if you want to stay here a while longer.'

'I've got to get back to the shop anyway,' Nell said.

'I might as well come with you, Em.' Tia looked at Sid. 'Feel free to take the rest of the cake – it's paid for after all. Consider it your first job perk.'

He looked pleased at this and began to fold each slice into a napkin to go in the shopping bag he'd brought with him.

'We're off!' Emma called to Darcie. 'Thanks!'

'Oh, wait!' Darcie rushed over and gave Tia a tentative hug. 'I didn't want to say before, but now that Nell's told Sid… Sorry, I overheard that bit… Anyway, I just wanted to say congratulations.'

Tia smiled. 'Thank you, Darcie.' Then she glanced at Emma and raised her eyebrows very deliberately. 'Wasn't there something we wanted to ask Darcie?'

'Oh yes!' Emma said. 'I nearly forgot! Darcie, the hotel is going to need a supply of baked goods – croissants, fresh bread, pastries, pies… that sort of thing. I can't think of anyone's better than yours at the café. I know you said your cousin bakes them – do you think she could supply us?'

'I think she'd love to!' Darcie said. 'I'll phone her today and ask!'

'Thanks, that's brilliant,' Emma said. 'Let us know what she says.'

Darcie beamed. 'I will!'

After saying goodbye to Nell and Sid, Emma and Tia began the walk back to the hotel.

'All things considered, I think that went pretty well,' Tia said.

'I certainly didn't expect Sid to say yes.'

'I think the only reason he did is that he's terrified of Nell.'

Emma laughed lightly. 'I think he quite liked the idea of being that important.'

'Probably. Em – do you think we've made a mistake?'

'Hiring Sid? I hope not. Although it does mean we'll have to look at that self-righteous moustache all day.'

'True.'

They walked for a while longer and then Emma spoke again.

'I'm going to miss you.'

Tia turned to her. 'I'm not going anywhere… Oh God, please don't tell me you're thinking of leaving again! Not now!'

'No, of course not. And I know you're not either, but once you're married things will be different. Have you thought about where you'll live?'

'I was kind of hoping we could still live at the hotel. But if not, June's cottage will be up for sale soon.'

'I'd be happy for you to live at the hotel if that's what you want. We might have to rejig the rooms a little…'

'Oh.' Tia blushed. 'Perhaps that's for the best. Though I hope the walls will be a bit thicker than they are at the cottage.'

Emma gave her a playful nudge. 'I'm glad you told him yes this time.'

'Me too. We haven't done much in the way of planning yet, but I know Aidan will be best man.'

'Of course.'

'Would you be my maid of honour?'

'Me?'

'I can't think of anyone else I'd rather ask.'

Emma threw her arms around her friend. 'I'd love to!'

'And we can have the wedding at the hotel, can't we?'

Emma smiled. 'I should hope so.'

As they walked together discussing dress styles, the best months to get married, whether Darcie's cousin would make the wedding cake,

Emma enjoyed the gentle spring sun on her face and the fresh breeze that swayed the long grass in the fallow fields and shivered the lines of daffodils in the hedgerows. There was a smell on the air that only came with spring, of new shoots and blossoms, like the land waking up. The night had brought a sharp frost and the day had begun with a low mist cloaking the hollows, but that was burning away now; although it was hardly tropical, Emma soon found walking got her so warm she needed to take off her jacket and carry it. As she and Tia revelled in their friendship, their plans for the future and their glorious surroundings, the journey had gone by so quickly that, before either of them had realised it, they were back at the hotel, greeted by the rumbling of a mechanical digger and a radio blasting over it. The boss of the landscaping company, Charli, came over to meet them.

'Did your meeting go well?' she asked.

'Great,' Emma said. 'Everything alright here?'

'Yes.' Charli hooked a thumb at the gardens. 'The boys are cracking on nicely. The company that's supplying the playground want to deliver a day early – think we can accommodate that?'

'I'm never going to complain about something being early,' Tia said. 'If it's alright with you, Charli, then it's alright with us.'

'I'll let them know then,' Charli said.

Emma's gaze ran over the grounds. It looked bare again, nature's sneaky little clumps of grass having been dug up and the remaining shrubs at the perimeter cleared, but it was a blank canvas now, waiting for some beautiful creation to grace it.

But then her forehead crinkled into a frown. 'What's going on over there?' She pointed to a man wearing a hard hat and goggles who was carrying a chainsaw.

'Oh,' Charli said, 'he's taking that tree down.'

Emma looked sharply at her. 'The apple tree?'

'Well, yes.' Charli looked confused. 'Your plan does say the playground is going there.'

'I didn't put anything in the plan about taking the tree down!'

'I did, Em,' Tia said. 'I didn't think it would matter.'

'No,' Emma said, 'I don't want the tree taking down!'

'But, Em—'

'It's King Edward's apple tree!'

'Emma…' Tia gave a nervous laugh. 'That's just one of Aidan's stories.'

Emma turned to her. 'It's the tree that broke my fall when I came off the roof!'

She began to march towards the man with the chainsaw. 'Not that! Come away – that stays!'

Tia ran after her, leaving Charli to watch open-mouthed.

'What about the playground?' she cried. 'Em, it's just a tree!'

'Move the playground,' Emma said. 'I don't care where to. The tree is far more important; it's a part of Honeymoon Station as much as the benches or the station signs; it's a part of the history… We can't chop it down!'

'You sound mental right now,' Tia hissed.

'I know,' Emma replied tightly. 'I don't care. I love that old tree and I want to see it here every day and I don't care who thinks I'm mad.'

Tia let out an impatient sigh. 'Fine.' She waved the gardener away. 'Give us a few minutes before you start,' she told him. 'We've got to sort something.'

'There's nothing to sort,' Emma said. She called after him, 'The tree stays!'

'Emma...' Tia nodded sharply towards the empty hotel. 'A word... in private.'

Emma marched in and Tia followed.

'What the hell was that about?' Tia demanded.

'Why didn't you ask me if the tree could come down?'

'Because Charli said it was in the way. You've never appeared so hung up on it before, and you weren't around to ask, so I thought it would be OK to tell her to chop it down. I don't understand why you're so upset – you haven't cared about anything else we've had to pull down.'

'But that's...'

It was Aidan's tree. It wasn't just any old tree, it was his. It was one of the first stories he'd told her, one of the first things his brave granddad would have seen as he arrived in Honeymoon as an evacuee – it was more than a tree; it was history, a part of this place, a part of the magic that Aidan's granddad talked about. The tree had saved Emma when she'd fallen off the roof. And when she looked at it she felt happy because it made her think of...

She stared at Tia, and she knew now what she had to do.

'Please,' she said. 'Don't touch it. For me. Take anything else out but not that.'

Tia looked confused and exasperated but then she nodded. 'If it means that much to you—'

'Thank you! I've got to go somewhere.'

'Where?' Tia called as Emma rushed out.

'I owe someone a story!'

Chapter Twenty-Eight

As Emma strode towards the village she pulled out her phone. She'd been so determined to see him that she suddenly realised she didn't have a clue where he was, whether he'd be working or if he was even in Honeymoon at all. But she knew now that she couldn't fight this anymore. She didn't even know why she'd been fighting it in the first place. She'd tell him, and then it was up to him what happened next, but at least she would never look back on this day and curse that she didn't take the chance.

He had to feel the same way as her – she was sure of it. She recalled now looks and words, and the times they'd spent together, and realised he'd been trying to tell her all along.

The phone was to her ear as she walked. Just as she'd given up on him answering, he picked up.

'Hey,' he said. 'Don't tell me your roof has fallen off already.'

'Can you meet me?'

'Sure,' he said, sounding taken aback but without hesitation. 'When?'

'Now?'

'Now?' he repeated. 'It's kind of… OK, where?'

Emma thought for a moment. She was close to the lane that led to one of the first places he'd taken her to.

'Mary's Stream?'

'Right,' he said slowly. 'And do I need to bring anything?'

'Just yourself.'

'I think that normally comes as part of the deal.'

'I'm on my way there now,' she said. 'Whenever you're ready… I'll wait. I'll wait for as long as you need.'

As Aidan pushed through the tree branches that hid the stream from view, he looked worried.

'Is everything alright?' he asked.

'Yes,' Emma said. 'Actually, I'm not sure. I just… I feel I owe you an explanation.'

'About what?'

'I'm going to find it hard so I thought I'd take a leaf out of your book.' She sat on a rock overlooking the murmuring water and he found a place to settle nearby. He turned an expectant face to her.

'You once asked me what my story was.'

'I remember,' he said, nodding slowly.

'And it wasn't that I didn't want to tell you,' she said. 'It's just that I often feel as if nobody would want to hear it.'

'You shouldn't ever think that.'

'If you want, I'm ready to tell it now.'

'I'd like that,' he said.

She drew a breath, as if drawing strength from the air, and began.

'There was a girl called Emma. When she was eight years old her mum died. She thought she had to fix the hole her mum had left. She had to be all things to everyone – a housekeeper and grief counsellor to her dad, mother to her little sister who'd never even known their real mum at all… Emma got so used to doing these things she didn't know how to stop, and when all the people who'd needed her at the beginning didn't need her anymore she let everyone else she'd ever met take advantage of that instinct to bend to the will of others. She put all the things she wanted aside and she was all things to everyone, and she thought that was how you got loved. She thought she didn't deserve anyone who wanted to be all things to her.

'Then one day something happened that broke her, and she ran away from that life, and she came to a village called Honeymoon. It was strange and it was new and she couldn't see that all the people who lived there wanted to welcome her because she was scared about what she'd done. She almost ran back to her old life, where she'd been unhappy but at least everything had been safe and familiar, but then a boy named Aidan stopped her from making such a huge mistake. He showed her that she did deserve someone who wanted to be all things to her and, in the things he did and said, he told her that it was him. But she was really stupid and she didn't understand, and she pushed him away and made him think she didn't want him at all. And now she thinks she might have lost him forever.'

She paused. He stared at her.

'The thing is,' she continued, 'I don't much like that ending. I was wondering if there was any chance I might still be able to get the proper ending; the happy one, the one where the girl gets the boy even though she's been a self-absorbed, whining, stupid cow.'

Aidan said nothing. He only stood and lifted her to her feet, and then kissed her with a kiss that contained every ounce of compassion and beauty and romance in his soul. Emma didn't need his words to tell her the answer, because he was telling her with his body as it moved with hers. All those months of longing, all those unspoken feelings, all that denial was in his kiss… and she wondered now as he caressed her what it had all been for. They'd wasted so much time… *She'd* wasted so much time.

But she had the most wonderful feeling now that they were about to make up for it.

Chapter Twenty-Nine

Tia raced into the reception.

'There's a car! In the car park! They're here!'

'Calm down,' Emma said, laughing as she straightened her blouse, the most delicious butterflies doing circuits of her tummy. 'They'll think we're mental and drive off again!'

Sid stood sentry at the hotel doors, looking officious and proud in his stationmaster uniform. He bowed as a couple in their thirties came in with a clutch of suitcases and bags.

'Welcome to Honeymoon Station Hotel!'

'Oh,' the woman said. 'Thank you.'

'Reception is just that way if you'd like to check in,' Sid said, sweeping an arm towards where Emma was standing behind the desk, with Tia alongside, looking as if she might explode at any moment.

'It's lovely in here,' the woman said to her husband, giving the interior an approving once-over.

'Thank you,' Emma said.

'You're actually our first ever guests!' Tia said.

'Really?' The man turned to her. 'Do we get a prize?'

'Oh…' Tia threw a confused glance at Emma, but the man started to laugh.

'Joking,' he said. 'You looked so worried then.'

The mood relaxed instantly. Emma started to go through check-in and had a quick chat with the couple about their journey and where they could visit in the surrounding area. Every so often she'd glance up and see Sid watching them like a hawk. Probably deciding if they were the sort of people Honeymoon wanted walking its streets – old habits died hard, she supposed. When she was done he showed them to their room and then, a couple of minutes later, he was back.

'Did they pass?' Emma whispered.

'I haven't decided yet,' Sid began, but then said no more about it, probably recalling Nell's threats.

'I'm going to get the bar ready in case anyone wants an afternoon tipple,' Tia said.

'No worries,' Emma replied, and then busied herself going down the list of expected guests and their estimated time of arrival while those naughty little butterflies did cartwheels in her stomach.

There'd been times she'd thought that this day would never come – too many of them – but here it was at last. As she looked down a list that showed the hotel would be close to capacity on its first ever weekend of business, it was enough to give her a smile that filled her heart completely.

The next person through the door was Darcie, carrying a huge basket of muffins.

Emma looked up from her list. 'We didn't order—' she began.

'I know,' Darcie said, lugging them to the counter. 'They're a gift to wish you good luck and to give to your guests when they arrive.' She smiled. 'And if they like them…'

'I'll know where to send them for more,' Emma said. 'Thanks, Darcie – they're brilliant.'

As Darcie hauled the basket onto the counter another party arrived – this time a mother, father and young daughter.

Sid bowed. 'Welcome to Honeymoon Station Hotel. Reception is just this way…'

Emma smiled at the family, but she made a mental note to have a word with Sid about the reception thing. It was fairly obvious to anyone who walked in that the desk was right in front of them. She'd said to tell people where things were if they asked…

The little girl bounced up and down. 'Are we sleeping in a train?'

'Yes,' her dad said with an indulgent smile. 'That'll be fun, won't it?'

'Yes!' she cried. 'Yes, yes!'

From the corner of her eye, Emma saw Darcie slip away. She guessed she didn't want to get in the way, and perhaps that old shyness had got the better of her, as it did from time to time. Emma resolved to call her later and thank her properly for the muffins.

After she'd checked in the latest arrivals, Sid took them out to the carriages, the little girl chatting to him incessantly the whole time.

Emma had set her phone to silent, but she had it under the counter where she could see if anything urgent came in. As she glanced at it now, she saw a message waiting that could only have arrived a few minutes ago.

Have you managed to insult any of your guests yet?

Emma tapped a reply to tell Elise she was a cheeky little so-and-so and that she ought to respect her elders.

A second later Elise replied: *Can't wait to come and visit next week. Can't wait to see you.*

I'll be thinking of you. Have a brilliant first day, and don't let dad drive you mad.

Emma was about to type a response when a voice made her look up.

'Got a room?'

'Jeez, Aidan! You made me jump!'

'Sorry,' he said with a sheepish smile, and at the sight of him there she couldn't help but melt. So sweet, so relaxed, so charming, so clever, so strong, so handsome… *so completely hers…* She couldn't imagine now why she'd ever tried to deny that she'd been hopelessly in love with him since the first day he'd told her one of his stories.

He leaned in for a kiss.

'Sid will be back in a minute,' she warned.

'So?'

'And guests are due.'

'Just one little kiss and I'm out of your hair for the rest of the day.'

'No.' She gave his arm a playful slap, though she wanted nothing more and to refuse him was torture. 'How's my dad?'

He leaned on the counter. 'All settled in.'

'Already?'

'He didn't bring that much down with him – says the rest is due tomorrow on the removal van. And yes, I'll go over to help him get it in.'

She smiled. 'I don't deserve you.'

'I know. So do I get a kiss now as a token of your appreciation?'

'No!'

Aidan shrugged. 'Though he picked a hell of a week to move in.'

'That's my dad. But, in his defence, once the contracts had been exchanged there didn't seem much point in hanging around. I still can't believe how quick that all happened. I mention casually to him that June is selling her house and the next minute he's bought it.'

'But you must be happier with him here.'

'Yes, where I can at least try to keep an eye on him.'

'Where *we* can keep an eye on him.'

'Ah.' She smiled. 'Now you deserve a kiss…'

'Welcome to Honeymoon Station Hotel!' Sid boomed and Emma, blushing furiously, almost threw Aidan out of the way to see Sid bowing to more arrivals. Aidan grinned. She'd say she was going to give him a piece of her mind later, but what was the point? He'd get round her anyway and it would only end in more kissing… and maybe some other things…

These thoughts left her head as she looked properly and saw who was coming through the doors.

'You made it!' she cried.

'We wouldn't have missed it for the world!' Patricia said, leaning across the reception desk to hug her.

'Of course not,' Dominic said, giving her a peck on the cheek. His gaze turned to the rosewood and the elegant wall lights and soft peach decor and the gleaming parquet floor and he gave a nod of approval. 'I have to admit to being very wrong. I never thought you'd get this done, but you did and it looks amazing.'

'We're so proud of you,' Patricia said. 'Your mum would have been too, and she'd have loved this.'

'I think so too,' Emma said.

Patricia and Dominic looked at Aidan.

'And how are you?' Patricia asked. 'You were the development we really didn't see coming… although' – she eyed Emma cheekily – 'we did wonder if there wasn't a bit of a spark there…'

'Did we?' Dominic said blankly.

Aidan laughed. 'It's good to meet you properly this time.'

'If you need a guide while you're staying here,' Emma said, 'Aid's your man.'

Patricia looked at him. 'Oh?'

'We're going to get some trips up and running for the guests,' Aidan said.

Emma took a leaflet from a rack on the counter and handed it to her aunt.

'*Tall Tales and Tragic Tours*,' Patricia read. She opened it up and scanned the page. 'People will love these.'

'We hope so,' Emma replied. 'Aidan fancied a change of career and we thought why not exploit the thing he's really good at?'

'I'm so happy to see things working out for you,' Patricia said, giving Emma a fond look.

Sid came up behind them. 'Could I show you to your room, sir and madam?'

Aidan shot Emma a private grin.

'We haven't checked in yet,' Patricia began.

'It's alright,' Emma told her. 'I'll check you in. Sid will show you to your room and we can meet again later in the bar.'

As they followed Sid, Emma booked them in. She heard Aidan chuckle and looked up.

'He's taking this concierge thing a bit too seriously.'

'Sid?' Emma replied. 'Yes, but I'd rather have him like this than sticking posters up telling everyone how much he hates us.'

'True,' Aidan said. He glanced along the counter. 'Muffins?'

'Darcie brought them over. They're freebies for the guests.'

'What about the staff?' he asked, swiping one.

'Oi!'

'And what about the flowers?' he asked, already munching on his ill-gotten gains.

'Nell,' Emma said, glancing at a huge vase containing peach and cream blooms that complemented the decor perfectly. 'We ought to be sending her flowers, not the other way around. She saved our bacon after all.'

'If it makes you feel better, I think you saved hers too. She's been bored to death running that shop for years; the hotel gives her something else to think about.'

'I never thought of it that way.'

'You never do, that's your trouble.' He popped the rest of the muffin into his mouth and chewed with the deepest contentment. 'Always worrying about what you might be taking from others instead of recognising what you might be giving them.'

'It's a hard habit to break.'

'I know that,' he said, sneaking closer again, 'but I'm here to set you right now…'

Blake rushed in, causing them to jump apart yet again.

'Bro, there's an actual minibus pulling up in the car park! Did you know that?'

'Oh, I thought…' Emma checked her schedule. 'They're not due for another two hours!'

'Tia!' Blake shouted.

She ran from the bar and frowned when she saw there was no actual fire. 'Stop shouting like a moron!'

'Sorry…' he panted. 'Loads of people arriving! Right now!'

Aidan began to chuckle. 'Stop panicking. There are four of us standing here – I'm sure we can manage a few early guests; after all, we've tackled way bigger.'

Emma looked at Tia. Tia looked at Blake. Blake looked at Aidan and Aidan looked at Emma. They all looked at each other and grinned. They *had* tackled way bigger and they'd won.

Emma straightened her blouse and faced the entrance just in time to see Sid back at his post. As the busload of guests started to arrive at the doors, he gave a low bow and in his most regal voice announced: 'Welcome to Honeymoon Station Hotel.'

Emma's heart swelled. If any of these people saw half the magic of her home that she did, they'd leave very happy people indeed.

A Letter from Tilly

I want to say a huge thank you for choosing to read *The Hotel at Honeymoon Station*. If you did enjoy it, and want to keep up to date with all my latest releases, just sign up at the following link. Your email address will never be shared and you can unsubscribe at any time.

www.bookouture.com/tilly-tennant

I'm so excited to share *The Hotel at Honeymoon Station* with you. It was a welcome distraction for me as I worked on it, particularly as the UK was in yet another coronavirus lockdown. I hope it's just as welcome a distraction for my lovely readers, and that a little fictional trip to beautiful Dorset offers a few hours of escape.

I hope you enjoyed *The Hotel at Honeymoon Station* and if you did I would be very grateful if you could write a review. I'd love to hear what you think, and it makes such a difference helping new readers to discover one of my books for the first time.

I love hearing from my readers – you can get in touch on my Facebook page, through Twitter, Goodreads or my website.

Thanks,
Tilly

tillytennant

@TillyTenWriter

www.tillytennant.com

Acknowledgements

I say this every time I come to write the author acknowledgements for a new book, but it's true: the list of people who have offered help and encouragement on my writing journey so far really is endless, and it would take a novel in itself to mention them all. I'd try to list everyone here regardless, but I know I'd fail miserably and miss out someone who is really very important. I just want to say that my heartfelt gratitude goes out to each and every one of you, whose involvement, whether small or large, has been invaluable and appreciated more than I can express.

It goes without saying that my family bear the brunt of my authorly mood swings, but when the dust has settled I always appreciate their love, patience and support. This year, due to lockdown restrictions, like so many other people I've spent a lot of time struggling to keep working while in a small house surrounded twenty-four/seven by my family, who all had their own things to do too. They've been truly amazing, however, as supportive and patient as ever, willing to give me space and time to do what I needed to – even when it meant they had to sacrifice space and time of their own. It's testament to them that any of the books I've written during this time ever got finished at all.

I'd like to take a moment here to remember Storm Constantine of Immanion Press, who passed away this year. She gave me my first editing job, the opportunity to see my very first book in print, pushed me to follow my dream when others told me I couldn't do it and never asked for anything in return. She was one of those rare people who was never less than herself and offered no apology for it, and was all the more wonderful for it. She championed me and so many other authors and I'll always think of her fondly.

I also want to mention the many good friends I have made and since kept at Staffordshire University. It's been over ten years since I graduated with a degree in English and creative writing but hardly a day goes by when I don't think fondly of my time there.

I have to thank the remarkable team at Bookouture for their continued support, patience and amazing publishing flair, particularly Lydia Vassar-Smith – my incredible and long-suffering editor – Kim Nash, Noelle Holten, Sarah Hardy, Peta Nightingale, Alexandra Holmes, Cara Chimirri and Jessie Botterill. I know I'll have forgotten someone else at Bookouture who I ought to be thanking, but I hope they'll forgive me. I'll be giving them all a big hug at the next summer bash whether they want it or not! Their belief, able assistance and encouragement mean the world to me. I truly believe I have the best team an author could ask for.

My friend Kath Hickton always gets an honourable mention for putting up with me since primary school, and Louise Coquio deserves a medal for getting me through university and suffering me ever since, likewise her lovely family. I also have to thank Mel Sherratt, who is as generous with her time and advice as she is talented, someone who is always there to cheer on her fellow authors. She did so much to help me in the early days of my career that I don't think I'll ever be able to thank her as much as she deserves.

I'd also like to shout out to Holly Martin, Tracy Bloom, Emma Davies, Jack Croxall, Carol Wyer, Clare Davidson, Angie Marsons, Sue Watson and Jaimie Admans: not only brilliant authors in their own right but hugely supportive of others. My Bookouture colleagues are all incredible of course, unfailing and generous in their support of fellow authors – life would be a lot duller without the gang! I have to thank all the brilliant and dedicated book bloggers (there are so many of you but you know who you are!) and readers, and anyone else who has championed my work, reviewed it, shared it, or simply told me that they liked it. Every one of those actions is priceless and you are all very special people. Some of you I am even proud to call friends now – and I'm looking at you in particular, Kerry Ann Parsons and Steph Lawrence!

Last but not least, I'd like to give a special mention to my lovely agent, Madeleine Milburn, and the team at the Madeleine Milburn Literary, TV & Film Agency, who always have my back.

Lightning Source UK Ltd.
Milton Keynes UK
UKHW011037241121
394475UK00004B/1386